DESCENT

NATASHA KNIGHT

PROLOGUE 1

PERSEPHONE

I close the bedroom door, muffling the sounds of the party downstairs. My hand still on the doorknob, I tell myself to exhale, to relax, but it doesn't do any good.

He's here.

He's come home.

Why? Why now?

The beeps and clicks from inside still sound foreign to me. Unfamiliar. Like they don't belong because they *don't* belong.

I steel my spine and take a deep breath in, preparing to turn around. To face this new reality.

But there's something else foreign here tonight. Someone else who doesn't belong.

My heart races as I inhale, smell the aftershave.

No, not foreign.

Familiar.

But he doesn't belong.

Ice clinks against crystal and I turn. The silvery glow of the moon casts a haunted look over the sick bed. The machinery. But it's not that I'm looking at now.

It's him.

Sitting in my father's favorite chair, drinking my father's favorite whiskey, and that moonlight, the glow is almost eerie on the chiseled, hard lines of his face.

For a long moment, the only thing I hear is that rhythmic beep, beep, beep. Six months of it, the machines never once breaking their cadence, the sound driving me mad.

He clears his throat, interrupting that rhythm. Even that, the sound of him clearing his throat, it makes my heart beat faster, raising goosebumps along my bare arms.

And then he speaks.

"Persephone."

One word. My name. He draws it out, voice gravelly, thick, like he hasn't spoken in a long time

I shudder. I haven't heard his low, rumbling voice in years, and I've forgotten what it does to me.

He's the only one who calls me by my given name, and it stirs something inside me I wish it didn't. It has a power I wish it didn't.

"Hades," I say, using the name I'd given him when I'd first met him as a child, back when my head was full of fairy tales and mythology and heroes and gods and happy endings.

Now, well, now, things are different.

He chuckles.

I'm grateful it's too dark for him to see my face, to see how his presence after all this time affects me.

"What are you doing here?" I ask, somehow managing a level tone.

"Waiting for you."

Waiting for me. Of course, he is. I knew he would be, didn't I? From the moment I heard he was back in town.

I force my legs to move. To walk to the side table where my father kept his collection of liquor—where he *keeps* the bottles—on top of a mirrored tray. I have to remember to speak in the present tense. He's still here. He's not gone.

I pour myself a vodka, taking my time while I have my back to Hades, the intruder, the unwanted, while I try to check my emotions. I swallow the contents of the glass, savoring the burning sensation as I pour another, listening to liquid spill into crystal. Listening to blood thud against my ears as my heart races.

Leather creaks and I stiffen.

He's up.

He walks too quietly for me to hear but it doesn't matter. I don't have to hear him. I *feel* him at my back.

The hair on the nape of my neck stands on end and I wish I had more protection than this dress with its open back offers.

"Vodka still your drink?"

Heat radiating off him roots me to the spot before he even touches me. Before the knuckles of one hand brush the exposed vertebrae of my spine leaving goosebumps in their wake.

I remember the last time he touched me. I wish I didn't, and I try very hard to push the memory away as my body craves something it can't have. Something it will never be allowed to have.

"Time."

The word has an energy all its own and it makes me think about Hades and Persephone.

The abduction of Persephone.

Hayden closes his mouth around the beating pulse at my throat and I stop breathing.

My glass slips from my hand. It bounces on the thick carpet, unbroken, splashing vodka against my legs.

He dips his head closer as I turn mine ever so slightly. I inhale deeply, taking in his scent and for one crushing moment, I close my eyes and I feel him.

I just feel him.

He makes a sound, something primordial. And when he moves, the scruff of his jaw brushes my cheek, warm breath tickling my neck.

I hear his moan before he pulls away and I stagger at the loss of him. I shift my gaze up to his, the green-gold glinting in the moonlight. I force myself to breathe, command myself to be unaffected. I fail at both.

His gaze hovers at my mouth before returning to my eyes and I feel his body tighten.

And this is my power. This one thing.

He wants me as badly as I want him.

But Hades condemns Persephone. He tricks her and steals her away, carrying her to the underworld, to his Kingdom in Hell.

That's what Hayden Montgomery will do to me if I'm not careful.

And just like that, the spell is broken.

He knows it too.

I turn to face him as he steps backward and looks me over. His gaze stops at my left hand and one corner of his mouth curves upward when he returns it to mine.

"My brother couldn't keep that pussy happy?" he asks crudely.

I narrow my eyes, tilt my head to the side and watch him swallow his whiskey.

"What do you want, Hayden?"

His eyes darken. "You really want me to answer that?"

"You can't be in here."

"I'm paying my respects to your father."

"Like hell you are. You're not welcome. Not in this room. Not in this house."

"Wasn't always the case, was it?" His gaze skims over me and he leans forward, trapping me between his massive body and the wall at my back.

I have to remind myself that he cannot see the pounding of my heart as it tries to beat its way clear out of my chest.

I have to remind myself that he's only human.

A man.

He is no more Hades, God of the Underworld, than I am Persephone, daughter of Demeter.

He's just a man.

Human.

The grin that spreads across his face makes me wonder if he'll prove me wrong as he brings his glass to his mouth and drinks, then sets it down on the mirrored tray beside us. I half-expect him to touch me. To kiss me.

But he does neither.

Instead, he walks to the door, places his hand on the doorknob and stops. He turns back to me, eyes narrowed. He looks me over once more and I shudder again.

"Time." He repeats it, that one word, and then he's gone.

I don't need to ask what he means. Just like I didn't need to ask what he wanted. I already know.

I knew it before either of us walked in here tonight.

PROLOGUE 2

The sound of the party below grates on my nerves the moment I'm in the hallway.

I walk down the stairs, ignoring the curious glances. I'm no stranger here. And I'm sure before I've even walked out the door, the gossips will begin spreading their poison.

Good. Let them. Let my family learn from them that I'm back.

I glance into the various rooms I pass on my way to the front door noting the furniture still inside the house. How opposite the bare rooms upstairs.

She's desperate.

And I won't let the opportunity pass me by.

Because it's high time the Abbots pay for what they did. Persephone will be sacrificed, but that can't be helped. It's fitting, actually. Almost poetic.

An eye for an eye.

A girl for a girl.

I pull the front door open, the gust of icy wind sobering as I step outside.

I climb down the stone stairs passing the handful of idiots freezing their asses off for a few puffs on a cigarette. I bypass the cars along the circular drive, bypass the paved walkway to the street. Instead, I make my way over damp grass to where our property lines meet. I stop there, glancing at the ruin of the chapel in the distance remembering the last time I saw Persephone Abbot.

She was sixteen.

Vodka was her drink then, too.

I remember carrying her home that night. Bringing her into her bedroom before all hell broke loose over our houses.

I shake my head, crossing the property line. I look up at what was once the Montgomery estate. Dark vines like long fingers claw almost every inch of what's left of the once beautiful stone walls as if taking it back into the earth.

I wish it would take the past with it. Take the ghosts that still haunt the damned place.

I turn to look back at the Abbot house.

My house now.

It will rot, too, the earth swallowing up our sins along with our homes. But not before I've had my fill of Persephone Abbot.

1

PERSEPHONE

T*ime.*

I shudder as the rumble of his voice echoes in my head, that one word carrying so much weight.

Time.

Time for the Abbot family's reckoning.

Time for Hayden Montgomery to collect what he thinks he's owed.

I still smell him when I inhale and some part of me is greedy to savor that scent before it vanishes, like he just did.

Here, then gone.

Like before.

I've known Hayden Montgomery since I was a little girl. I grew up with him next door.

The bastard son of the Jeremiah Montgomery. Bastard but first-born of a set of twins. Hayden and Ares Montgomery. He always thought that would mean something. That the fact he was first-born carried more weight than it actually did.

I bend to pick up my glass and set it on the tray. Instead of refilling it, I take the one he left behind. I bring it to my mouth, inhale the scent of whiskey as I put it to my lips. I swallow the last drops and when I do, I swear I feel his mouth on me. Feel his hands on my skin.

I was ten when I first met him. His sister Nora and I had been playing with my stepmother's antique doll. I knew we shouldn't. I'd been punished for it before and you'd think I'd have learned.

She'd told me the doll was one-of-a-kind. A gift from her mother, a woman I never met.

I remember the instant it slipped from my hand and I heard the crack as the head hit the pavement and broke in two. I remember sobbing because I knew I'd be in trouble. And in our family, my stepmother was the one to watch out for. My father was—*is*—the gentlest man I know.

That rainy morning was when I'd first met Hayden Montgomery. Already back then, he wasn't welcome at home and when he was there, he was only ever coming or going. Mostly going.

He'd walked out of his house and stopped when he'd seen Nora and I sitting on the curb trying to fit the two pieces together. He'd crossed our cul-de-sac and come to sit beside us.

He was a little scary back then. Well, he's still a little scary. But I'd had this strange fascination for him. The prodigal son. The one who I only ever saw shadows of.

Neither Nora nor I had had to say a word as he looked down at the doll and I remember studying the yellowing remnants of what I knew even then was a bruise along his jaw.

"What have you done?" he'd asked.

"We broke her stepmother's antique doll," Nora had whispered.

"Oh dear." He'd taken the doll and looked at it.

"She's going to kill me," I'd said, fresh tears forming.

"She can't kill you," Nora had tried to reassure me in that matter-of-fact way of hers that made her sound like an adult even though we were the same age.

"Nora's right. A murder on the street would send property values way down. Can't have that," Hayden had said.

Nora had giggled. I hadn't understood a word. But he'd smiled and the dimple on his cheek had made me smile too.

"This isn't too bad. I know someone who can help."

"You do?"

"My brother knows everyone," Nora had said proudly, her smile beaming. She'd always talked about him like he was some mythical hero.

"I won't be able to get it back to you until tonight though," he'd said.

"Don't worry, she won't be home until late."

"All right then." He'd stood and held out his hand. "I'm Hayden Montgomery by the way. I'd better know your name if we're to be co-conspirators."

"Hayden." I'd stood too. He was so tall the top of my head came to the middle of his belly, so I'd stepped up onto the curb. "Like Hades."

I'd thought myself in love at that moment. I still remember it so vividly.

He'd just looked confused. But then I'd placed my hand in his and introduced myself. "I'm Persephone Abbot. But everyone calls me Percy."

"Ah, I see. Well, I'll call you Persephone. Now go inside. You're already soaked through. And Nora you'd better get home. Your mother's looking for you."

"You'll bring her back?" I'd asked him.

He'd nodded. "I'll meet you here at eight o'clock sharp."

"Thank you, Hades."

I exhale at the memory, put the glass down. "You're not a little girl anymore," I remind myself and walk to my father's bed.

He's mostly unchanged, his still-handsome face just a little older. His salt-and-pepper hair more salt than pepper now. I tuck him in and give his hand a squeeze.

"I love you, dad." I bend down and kiss his forehead.

No change. But at least he's alive.

I walk out of his bedroom, pausing at the top of the stairs to look down at the party my stepmother is hosting just six months after the accident. With my father up here like he is. With our finances what they've become.

But I guess this is her show of defiance. Her revenge against me because my father left me in charge of the estate. Of Abbot Enterprises. Of everything.

Not that it matters. There's nothing left.

I catch her eye in the foyer down below. Her mouth is moving, she's talking to one of her nasty friends and even now, she still manages to express her feelings toward me in just that glance.

She must say something about me because her companion's gaze shifts up to mine.

I don't meet it but turn away, walk down the hall and toward my own bedroom at the opposite end of the corridor. I close the door and stand there, inhaling, smelling that hint of aftershave here too.

He'd come in here before going to my father's room. I wonder what he'd done. If he'd opened my drawers, snooped through my things.

No. That's not his style.

He'd pulled the blanket on my bed back and left a package for me on my pillow.

I go to the bed. I pick up the thick, black envelope with

the stack of legal paperwork awaiting my signature, handy sticky notes pointing to where I should sign. Where I'm to put down my name and give up my family's future, our legacy.

The words hostile takeover ring in my ears, our attorney's warning.

"Fifty-one percent. It's that or you lose the company."

It's lost if Hayden Montgomery holds controlling shares anyway.

And it's not just that.

I lean my head back against the headboard and look around the almost bare room. Just the bed and an old dresser left in here. Even the nightstand is gone. The lamp looks homeless on the floor.

Homeless.

That could be us. If I don't sign these papers or come up with the money I need to save the house, not to mention the company.

I set the stack of paperwork aside. The thick, gold-embossed black card slips off the pile and onto my lap. I touch the lettering, his name in its elegant font. On the back someone wrote a time and a place. No phone number to decline the invitation because this isn't an invitation. It's a summons.

Eleven o'clock.

Hades Gentlemen's Club.

But I don't like being summoned.

I rip the card in two. Do the same with the documents. I drop them to the floor and make a point of stepping on them, my heel digging a hole into the pages as I make my way into the bathroom.

I slip my dress off my shoulders as I move, letting it fall to the bare hardwood floor. I step out of my heels and slide my panties off, then switch on the bathroom light. I run the bath and turn to my reflection in the mirror. Taking the irritating pins out of my hair, I drop them into the sink, pile the dark mass of waves on top of my head and use a soft tie to make a messy bun. I scrub my face clean of makeup and when I look in the mirror again, I see the dark circles under my eyes.

These last few months have been hard. I don't remember the last time I slept a full night since my father's accident. Since learning the true state of things.

Opening the medicine cabinet, I take out the prescription sleeping pills and pop two into my mouth, although I seem to be immune to them. I slip into the hot tub. Turning the tap off, I lay my head back and stare up at the colorful glass chandelier hanging from the ceiling. It's from Venice. My dad ordered it for me after a trip there when he'd seen how much I'd loved the glasswork.

Money. I've lived without it. The first eight years of my life I lived without it.

Then my mother died, and I learned who I was. Learned who my father was. And coming into this house was exactly as I imagined, a Cinderella story. Although I've never allowed myself to feel sorry for myself. I have more than most, after all.

I have a sister. Well, half-sister. And a father who, as soon as he learned of my existence, loved me.

My stepmother is a bitch, but hey, you can't have it all. The fact that I look like my mother doesn't help. Neither does my father mentioning it every time he sees me.

The thought of my father lying in that bed makes me sad, but I can't let it. He needs me now. I need to be there for him like he was for me when mom died.

And that means facing Hades tomorrow.

That means swallowing my pride and doing what I need to do to save our home, our legacy.

2

HAYDEN

I'm having breakfast when Peter enters through the dark, carved-wood doors. I look up from my paper, drink a sip of coffee.

"Ms. Abbot is here, sir."

I glance at the antique clock over the door. Ten past eleven. She's late.

Folding the paper, I lean back in the comfortably worn leather chair. "Bring her in."

Peter nods.

One of the older men at the table across the room rises, nods his greeting to me and shakes his companion's hand before leaving. It's only a moment after he's gone that Peter is back. He opens one of the double doors and stands to the side.

Persephone enters.

The restaurant is only half-full, but every man turns his head when she steps inside. I understand why. She's a beautiful woman.

I study her as she looks around. She hasn't spotted me yet. I'm in the far corner at my usual table.

She takes in the space. The restaurant is a good size with several alcoves leading to other rooms. Heavy velvet onyx curtains separate the spaces. Dark wallpaper with the repeating letter H in gold leaf adorns the walls and sconces cast a soft light throughout. The large windows are tinted slightly so the interior is wholly separate from the outside world. The curtains that drape them are tied back with thick golden ropes.

A uniformed bartender stands polishing a glass behind the antique bar and soft music plays in the background.

When she finally spots me, she stops as if startled. As if she didn't expect to see me.

I get up, button my jacket, nod my greeting.

It takes her a moment and I see her stand up a little taller, steeling her spine in preparation for our meeting, I imagine.

She's wearing a cream-colored suit jacket and a matching pencil skirt. Beneath her jacket is a white blouse with lace ruffles. Those ruffles flutter out at her wrists, too. Her dark hair is pulled back tightly from her face and she's clutching a leather bag too small to hold the documents I left for her.

Her heels click delicately, and I don't miss how the eyes of every man in here slide over her lithe body. Hell, I don't blame them, but the predator inside me is rattled.

Mine.

She stops before my table and her unreadable violet eyes lock on mine.

I remember those eyes. I know how they look when she's aroused. I know how her lips part just so as she pants.

I clear my throat when what I need to do is adjust my cock.

"Hades," she says, her voice like smooth ice. She's a

woman now. No hint of the girl who first named me Hades. The one I carried out of the chapel that Halloween night.

"Persephone." I make a point of letting my gaze slide over her before returning my eyes to hers. "Welcome."

She snorts, pulls out her own chair and sits before she's invited to.

I sit too as a waiter appears. "Sir."

"Something to drink?" I ask her.

She looks up at him. "Coffee, please."

"Clear my plate and bring us some coffee," I tell the server.

Persephone snorts again, studies me. "Let me guess, they don't take orders from women."

"Correct. It is a gentlemen's club."

"You're using that word loosely, then?"

I smile, lean back in my seat and study her. Apart from our short meeting last night, the last time I saw her was five years ago. And I remember it like it was yesterday.

She holds my gaze and I wonder if she's remembering that night too. And I know she is when her cheeks flush red and she clears her throat, busying herself with whatever is inside her bag.

The waiter returns with coffee. After laying everything out, he picks up the silver carafe and pours us each a steaming cup.

"That'll be all," I tell him without looking away from her. I pick up my cup.

She moves the coffee to the side and takes a stack of papers out of her bag. She sets them on the table and pushes them toward me. They're the contracts I'd delivered last night. Ripped in two.

I'm not surprised. I never expected her to sign them.

That's not the contract she'll be signing at all today. Ultimately, yes, but not today.

"I'm not handing over my family's company to you."

"Then hostile takeover it is."

"That is your M.O., isn't it?"

"I've already spoken with members on the board. I have the votes I need if you insist on forcing my hand."

She grits her teeth and glares at me. "Who?"

"You'll lose more than you would accepting my offer," I add on, choosing not to answer her question. "I've been generous."

"Generous?"

I take another sip then set the coffee down. "When are you moving out?" I ask, taking up the question of the house which I now own.

At that, she falters, fidgeting in her seat before pouring cream into the coffee she won't drink and stirring for what seems like an eternity.

When she finally looks up at me, it's not the confident businesswoman who walked in here just moments ago. It's the little girl I first met crying over her stepmother's broken doll.

But that's gone as quickly as it came as she narrows her eyes at me.

"What do you want?" she asks.

I gesture to the contracts on the table. "You know what I want."

"Why? You don't need the money. Your businesses are profitable enough for a hundred lifetimes. You don't need to take over my family's company."

She's done her research. Good. "No, I don't *need* to, you're right. I just want to. When are you moving out?"

"What would Nora think if she knew?"

My jaw tightens. "Nora would say it was about time. But she can't say anything anymore, can she?" I lean toward her. "Do not bring up my sister again."

She exhales, shifts her gaze sideways. Thick lashes shield her eyes momentarily. That was a low blow and she knows it.

"That house has been the Abbot family home for generations," she says.

"I know your history."

"My father isn't in a position—"

"Your father made poor business decisions which left you vulnerable." He'd taken some gambles in his career. I don't mention my part in those gambles. But then he'd gotten involved with the wrong people when he needed capital. I'm not even certain it was an accident that left him lying in that coma.

"And let me guess. You saw an opportunity," she says.

"I am a businessman."

"What is it you really want, Hades?"

"I like how you say my name, Persephone."

"Then I won't say it again. Although it fits, doesn't it? God of the underworld. Satan himself."

"That's not quite right. You need to brush up on your mythology. And here I thought I was helping you."

"By stealing our business and our home out from under us?"

"Who broke off the engagement?" I ask out of the blue. "You or Jonas?" Jonas is my asshole stepbrother.

She falters, her face flushing. "That's none of your business."

"So, it was him?"

She opens her mouth, closes it. Her jaw tightens as she grits her teeth.

I grin, oddly proud of her. "No, not Jonas. It was you."

"Why does it matter to you?"

"I'm just glad you came to your senses."

"This is none of your business."

"I think it is my business. We share history, remember?"

Again, she shifts her gaze.

"Or don't you want to remember?"

"Stop."

"You looked beautiful last night, by the way. I don't think I mentioned it."

"Well, thanks. That just means the world to me. Asshole."

"I prefer that dress to this suit. Leaves more of you for the eye to enjoy."

"Fuck you."

"Is that an invitation?"

She tilts her head to the side. "Are you hard up for a fuck? Is that what this is about? You want to get in my pants, *Hayden*?"

I lean toward her. "Been there, sweetheart."

She flushes a deep red and has no comeback as she glances nervously around.

"Back to my question. When are you moving out?"

"I can't move my dad out."

"Why not? It's not like he'd know. He's a fucking vegetable."

"He's not. He's breathing on his own and there's brain activity."

For a moment, I feel sorry for her. But then I remember who she's talking about. What kind of man he is. What he did.

"I'll tell you what," I start. "I'll arrange for him to be

moved. You won't be able to afford that given your current financial situation."

"If you're trying to shame me, remember I lived half my life poor."

"The wrong half."

"Do you want me to beg? Is that it?"

"Would you? Would you get on your knees right here and beg me to let you stay in *my* house?"

"You'd make me do that?"

"Oh, sweetheart, I'd make you do a lot worse."

"Why do you hate us so much?"

I grit my teeth, wishing my coffee was a whiskey. "How rude of me," I start. "I haven't even asked how Lizzie's doing." Lizzie—Elizabeth—is her younger sister. A handful from what I've heard, one her mother, Irina, shipped off to boarding school as soon as the girl could walk. "She's back home, isn't she?" The only reason she's back is the old bitch couldn't make tuition.

"Home is where she should be. Where she belongs."

"I'm sure Irina is thrilled with that."

"She isn't."

I study her as she picks up her coffee, brings it to her mouth, then sets it back down. I wait for her to make the next move. To set the real play in motion.

"I can pay you," she offers.

Here we go. I raise my eyebrows.

"I mean, I can buy the house back. I can make payments and—"

I chuckle, shake my head. "You won't have a job when I take over Abbot Enterprises."

"I have money. I can get—"

"Sweetheart, you're embarrassing yourself."

"And you care? It's what you want, isn't it? Me on my knees? Quite literally."

"I wouldn't mind you on your knees, but I'd keep you busy doing something more...enjoyable."

Her eyes lock on mine as she understands my meaning. She shakes her head, does that snort thing again. She's a snob. Has been since she set foot in her daddy's big house.

She leans toward me. "You want me to suck you off? Is that what it will take for you to back off? You want that here too? Here and now? Me on my knees under the table getting my face fucked by the great Hayden Montgomery for everyone to see?"

"The idea does appeal."

"You're unbelievable."

"But it's not enough. And besides, I'm not interested in my brother's sloppy seconds."

"I'm not...we never..." she falters, starting but stopping. She looks around, her cheeks flushed. "How dare you?"

"Oh, I dare." But I'm surprised to have struck a nerve. Noted. "You're not what?" I probe, my mind working to fill in the blank spaces she leaves.

Her eyes narrow, jaw tight.

"Sloppy seconds?" I ask.

Her cheeks burn.

I study her reaction. It takes me a moment to process.

She rubs her face with both hands and when she looks at me again, her eyes are watery. Tears make them shine, make them sparkle like jewels. I'd forgotten that detail. Forgotten how pretty she is when she cries.

Fuck. My dick's getting hard again.

I raise my hand and a waiter appears.

"Whiskey."

He's gone and back in a minute. I pick up the glass and drink a big swallow.

"Early for that, isn't it?" she asks.

I check my watch. "I have a meeting," I lie. "Let's wrap this up. You want a reprieve? Time?"

She swallows, nods.

"Then you finish your sentence. You never what with Jonas?"

She sits ramrod straight in her seat, eyes hard. "You're a smart guy. I'm sure you can figure it out."

I lean back, tilt my head to the side. "You never fucked?"

She clears her throat, unable to hold my gaze. Her shoulders collapse a little.

I let out a chuckle, more out of disbelief than anything else. "But you were engaged."

"We didn't. Period."

My body relaxes a little. I didn't realize it was tense. I clear my throat. "I know Jonas and I don't believe you."

"What I don't believe is that I'm even having this conversation with you," she mutters, obviously flustered. She lowers her lashes momentarily, again picking up her cold coffee, even taking a sip this time before facing off with me again. "This isn't any of your business."

"Then why mention it?"

"You suggested I was...sloppy seconds. That's a disgusting term by the way."

"Why did you come to me with the contracts torn?"

"What?"

"You want to make a deal? A different deal? Is that it?" I drink a sip of my whiskey and watch her. "How far are you willing to go to save your house?"

She stares at me and I see the battle inside her head, the

urge to tell me to go fuck myself warring with the knowledge that her options are very limited.

"How far?" I probe.

She sits up taller, takes an audible breath in. "This is insane, and I don't like what you're suggesting."

"What am I suggesting?"

She seals her lips shut and folds her arms protectively across her chest.

"You want to play with the big boys, you'll need to grow up, Persephone." I push my chair back and stand. "Be out of the house before the end of the week." I take a step away.

"Wait."

I stop.

She looks beyond me, shakes her head as if having an internal conversation with herself. Her forehead furrows and it takes her a long time to speak. "I'm telling you the truth about Jonas and me."

"You never fucked."

She rubs her forehead, her hand trembling when she does. When she looks back at me, I don't see anger. What I see is fear. And desperation.

"Are you going to ask me to prove it next?" her voice falters, trembles like her hand.

"I could check..." I start because I can't resist.

"You know what? Fuck you!" She's on her feet so fast she almost knocks her chair over. "Just fuck you, Hayden Montgomery!" She bends to pick up her bag, takes a step away then changes her mind and turns back to me. "When I first met you that day on the curb, you know what I thought?"

It takes me a moment to follow her train of thought. She means when I'd found her and Nora with that broken doll.

"What?" I ask. I shouldn't care what she thought but I do. Always have.

"I thought you were going to be my hero. Hades come to steal me away from my wicked stepmother."

"You're mixing up your fairytales."

"Oh, you know what I mean."

She holds my gaze and all I can think is how those eyes used to look at me and all that talk about used goods, it doesn't matter. Never did. Not with her.

But her revelation changes things.

Changes the past.

"Sit down," I tell her.

"And then there was the other time."

Every muscle in my body coils at the memory of that *other time*. "I said sit."

She sits. Her eyes glisten with unshed tears. "But I was wrong."

"That's one thing we can agree on. You were wrong."

She suddenly looks so tired and I'm not surprised. She's carrying the bulk of the burden of her father's situation, not to mention the financial consequences, on her shoulders.

And then there's what I'm doing.

"Yeah, I was wrong. And now, I'm desperate and you know it." She swallows. Those unshed tears must be burning her eyes.

"Are you putting yourself on the table?" I ask because I cannot and will not let those tears sway me.

"Is that what you want?"

"Let's be very clear. You own this. Answer my question."

"I have no choice."

"Don't play the fucking victim, Persephone. That's weak. And it's not who you are." We study one another for a long minute before I speak. "At least not who you were. You have a choice. Always. Now answer my question but think carefully first. I'm not playing games."

She takes a long minute to answer and I know that some part of her knew she'd use this today, she'd bargain with this one thing, even if she couldn't consciously acknowledge it.

And I can see it's easier to paint me as the villain. Make me the man who took her to his bed against her will. But fuck that.

"Yes," she finally says.

I nod. Stand. "You'll have a new contract today."

Her eyes grow infinitesimally wider like she can't believe this is actually happening.

"Go home. I'll be in touch," I say.

"Is that my dismissal?" she almost recovers, that cool arrogance back.

"I don't think you're one to be dismissed."

She bites her lip and can't hold my gaze. She pushes her chair back and takes a deep breath in.

She stands and busies herself with something inside her bag and I think she's talking herself into not crying. Not here. Not in front of me.

Without a goodbye, she turns to leave.

"He stole her away simply because he wanted her," I call out before she's taken two steps away.

She stops.

"Not to save her from anything," I finish.

She turns back to me, studies me with those shimmering jewel-eyes. "You forget one thing," she finally says.

"What's that?"

"Hades loved Persephone."

3

PERSEPHONE

Hades loved Persephone.

I am an idiot. And a masochist to be considering making a deal like this with that man.

My drive home is a blur. I take in the Montgomery house as I turn into our driveway. I remember when it was beautiful. Since the fire, it's almost as though the earth around it has come to life. Like it's determined to take back what it believes belongs to it.

The Montgomery and the Abbot families share a cul-de-sac. Two massive mansions bound together but seemingly set apart from the rest of the world.

I push the button and the gates slide open. I see my stepmother, Irina's, car parked at the front door. My father's nurse, Celia, is here too. Her older model Honda looks out of place in this neighborhood.

I pull into my usual spot and climb out, hugging my coat to myself. I take a moment to look at the darkening sky. They're predicting snow. Several feet of it.

Movement catches my eye at the Montgomery ruin but when I turn to look, I see nothing. No one.

Maybe it's Nora or her grandfather.

They died within days of each other. He in the fire that destroyed the house, she in the chapel by her own hand.

I shake off the chill that accompanies the thought. They've been dead for five years and there's no such thing as ghosts.

It's what I tell myself every time I think I see something.

I wonder where Hayden is staying. Maybe at his club?

Hayden's grandfather had left him the building when he'd passed away. That was one of the things that had turned father against son in an already tenuous relationship. Hayden's father, Jeremiah, had believed it his right to inherit the dilapidated building along with the rest of the Montgomery fortune, which was built on real estate, much like the Abbot fortune. My father was the third of the Abbots to add politics to his résumé.

Hayden was Jeremiah's first-born. Jeremiah was a senior in high school, his sweetheart a sophomore. She'd gotten pregnant and given birth to Hayden and his twin brother, Ares, just before she turned seventeen, and then she'd disappeared. Word was that she and her parents were paid off by Hayden's grandfather to leave town without the boys and it made sense because Hayden's grandfather took them in.

Jeremiah met and married Carry, Jonas's mother, when he was closer to thirty. He formally adopted Jonas, who was only a year younger than Hayden, giving him the Montgomery name. They adopted Nora soon after that.

The Montgomery house belonged to Hayden's grandfather and he lived in the house with Jeremiah and his new wife and family. I remember how intimidating the older Mr. Montgomery was. How scary I always thought him, especially given the stories Nora told me.

I was sixteen when Hayden's grandfather passed away in the fire that Halloween night, two days before my father found Nora at the chapel. I remember my parents discussing it at the dinner table weeks later. Remember the rumors my stepmother never tired of recycling about my dead best friend.

Strange how similar mine and Hayden's stories are. We both have our wicked stepmothers. But my father never turned against me. And I love my half-sister.

Jonas and Hayden hate each other with a passion. Ares, the few times I've had contact with him, seemed better able to handle his father than Hayden ever did.

The front door of the house opens, and I watch Celia step outside. Irina is behind her, cigarette in her hand. She's still in a robe and looks a little worse for wear after the party. She watches me from the front door. I want to talk to Celia before she leaves.

"Celia," I say, walking quickly toward her. The temperature seems to have dropped since earlier this morning and a cool wind has picked up.

She smiles to me. "Percy, I'm glad I didn't miss you."

"How is he?"

She gives me that usual sort of sad look that says I'm denying the truth. "He's the same."

"Well, that's good, right?"

"Sure. Listen," she glances back at the house. "The cigarettes...she shouldn't smoke inside and certainly not in his room."

"She's smoking in his bedroom?" God. What is wrong with her?

Celia unlocks the car door. "I tried to tell her."

"I'm sure she was very receptive. I'll talk to her."

She puts her hand on my arm. "Don't, Percy. It'll just

upset you. And it doesn't matter. It's good you decided to move him. You're making the right decision."

"Move him?" I'm confused.

"Yes. That's what I was told at least. We'll be back later this afternoon." She looks up at the sky. "Before the blizzard, I hope."

"I'm sorry, what? Who told you we're moving him?"

She looks at me strangely.

"I haven't decided yet," I continue. "And I want to be close. Besides, I can't afford—" I stop.

Hayden.

My breathing becomes harder as my hands fist.

"Listen, I'll be honest with you. It's better for your father to be in a facility. It's better for everyone."

I can't hear her right now, though. How dare he?

She checks her watch. "I need to go. I'm late for my next patient. I'll see you later today. I'm coming back to help."

I nod because I can't speak.

"It'll be okay. You'll see." She gives me a hug and I realize how much I miss the warmth of another person.

When she's gone, I turn to climb the stairs to the front door which Irina closes before I get there.

I enter the big house and unbutton my coat. It's cool inside, although warmer than out there.

"Irina," I call out, following the waft of cigarette smoke up the stairs to her room.

I knock when I get to her door and open it when she doesn't reply. I find two open suitcases on the bed and a maid folding clothes into them.

Irina walks out of the closet carrying a smaller Louis Vuitton case.

"What's going on?" I ask.

She hands the case off to the maid and turns to me, taking a drag on her cigarette.

"I'm going on a trip. Should make you happy."

"Trip where?"

"Florida."

"Florida? Why?" She only goes to Florida to visit her plastic surgeon.

"Because I hate snow." The cigarette is down to a stub and she puts it out in the already full ashtray on the nightstand beside the bed.

All her furniture is still here. She refused to give anything up. I wonder how my father could stand her. She's the most selfish woman I know. But maybe he couldn't. They haven't shared a bedroom in years, and I did the math. She was pregnant with Lizzie when they got married.

"We can't afford any procedures. You do realize that?"

"It's not coming out of your tight wallet, Percy."

"Then whose?"

She grins. "Hayden Montgomery." She gives me a once over and I read the hate in her eyes. "I wonder what you did for him to have been so generous with me."

I open my mouth to tell her off but stop. If Hayden wants to pay to send her away, fine. I'm not going to argue that. That's between them. And she can think whatever she wants about me.

"What about Lizzie?" I ask.

"What about her?"

"You can't take her with you. She's got to go to school."

"Oh," she chuckles. "I'm not taking her with me. She's all yours. You always did think you knew best with *my* daughter."

I don't argue. It's true.

"Now you can deal with her. If you don't mind, my flight leaves in two hours."

"And dad?"

She walks up to me, gives me a wicked grin, takes my shoulders and squeezes hard. "He's a vegetable. Face it, Percy." Her stale coffee and cigarette breath make me nauseous.

"Well," I tell her, stepping backward. "I won't keep you." I turn to walk away but when I get to the door, she calls out my name and I stop.

"He'll bring you down a notch, you know."

I don't turn to face her.

"Like you deserve."

"Have a good trip, Irina." I walk out the door, refusing to engage. She spews poison. It's her special gift in life. I go to my father's room and am surprised to find it freezing as I approach. When I enter, I see Lizzie closing the window.

"Why is it so cold in here?" I ask, going to my father, pulling another blanket up over him.

Lizzie shakes her head and turns to me. "Mom said she wanted to air it out. Hide the fact that she was smoking in here is more like it," she says, looking at dad. "I turned the heating up. It'll warm up fast." Apart from this room, Lizzie's room and, of course, Irina's room, the house is cold. We can't even afford to heat the place anymore.

"Thanks Lizzie." I study my half-sister. She looks more like her mom than our dad, but she has his bright-blue eyes. "How are you doing?"

She shrugs a shoulder and turns to me, pulling the sleeves of her sweater into her hands and wrapping her arms around herself.

I think how much older than fifteen the makeup makes

her look but, in her eyes, I see a little girl. A sad, scared little girl.

"I'm fine. Happy she's leaving."

I'm sure she'd be happier to have Irina be a real mother to her. "Why aren't you at school by the way?"

"Canceled. Snow."

"Already?"

"Yeah. I'm spending the night at Marigold's." Marigold lives closer to their school. "I'll go over for dinner."

"Do you think that's a good idea? I mean with school—"

"You're not my mother, Percy," she snaps and walks to the door.

"I didn't mean—"

"I'll take the bus so you can stay with dad."

"I can drive you."

She shakes her head and stops, turns to me. "It's fine." She shifts her gaze over my shoulder to our father and I see how her eyes glisten with tears. "He knows we're here, right?"

"He knows. I'm sure of it." I'm not.

She walks out of the room without another word.

4

PERSEPHONE

Having changed into an old, worn hoodie and yoga pants, I'm on my way downstairs searching for a number for the club to find out what's going on with my father when the doorbell rings.

I check the time. Sotheby's is sending trucks to pick up the antique dining and living room sets today, but they're not scheduled to come until late afternoon. I wonder if it's the snow that's got them out here early.

But when I get to the door, I don't see a truck. Instead, a man in a suit is standing at the front door. He looks vaguely familiar, but I don't know from where and I wonder if I shouldn't have left the gate open.

I open the door and he stands up taller.

"Yes?" I ask. "Can I help you?"

He holds out a large black envelope with the letters HM embossed in decorative gold at the center.

"Ah," I look up at the man again and I remember. "You work at the club." He's the one who'd let me in this morning.

"Yes, Ms. Abbot. Mr. Montgomery sent this. He said you'd know what it is."

"He didn't waste any time, did he? I was just searching for his phone number."

"You'll find what you need inside. I need to get back." With that, he turns and begins his return to his car which I can see now is parked along the curb.

"Wait. I need to get in touch with Hade—Mr. Montgomery."

"He's left instructions."

Before I can get another word in, he's gone and I'm standing in the doorway holding the ominous black envelope.

I glance over at the Montgomery house next door, thinking how beautiful it once was. I shake my head, closing the door behind me. Walking inside, I go straight to my father's study. Since the accident, I've taken it over. I sit behind the desk and open the envelope, take out the single sheet inside.

In the few minutes it takes me to read it, I feel my ears burn with growing rage.

"No wonder it didn't take him long to draw this up," I say out loud, turning it over, looking for a phone number. When I don't find one, I peer inside the envelope for a card but it's empty.

His instructions, however, are clear, and the reality of what I did—our conversation from this morning—slams me in the face.

This new contract gives him exclusive rights over me, my time, and my person in any capacity he chooses. I am to submit to his commands and make myself available for his pleasure.

For his pleasure!

In exchange, I will be given the right to live rent-free in my own home as Mr. Montgomery's *guest*.

"How generous, you fucking asshole."

The doorbell rings again.

I get up, fist the contract in my hand, assuming it'll be the same man who just delivered this. But when I get to the door, I find two men from Sotheby's standing outside. The shorter one is holding a clipboard and smiling at me.

"Ms. Abbot?"

"Yes, you're from Sotheby's," I say, my mind on that idiotic contract. He wants me to be his whore in exchange for living as *his* guest in *my* house! "Come in."

"We're here to pick up the dining and living room sets and—"

"It's fine. Just...I need to do something."

"If you can show us where the things are, we can take care of it."

Lizzie appears at the top of the stairs. I look at her, see how her face falls at the sight of the men here to take our things. This isn't their first trip out here. I'd left her room as intact as possible, but we'll need to sell everything.

Unless I sign the contract in my hand.

"Lizzie, I need to go. Can you help these men?"

"Where are you going?"

"Into town."

"But I told Marigold I'd be there by five. I don't want to be late."

"I'll be back in time and I'll take you. Please don't leave dad alone."

"I wouldn't. Christ, Percy. I can't believe you think I would!" Annoyed, Lizzie turns to the men. "This way."

I grab my coat, slip into a pair of running shoes and head out to the driveway, dreaming of telling him exactly where he can shove his contract even though I know what I'm going to have to do.

It takes me twice as long to get to the club with the snow that's falling in thick flakes now. But the man who showed me in this morning and dropped off the envelope just a little while ago doesn't seem surprised to see me again.

I realize when I leave my car with the valet that I forgot my purse and phone. I just came clutching that stupid contract.

"Where is he?" I ask, peering back to the entrance of the restaurant where we'd met earlier.

The man blocks my path. "If you'll have a seat, I'll let Mr. Montgomery know you're here."

"I'll let him know myself." I walk around him, and he follows close on my heels, telling me to wait as I push the curtain back and reach for the doorknob. I open it, and, opposite this morning, almost every table is full, and all the men seem to stop their conversations and look up at me when I enter.

"Ms. Abbot," the man on my heels says again, this time a bit more forcefully. "If you'll wait, I will find Mr. Montgomery for you."

I look at the table on its raised dais where we'd sat earlier but it's empty. I guess that one's reserved for his exclusive use. How arrogant to have it raised as if it's a throne and he's the king.

Although I guess here, he is king.

I walk toward the curtain I saw earlier behind which I hear more sounds, men talking more quietly, then something else. Something different. A slap?

"Miss," the man closes his hand over my arm to stop me when I reach for the curtain.

I look down at where he's touching me, open my mouth to protest, but suddenly, I don't have to.

"Peter," comes Hayden's deep voice.

Peter and I both turn to find Hayden stalking toward us, looking every bit the predator he is with his dark suit and narrowed eyes on Peter's hand which is still closed around my upper arm.

"Sir," Peter says, clearing his throat and releasing me instantly. "I was..." he falters.

Hayden looks me over. I look down at myself, at my open coat, the hoodie that's really meant more for inside the house than outside it, yoga pants and—shit—mismatched sneakers.

In my haste, I'd put on one of mine and one of Lizzie's. How?

And why now of all the days?

I clear my throat when his eyes return to mine.

He arches his eyebrows.

I tuck my hair behind my ear. I'd let it down but hadn't bothered to brush it out and am suddenly very conscious of it. I hadn't even looked in a mirror before I'd stalked out of my house and come here to tell him off. All the while, he still looks perfect, impeccable in his tailored suit. Looking right at home in his expensive club, with his initials in gold all over the walls.

"Narcissist," I say.

He cocks his head to the side but either ignores my comment or knows it's true so doesn't bother denying it. "Were you anxious to deliver the contract in person?"

I step toward him, hating how I have to crane my neck to look up at him. He's at least a foot taller than me and now that I'm not wearing heels, the difference puts me at an even greater disadvantage.

I steel my spine when he doesn't budge, his eyes sparkling with amusement and his lip quivering with suppressed laughter.

"No, not anxious to deliver it. You didn't include your phone number anywhere. I can't call you."

"I will happily give you my phone number. I didn't realize you were interested," he says with a wink.

"I imagine it's hard for you but try not to be a dick."

I notice heads snap toward us, but he doesn't seem bothered. His smile widens, in fact. Like the cat who just swallowed the canary.

I clear my throat. He may not be embarrassed but I certainly am.

That slapping sound comes again from behind the curtain followed by a girl's moan. "What the hell's going on in there, anyway?"

"This isn't a good time," he says. "I have an appointment—"

"You have an appointment? I have a life! Sorry to be an inconvenience while you take it over."

"Go home. We'll do this later."

"No." I dig my heels in.

He pauses, smirks. "No?"

"No. We'll do this now."

"Fine, if you insist."

He takes my elbow and steers me away, tightening his grip when I try to free myself.

"Let me go."

"It's a gentlemen's club, Persephone. Not for ladies. And you're causing a scene."

"Like you care."

"I don't, but I thought you might. Isn't Senator Barnes a family friend?" he asks, gesturing to the senator sitting a few tables away watching us.

I'd been so angry I hadn't even looked around. Now that I do, I see more than one face I recognize.

"Smile and nod," Hayden says.

I do.

He leads us to an elevator that I don't even recognize as one until the wood paneled doors slide open and we step inside. He only releases me once the doors close. He punches some numbers on the keypad and the elevator begins its ascent.

I turn to him, catch a glimpse of myself in the mirror against the wall. I look at us together.

I look like something the cat dragged in.

He, on the other hand, well, he's the cat who did the dragging.

"Where are we going?"

"My office."

At the thirteenth floor, the elevator dings and the doors slide open.

"I thought buildings didn't have a thirteenth floor. Bad luck or something."

"Good and bad are a matter of perspective."

I look around the large room with windows overlooking the city. The furnishings are dark, like in the club, leather and polished wood and chrome. Masculine, like I'd expect. There's nothing soft in this room.

At least the walls aren't plastered with his initials here.

"Drink?" he asks.

I turn to find him pouring himself a whiskey.

"No, thanks." I need to keep my wits about me.

"You sure? You look like you could use one. When's the last time you slept?"

"I look like this because I got home to learn from my father's nurse that he'd be moved today. Then had a conversation with my stepmother about her sudden trip to Florida, compliments of you. Then, after trying to talk to my sister who is lying to me about skipping school, my doorbell rings and I think it's the men from Sotheby's come to pick up our things but no, it's your errand boy," I say, waving the contract around. "And when I ask for a phone number, he runs off, telling me all I need is in that envelope. And this," I shake the paper at him. "This contract is...is insulting and degrading and—"

"What did you think we were doing exactly, Persephone?" he cuts me off casually and I watch how relaxed he looks. His arm on the mantle of the fireplace where the fire crackles softly, drink in his hand, his sly predator's eyes on me.

"What did I think we were doing exactly?"

He nods, sips his drink.

I shift my gaze, scratch my head, shake it, then turn back to him. "Do you snap your fingers and people just do what you tell them?"

"Yes."

"Unbelievable. You're an arrogant son of a bitch, you know that?"

"I never knew my mother so I can't say." He's casual, watching me over the rim of his glass, but I don't miss how his posture just stiffened. "Let me get you that drink before you say something you'll regret." He walks to the bar and pours me a vodka.

I don't refuse it when he hands it to me. Instead, I drink a big sip. "I don't drink during the day," I tell him.

"Clearly."

"This isn't...I'm not—"

"Are you going to miss Irina?" he asks.

"Well, no."

"But you're upset I sent her away?"

"I'm upset that you just inserted yourself into my life and

not only sent her away but then you're taking my father away. Not to mention the house or the company."

"I'm not taking your father away. I'm getting him the care he needs. The care you can no longer afford."

"You don't give a crap about him. You said yourself he's a vegetable."

"You're right. I don't care about him. I care about me. I'm clearing my own path. I don't want anything getting in the way of having you in my bed, Persephone."

5

HAYDEN

S he's clearly taken aback.

I watch her swallow the rest of the vodka. The way she looks right now with her mismatched shoes, messy hair and tired eyes, she's a little lost. No, a lot lost. And out of her league.

"Take off your coat and sit down."

She inhales deeply, walks to the couch and sits but keeps her coat on.

"Have you eaten today?"

"What?"

"Have you eaten anything?"

She presses the heel of her hand to her forehead, squeezes her eyes shut. "I don't remember."

"You need to eat."

"Please don't pretend to care."

"I'm not pretending."

Her eyes narrow.

"I take care of what's mine," I add, just to be clear.

She snorts, leaning her head against the back of the couch and folding her arms across her chest.

I walk to my desk, push a button on the phone. Peter answers immediately. "Get some food up here. A sandwich. Something substantial." I stop, remembering. "Are you still a vegetarian?"

She nods.

"Vegetarian," I amend.

"Yes, sir," he replies, and I disconnect the call.

She finishes her drink. "I want to be close to my father."

"The facility is a half-hour drive away."

"You had no right to do it behind my back."

"It wasn't behind your back. I believe I mentioned it. This was simply efficient."

She sighs, sits back and looks at the contract still in her hand. The elevator dings and a few moments later, the doors slide open.

We both turn to watch Peter and a waiter enter. The waiter carries a tray inside and sets it on the coffee table. He takes the cover off the plate and at my nod, they both leave.

"Eat," I tell her.

She looks at the sandwich, a baguette with brie and some greens, with a small side salad. She then slides her arms out of her coat and picks up the sandwich, takes a bite, making a point of looking at me as she chews.

I drink my whiskey and watch her.

She'll be turning twenty-one soon. Last time I saw her she was sixteen years old and too drunk to stand on her own. Although Jonas wouldn't admit it, I think he'd put something in her drink. And the way she was with me afterward, when I brought her home, that's not just alcohol.

It was Halloween night. I still remember the lightning storm. It's what had caused the fire at our house.

After overhearing the argument between my grandfather and father, I'd gone out to the chapel ruins avoiding the party. It's where I always used to go on nights I felt shitty. But that particular night was different. I'd heard my grandfather angry, but I'd never heard him sound like he had that night.

As I approached the chapel that straddled both Abbot and Montgomery properties, I saw the light of lanterns burning inside. I might have changed direction if I hadn't heard her. I might have opted to leave. But I had heard her, Persephone, and she'd sounded wrong.

She wasn't screaming for help or anything like that, but she sounded off, like she couldn't scream. And she sounded scared.

When I'd gotten close, I'd seen the three of them through the glass-less windows. Jonas, Nora and Persephone. Nora and Jonas didn't see me right away, but I remember how Persephone had looked at me when she did. She turned her head as I got near like she felt me coming before I even stepped out of the shadows.

Jonas and Nora wore strange black cloaks. I remember how dark the circles under Nora's eyes were, thinking it must be Halloween makeup. She didn't look like herself and it struck me strangely.

"Don't let her up," Jonas had told Nora.

Persephone's mouth was open, jaw slack, and she just looked out of it. She was lying on the altar, trying to get up, but Nora had her hands on her shoulders, whispering something to her. I remember how strange I thought it was that Nora would be keeping her down on Jonas' command. How not like my sweet sister.

The skirt of Persephone's costume—because they'd come from the party at our house—was raised to her belly. I still remember my stepbrother's hand bruising her thigh.

I remember how enraged he'd looked when I'd slammed the door against the stone wall and stalked into the church.

I wonder how much of that night she remembers. How much of what happened after.

"Happy?" Persephone asks, drawing me back into the present.

She's eaten about a quarter of the sandwich.

"I'd be happier if you ate the whole thing."

"Why are you back? I mean, why now?" she asks, ignoring me.

I've been away for five years. That's not to say I haven't been here in those years, but when I was, I always stayed at the club. Never went anywhere she'd see me.

"It was time."

"You waited until after my dad's accident to make a move on Abbot Enterprises."

"That's not true. Plans were in the works for some time before the accident. Your father knew."

"He never mentioned anything."

"No, I guess he wouldn't. He was ridiculously optimistic about trying to save the company, the house and his reputation."

"He's not ridiculous."

"Ridiculously optimistic. There's a reason I was able to do what I did, Persephone. He left himself wide open and if it wasn't me, it'd be someone else."

"No one would take our home from us."

"The bank would. Isn't it better off on my watch?"

"Nothing's better off on your watch."

"No? I remember a night when you were grateful for it."

She goes quiet, shifts her gaze away. Her cheeks flush and she takes a deep breath in. "Just tell me why you're doing this."

"It wouldn't change things."

"Tell me. I deserve to know."

"Deserve," I snort. "Does Nora deserve to be in the ground?"

"What?"

I swallow my drink, let it burn. "You couldn't handle the why, Persephone," I say more harshly than I intend. I pick up her glass and refill both. I set hers back down on the table before her.

"What does that mean? What you said about Nora?"

"Let me give you some advice. Trust me when I tell you to leave it alone."

"But I don't trust you."

Her words make me flinch. I watch her drink a sip of vodka and tell myself I'm right. That learning the truth would destroy her.

But isn't that what I want? The destruction of the Abbot family just like Quincy Abbot destroyed the only good in mine?

"Why did you break off the engagement to my brother?" I ask because I need to know.

She glances at the glass in her hands and when she looks back at me, her eyes are darker. Sadder. She puts the drink down and picks up the contract which looks abused now.

"You said you'd give me back the house," she says, not answering my question. I'm not the only one keeping secrets.

"I don't think I ever said those words."

"You inferred them."

"I disagree. The house belongs to me. Period. But I'm not unreasonable. I have my own home. You sign the contract and you'll be allowed to carry on with your life in the house like you always have."

"But it will still be in your name. *You* will own it."

"Correct."

"As you said, you have your own house. What do you want with ours?"

"I haven't decided yet. We were discussing the contract itself."

"You're the one who brought up my engagement to Jonas."

"Which you don't want to talk about."

"Fine." She looks down at the contract. "I'm not going to give you, how did you put it, *my person*," she reads. "And make myself available *for your pleasure* so I can continue to live in my house with you as what? My landlord?"

"Rent-free," I add with a grin, and watch her eyes burn as she grows angrier.

"I want the house back in my father's name."

"No pussy is worth that much."

"You're crude."

"You're arrogant."

"What's the difference? I mean, you don't want the house to live in it."

"But I do want the house."

"And what happens if you tire of me?"

"Don't let me tire of you."

"Are you just going to dangle that in front of me as I..." she looks at the contract again. "*Submit to your commands.*"

I grin. "I do like that language."

"It reads like something you'd say. Did you write it up yourself?"

"I did."

"That wasn't meant as a compliment."

"No, I didn't think it was. What's your decision?"

She exhales, her shoulders slumping a little. "What about the company?"

"I want fifty-one percent. Non-negotiable if you don't want a hostile takeover on your hands."

"I hate this."

"You're in debt up to your ears. I saw your house. I saw the state of things. You're having the furniture you have left auctioned off to pay your creditors and even if you got top dollar on every single piece, you wouldn't have enough to do it. Take my offer. It's a good one. A fair one."

"And what do I tell my dad when he wakes up? I sold him out to his enemies?"

I don't reply. Thing is, he isn't going to wake up, and if by some miracle he does, he won't be the same. Not with an injury like he sustained.

Karma's finally paying him back. I do wish I were the one who dealt the blow, though.

"The name of the company stays the same," she says.

I nod.

"And whoever you hire to take my father's place has to consult me on any major decisions."

I snort. "I don't think so."

She grits her teeth. "What about my job?"

"You want to keep your job?"

She nods.

"Fine."

She quiets. "Fine?"

"You'll report to me."

She's hesitant. "I don't like this."

I shrug a shoulder. The odds are stacked against her. She'll agree. "This is entirely up to you. You can walk away. Right now."

"And pack my bags? Tell Lizzie we have nowhere to go?"

"I told you once before not to play the victim card. It's not who you are. Not someone I'd offer a deal like this to."

She quiets and I listen to her breathe, watch her think. "So, you just expect me to sign this?"

"Yes."

"This isn't right."

"Right and wrong, like luck, are a matter of perspective. I'm making a concession. You get to keep your job."

She takes a moment then gets up, walks past me to my desk. She bends to pick up a pen and my gaze shifts to her ass in those tight pants. She amends the contract to state her position at the company then scratches her signature on the contract and something feels different. Not better. Not worse. Just different.

Taking her family down has been the thing that's driven me for the last five years. I'm half-way done.

But with her, there's something else.

I want her. She and I, there's always been something between us. But it's not just some romantic bullshit.

Persephone Abbot belongs to me. She always has. And now, she belongs in my bed, too. And I'll make sure she stays there no matter what I have to do.

She closes the lid on the pen, sets it on top of the contract and turns to me. "What happens now?"

"What happens now?"

She nods.

"You take off your clothes."

6

PERSEPHONE

"What?"

"Take off your clothes," he says more slowly, as if I'm hard of hearing or slow to follow.

I stare at him while he moves to sit down on the leather armchair.

He raises his eyebrows and crosses one ankle over the opposite knee.

"We're doing this here?" I hear the slight tremor in my voice. Does he? "Now?"

He gives me a slow nod while his gaze slides over me. "You insisted, remember?"

Okay. Well. It's going to happen sooner or later. What did I expect? A date? Dinner? I guess he did give me lunch.

But it's hard. Harder than it should be, maybe. At least harder than I thought it would be with him.

I pull the sleeves of my hoodie into my palms and shift my gaze out the window. Snow is coming down hard, melting as soon as it hits the window, leaving wet streaks on the glass.

I can't do this. Not like this.

Traffic has slowed. I don't hear it—I don't hear any noises from outside—but I see it in the blinking red brake lights.

Why did I think I could do this?

"Problem?" comes his deep voice.

Gasping, I jump. I didn't realize he'd gotten up. Or that he's so close behind me that when I turn, I crash into his chest. I can't help but inhale his scent. Powerful and dark and reeking of man.

I can't do this.

His gaze sweeps my face, pauses at my mouth before returning to my eyes. He raises his hand, fingers light as a feather against my temple when he pushes a lock of hair back. He doesn't speak, not right away.

If I do this, I'm finished.

"She wasn't the same when she came back," he says, voice so low it's almost a whisper.

"What?"

"Persephone. She was different."

I lick my lips, swallow.

"Hades stained her," he adds.

I blink, taking in his words, trying to breathe as his dark eyes devour me.

"Like you're going to stain me," I say weakly.

He studies me, and I see the past in his eyes. I see that night. The Halloween party. The drink. Jonas. Nora.

I remember him coming into the chapel. Remember the broken door slamming against the stone wall and the icy, wet wind. I remember shivering on that stone slab.

He'd looked like an angel that night. One who'd fallen lifetimes ago. The darkness that surrounded him, I remember that too.

I see how he looked at Jonas. And I see how he looked at me lying there. Being made to lie there.

Rage.

Like he would murder Jonas.

After he lifted me in his arms, there was lightning, then my memory goes dark for a while. I don't recall the walk back to the house. Don't recall him laying me in my bed or undressing me. I know I couldn't stand my clothes, my skin burning, itching like a million ants were crawling over me.

But I do remember how he looked at me when I was naked.

And I can still see him afterward.

An animal licking his lips after feasting. Me beneath him my legs open. My body slick with sweat and chilled with rain at the same time on that icy night.

"What if I say no?" I ask.

"You won't," he says, and he's not mocking me. Just talking. "It's what you've always wanted. I'm giving you what you've always wanted. What you're too weak to ask for yourself."

"I'm not weak." But he's right.

Hades and I, there's something that binds us. It's always been like this with us. Like a moth to the flame.

Except that I don't know which of us is the moth and which the flame that will burn the other.

He grips my wrists roughly, pushing them behind my back, holding them in one of his hands. His gaze burns with hunger. He's ravenous. But does he know that hunger will devour us both?

"I made a mistake with you," he mutters, eyes out of focus. I think he's talking more to himself than me.

"What?"

He shakes his head and his eyes come back into focus.

And when they do, they're harder. He grips the zipper of the hoodie and his tone is different. "When I tell you to take off your clothes you take off your clothes." He unzips me as he speaks and in moments, the hoodie is hanging open leaving me exposed in just a bra.

He doesn't look down as he pushes his big hand into the waistband of my yoga pants.

"Hayden," I start, trying to wriggle free of his grasp.

I should tell him now.

He slides his hand deeper and I gasp when his fingers slip into my underwear, into the neat mound of hair there before they curl around my sex.

Predator.

Run.

But he has me and I can't. I wouldn't if I could.

"You should...I..."

He flicks his thumb across my clit and my breath catches. He watches me, eyes locked on mine while two fingers slide inside me.

I rise up to tiptoe.

He pauses, a look of surprise crossing his features. He moves his fingers again, testing.

I grit my teeth, not sure what I expect him to do.

He tilts his head, a question in his eyes.

I swallow.

He tests again.

"Persephone?"

I just stare up at him feeling my face burn.

"Are you a virgin?"

Should I lie? Does it matter? I mean, he can tell, obviously he can tell.

He moves his fingers again, pressing against the barrier.

"Persephone?" His eyebrows furrow.

"Does it matter?" I'm trying to sound just a little in control but my voice quakes. "I mean, it's proof I wasn't lying about Jonas at least," I try to sound casual while I'm anything but.

"Persephone—"

"Is it off? Our deal?" I'm not sure a man like him has much use for a virgin when he can bed any woman he wants and preferably an experienced one.

He studies me wordlessly and all I can do is stare up at him, at the green-gold ring around dilated black pupils.

"Is it?" I ask again.

He shakes his head, pulls his hand free. "No."

7

HAYDEN

She's a virgin.

Fuck.

This changes things.

The elevator dings.

Persephone gasps, turning as the doors slide open. I look at my brother's face as he steps into my office. I register his momentary surprise, but he's quick to hide it and a grin spreads across his face.

Ares and I are identical twins, each a mirror image of the other. I wonder if she notices the small details. The cleft in my right eyebrow, my brother's matching one in his left. The dimple in my right cheek, his on his left.

"Didn't realize you had company, brother." Ares says. He doesn't step back onto the elevator, and he isn't subtle as his gaze sweeps a partially undressed Persephone before I can shield her from his view.

"What's going on?" Persephone asks, panicked as she adjusts her yoga pants.

"I told you this wasn't a good time, didn't I?" I tug her hoodie together and zip it up. I lean into her ear. "Were you saving yourself for me?" I whisper so only she hears me.

"What?" She draws back, confused and embarrassed.

"You remember my brother, Ares?" I ask, stepping to the side once she's covered.

She stares at him as if she can't believe this is happening.

"Ares, Persephone," I say to him.

Ares pours himself a whiskey and gives her a one-sided grin. "Percy Abbot. You were always a pretty thing. Although seeing this, I do have to wonder about your taste in men." He winks.

Her cheeks burn red as she fumbles with the hoodie's zipper, trying to tug it even higher.

I drink a sip of whiskey. "You're early," I tell Ares.

He shifts his gaze to me, and the playful smile vanishes. "I have shit to do. I don't work for you, remember. Don't expect me to appear at your summons."

Persephone grabs her coat, puts it on and hugs it to herself. Her face is still fiery red when she turns back to me.

I take her elbow and walk her to the elevator where the doors open immediately. "Shane will take you home. I'll pick you up for dinner at eight," I tell her, pushing the button for the lobby.

"I'm not—"

The doors slide closed. "There's also an auction you'll attend with me tomorrow night. I'll send some dresses. Pick one."

"What auction?"

"Be ready." The elevator doors open. I hold the door open and watch her.

"So that's it?" she asks.

"What did you expect?" I look over her head to Peter. "Have Shane take Ms. Abbot home."

"I have my own car," she says as Peter confirms.

"It's snowing."

"I'm capable of driving in snow. I drove here."

I look her over. "My point."

"I'll drive myself."

"I take care of what's mine."

"You mean you humiliate what's yours. And *temporarily* yours, by the way."

Temporarily. My eyes narrow. I step toward her. "I warned you it wasn't a good time. You insisted."

"And also, I'm not *yours*. We don't live in the dark ages."

"Yes, you are. Accept it." She opens her mouth as I check my watch. "You'll want to hurry if you want to be there when they move your father."

"What?"

"They'll be at your house in a few minutes."

"But—"

"Take a nap, too. You look like you need some rest."

"You're a real jerk, you know that?"

"Miss," Peter says.

She turns to him, then back to me.

"Shane is outside."

She opens her mouth to say something, but I speak first. "Goodbye, Persephone."

I'm not sure what's making her cheeks burn so red, the fact that she's embarrassed or that she's angry, but I pull my arm back and watch her until the elevator doors slide closed and she disappears from view.

8

PERSEPHONE

S hane doesn't speak a word while he brings me home and someone else follows driving my Jeep, parking it on the driveway just out of the way of the ambulance standing there.

I slip out of the car and head to the house. A man opens both front doors before I even get up the stairs. He's in a medical uniform.

Celia walks outside, smiling when she sees me. "Percy, I'm glad you made it! I wasn't sure you would, and I know you wanted to be here for this."

Behind her I see my father's already been arranged on a gurney, the equipment he's attached to close behind.

"How is he?" I ask, going right to him. I pull the blanket up a little higher and fix his hair. "I should have cut his hair," I say absently. "I left it too long."

Celia's hand is on my shoulder. "We'll take care of it, don't worry."

I turn to her and she wipes a tear from my face. I didn't realize I'd started crying.

"It's going to be okay, Percy. I know this is better for him and for you and Lizzie. I would tell you if it weren't."

"I know. It's just...I hate seeing him like this. I guess I'm still not used to it."

"I understand. But you need to leave him with us now. You can visit as often as you like." She glances down but doesn't mention my mismatched sneakers. "You have to look after yourself, too. And Lizzie, I guess, with Irina leaving."

"Where is Lizzie?" I ask, not seeing her here.

"She went to her friend's house. I thought it'd be okay since I was here."

"She already left? I told her I'd drive her."

"I think it's hard for her to see her father like this."

I look down at him again. He's shrunk a little, I think. He was so vibrant. Larger than life.

When I turn back to Celia, she's nodding, smiling sympathetically.

"We'd better get him in the ambulance," one of the men says.

"Yes," Celia answers. "Before he gets cold."

I nod, lean down to kiss my father's forehead. "I'll come as soon as I can. I promise," I whisper, holding onto his hand.

There's no response. No squeezing of my fingers, no blink or anything to acknowledge if he's even heard me.

Celia pats my shoulder and I step backward. The men roll him out, lifting the stretcher to carry it down the stairs while two others follow with the equipment.

"In addition to mine, here's a phone number you can call anytime," Celia says, handing me a card.

"You'll still be his nurse?"

"Yes." She's still smiling. "Listen, Percy, get some rest and think things through. Think about your future. What you want. I know you've been worrying. What's happened is a lot for anyone to manage and you have Lizzie to look out for on top of everything. It's time you planned for yourself and for her. Let us take care of your father and you take care of yourself."

I'm going to full on sob if this continues. I know what she's trying to say. It's just a message I don't want to hear and so I nod and wipe the heels of my hands across my eyes.

"Ready," one of the men says.

"Coming," Celia says. She turns to me. "I'll call you once he's settled."

"Thanks. For everything."

"You're welcome. You're doing the right thing."

She walks out and a few minutes later the driver pulls away. I stand there and watch as snow sticks to the grass and the street, only closing the door once the ambulance is out of sight.

Turning back into the house is strange. It's so eerily quiet now with Irina and Lizzie gone. With dad and his machines gone. I didn't realize I'd always paid attention for them down here too. Always aware of the soft sounds of the monitors, waiting for any change.

I walk into the kitchen, seeing in my periphery the empty living and dining rooms, trying not to think about it.

I've bought us some time and I have my job.

And all I had to do for it was sell my soul.

I remember the look on Hayden's face when he realized I was a virgin. It was strange, like it meant something.

But then the image of Ares walking into his office flashes across my mind and I close my eyes against it. Hayden knew he'd come. He knew it and still humiliated me. I guess he was teaching me a lesson.

I make a cup of tea and stand at the counter drinking it,

watching the snow as it thickens and becomes denser. I drink half of it before thinking I should check on Lizzie.

My purse is still in the study along with the black envelope on the desk. I ignore the envelope and dig for my phone in the bag. I see a text from Lizzie when I pick it up.

"Battery's low and I forgot my charger, so I'll see you when I'm back. Probably wait out the snow here. Dad's fine. Celia was there when I left."

I text her back. "Have a nice night. See you tomorrow." I don't want to pester her about the fact that I'm sure at least one other person at Marigold's house has an iPhone charger she can borrow.

I see a missed call from Jonas. I'm surprised. He hasn't tried to call me in months.

At first, after I broke off the engagement, it was nightly. He was always drunk. I finally stopped picking up, so he left messages. He only stopped leaving those when I threatened to go to the police. I never want to see Jonas Montgomery again. Just the thought of him makes my skin crawl.

I delete the message without listening to it, finish my tea and am about to go upstairs when the doorbell rings.

With a sigh, I go to the front door to open it. I have to remember to close the gate.

Outside are two men each carrying two large black boxes with gold ribbons around them.

"Persephone Abbot?"

"Yes."

"These are for you." Without waiting for me to invite them in, they enter, and I step aside as they set the boxes on the floor when they don't find any tables to put them on. Apart from the coat rack and an old grandfather clock I couldn't bring myself to part with yet, it's empty.

I don't need to ask who the boxes are from. I know.

"If you can sign here," one of the men says, producing an electronic device out of his pocket.

I sign and once they're gone, I take the card that's tucked between the ribbon and the first box, recognize the name of the boutique.

These cost him a pretty penny, but I guess he has enough pennies.

I open the letter and read it.

Looking forward to the fashion show.

Hades.

He refers to himself as Hades. Should I find it strange?

"Arrogant bastard," I mutter to myself and balance the boxes to carry them up to my room in one go. I lay them on the bed and pull the ribbon off the first one. I hate to admit that I'm curious.

I fold back layers of perfumed black tissue paper to unwrap a stunning deep red lace dress. I take it out of the box and hold it up. It's a mermaid style with a deep V cut down the front and a deeper one at the back.

The size is right, and I have to admit, it's gorgeous. I try to remember the last time I wore red. Or a gown like this. The dress I'd worn last night—was it just last night—was beautiful but nothing as extravagant as this.

The next one is a deep emerald green silk that feels amazing. It's floor length and off the shoulder and will hug every curve.

The third is a halter dress in rich sapphire that has a back so low, I'm not sure it would be decent to wear out.

The final box contains matching high-heeled shoes and accessories to go with each dress.

Pretty penny, indeed. I guess he wasn't taking any

chances on my wardrobe considering what I looked like showing up at the club today. I wouldn't either if I were him.

But before I have to think about dinner or the auction or anything else, I need to get some sleep. I'm so over-tired, I can't think straight.

9

HAYDEN

The gates stand wide open when I drive the Range Rover up to the house to park along the circular drive.

It's snowed all afternoon and it's already a foot deep when I step out. I open the trunk to lift out my duffel bag and climb the stairs to the front door. I slide my key into the lock, but find it unlocked.

Opening the door, I shake my head and walk in. I hang my coat on the rack, noticing hers there along with several others. At least one is her father's. She should clean his shit out of the house. He's not coming back. She has to know that.

The house is quiet, and the only light is coming from the kitchen. I check the time. It's about fifteen minutes before eight.

My footsteps echo as I walk toward the kitchen, but no one's here.

I peer into several rooms, finding most of them empty. They were furnished last night but I remember her telling me Sotheby's would be back today.

The study is the only room that still seems to contain most of its furnishings.

I climb the staircase up to the first floor. It's quiet here too.

Irina's gone and good riddance. She jumped at the chance to get out of here and it's worth every penny. I can't stand that woman. Never could, even before Persephone came into the picture.

I don't knock when I get to Persephone's bedroom. Instead, I open the door and step inside, remembering how it looked last night when I'd left the envelope on her pillow. How even the carpet was gone, only the bed, a lamp and an old dresser left.

Quincy Abbot fucked up and his family is paying the price. This isn't how I wanted it. Not the sequence at least. I wanted him to witness the destruction of his family.

I set my bag down when I see her. She's lying on her side, her back to me. The boxes containing the dresses I sent are on the floor but at least she's opened them.

I check the time again but I'm not wrong.

I go to the bed, look down at her.

As if feeling my presence, she moves, rolling onto her back. I think she's going to open her eyes, but she doesn't.

Well, I did tell her to get some sleep.

She stretches an arm over her head. She's wearing a tank top and her hair's strewn wildly about the pillow. Her face is relaxed, soft and sweet and I'm tempted to strip off my clothes and get into the bed.

But I need to remember why I'm here and why she's here.

I think about what we talked about. About Hades staining Persephone. I want to stain her. I've never wanted to mark a woman more than I do her. It's always been like this with her.

I think about her earlier today. My fingers inside her. The shocked look on her face which makes sense now.

A virgin.

I smile. I didn't think it would matter but it makes a difference, this piece of knowledge. I sit on the edge of the bed. She still doesn't stir which I find strange.

And when I see why, a brick settles heavy in my gut.

Bending, I pick up the bottle of prescription sleeping pills lying on the floor beside the lamp. I recognize the name of the pills and my heart hammers against my chest.

What the fuck is she doing with these? These of all the options out there?

But I keep reading. They're not hers. They're Irina's.

"Christ."

I twist off the lid and look inside, count the half-dozen pills then pocket the container and look at her again.

"Persephone."

Nothing.

I peel back the blanket. She's in a silk tank top and panties and I take in all that skin, those long limbs, the expanse of taut belly between her panties and top.

She makes a sound, scrunches up her forehead. She draws her arm down. She must be cold. I get it. It's fucking freezing in the house.

"Persephone," I say again, this time a little more forcefully. I take her shoulders, give them a squeeze, a shake.

She groans but settles back into sleep and I wonder how many of the pills she took. Wonder what the fuck she was thinking.

"Time to wake up," I tell her, pulling her to a seat.

"Mmm." She flops onto my shoulder, arms useless at her sides.

I smell her sweet skin, pick up a hint of vanilla.

"All right," I say, standing, taking off my jacket and tossing it on the foot of the bed.

She rolls onto her side and I get a view of her ass, the fabric of the panties not covering much.

Leaning down, I lift her up in my arms.

"Hades," she mutters. Her head lolls against my arm.

"How many of those pills did you take?"

She wriggles in my arms as I carry her into the bathroom. When I switch on the light, she tries to hide her face in my chest.

"How many pills, Persephone?" I ask, setting her on the edge of the tub, keeping hold of her as her head flops forward and she goes quiet, her breathing leveling out.

"Fuck. Look at me. Open your eyes and fucking look at me," I tell her, holding her by her jaw and tapping her cheek in an effort to wake her. "Persephone. Look at me."

When she doesn't respond, I reach around her to keep hold of her and undo the cufflink at my right wrist, then left. I pocket both, then roll the sleeves up to my elbows.

I reach to plug the tub and switch on the cold water, my arm still around her back.

"Here we go," I say, picking her up. "You are not going to like this."

I slide her into the tub and her reaction is instant.

Her eyes fly open and her shocked gasp is almost a scream as she turns her body toward me, hands clawing at my arm to get out of the cold water.

"Awake now?"

She looks up at me, her expression one of confusion, disorientation.

I splash water at her face.

She sucks in a shivering breath. "Stop! What are you... are you insane?"

"How many pills did you take, Persephone?"

She's trying to get to the tap to turn it off herself.

I grab her wrist, make her look at me. "How many?"

She shakes her head. "I don't know. Four. Five maybe."

"Never these. Do you understand me? Never these!"

"You're hurting me!"

I look down at where I'm holding her wrist. Hard. I clear my throat, loosen my hold.

"They don't work anyway," she says.

"Fuck." I switch off the water. I take a towel from the rack and turn to find her trying to climb out. "Jesus Christ. Wait a fucking minute," I say as she slips, and I catch her just before she knocks her face against the side of the tub.

"What are you doing? Are you trying to freeze me to death?"

"No, you're doing that yourself with the heating switched off during a fucking blizzard." I wrap the towel around her. I pull off my own shirt, which is pretty much soaked, and hold her to me to warm her up.

She's shivering and doesn't fight me, but tucks her arms between us, laying her cheek on my chest.

"I'm so cold." Her teeth chatter.

I draw her back, pull the wet tank top from her, then wrap her tight in the towel and lift her up.

"Why isn't the heating switched on? And why the fuck are you taking Irina's sleeping pills? And four or five? You don't even remember how many you took? If you're trying to hurt yourself, you're being a fucking idiot."

"Hurt myself?" she asks, blinking heavily, rubbing her eyes.

I stand her before the bed to drag her soaked panties off and toss them aside before I sit and pull her onto my lap, holding her against my chest.

"Yes, hurt yourself." I hear it myself, understand its meaning.

Is history repeating itself?

She draws back. "I'm not. I wouldn't." She shakes her head, clearly upset by what I just said. "I just...I can't sleep. The pills don't work so I...I took a few more." She glances away, pushes her fingers into her hair.

"Well, that's fucking stupid. No more pills and certainly not these."

She looks up at me and I see the moment she realizes that she's naked on my lap.

"I wasn't trying to hurt myself. I wouldn't," she says, trying to extricate herself.

"The front door was unlocked, the gates left open. Anyone could walk in here."

She opens her mouth but closes it again because she knows she's being stupid not closing the gates.

"And why is it so cold in here?" But I realize why as soon as I ask it. "Fuck."

Tears fill her eyes and she pushes against me. "Let me go."

"No."

"I said let me go." She shoves harder.

"Fine," I drop her on her ass on the carpet.

She's surprised but recovers quickly. Stands.

"You want to know why it's cold in here?" she asks wrapping her arms around herself. "It's fucking cold because we have no money, remember? In case you haven't noticed, the house is almost completely empty of furniture and just today, I signed a contract selling myself to you so I could buy time. So I wouldn't have to tell my fifteen-year-old sister that we're homeless."

"Homeless is an exaggeration."

"Is it? It's fucking freezing because you stole our house out from under us. You stole everything while my father lies dying in that fucking hospital bed!"

I'm on my feet in an instant feeling a familiar rage. One that I know doesn't belong to her.

Persephone takes one look at me and turns to run. But I'm blocking her exit and she corners herself when she backs away. When her back is to the wall, I slam my hands against it, making her jump

"I didn't steal anything," I say, my voice low and tight. "Everything I did was legal."

"Legal but cruel."

"Your father wasn't the man you thought he was."

"He was a kind man. That's all I need to know." She shakes her head. "He *is* a kind man!"

"Bury your head in the sand. It's easier that way."

"Fuck you!"

"Fuck me?"

"Fuck. You."

"You don't know anything."

"I know you're a monster. That's all I need to know."

"Be careful, sweetheart."

"I'm not scared of you, Hayden Montgomery!"

"No?" I lean my head down so my forehead is touching hers. "You're not scared of me? Maybe you should be."

I watch her throat work as she swallows. Watch how her hands have fisted at her sides.

"Get on the bed, Persephone."

She stares up at me.

"I said get on the goddamned bed. Don't make me make you. I was gentle this morning."

"Gentle?" Her forehead furrows, any rage-fueled confidence vanishes as she processes. "You humiliated me."

"Your pussy was wet."

"I—"

"Get on the bed."

Her pulse races at her throat and for a moment, I'm not sure if she's going to do it or if I'm going to have to make her. I'm not sure which I want.

I lean away, give her an inch of space.

She glares up at me, and when she drops her head, her hair falls like a veil between us. I look at her like this, shoulders slumping in a little as she hugs her arms around her middle before shifting her gaze back to mine.

This is hard. This is fucking hard. Looking at her like this. Watching the sheen of tears glaze her violet eyes.

But she steels her spine, her hands fist as she forces them to her sides.

"You're going to have to make me," she spits the words and before I've even processed them, I'm on her. I'm gripping that hair and dragging her backward like a fucking caveman as she stumbles, arms windmilling to keep her balance.

I think she's calling for me to stop. Calling my name. But I can't hear her, not right now. I deposit her on her ass on the bed and set one knee between hers.

I make her look up at me, holding her head at what I'm sure is a painful angle, because I want to be sure she hears me.

"When I say jump, you fucking jump."

"And when you say for me to spread my legs, I spread my legs?" she says through gritted teeth.

"Exactly."

"You're a monster. A fucking monster."

"You agreed!"

"It doesn't matter anyway, does it? You'll take even if I don't give!"

"What?"

"You heard me."

"You think I would take *that* from you?"

She pauses, sucks in a choked breath. "You're hurting me," she finally says.

I look down at her and I see us. See me holding her. Overpowering her. She's no match for my strength.

I let up a little, release her altogether.

"Christ." I back away, give her space as I run a hand through my hair.

She's right. I am a monster. But I'm not that kind of monster.

When I look at her again, I find her sitting on the very edge of the bed, wide eyes on me, arms covering her breasts. Her wrists are tucked between her tightly closed knees. I can hear her short breaths and watch her shudder with cold or fear or both.

Fuck.

I go to her and she leans away just a little. I look at her, brush her hair back from her shoulder. I don't know what it is with her. No other woman has ever stirred such havoc inside me. Not a single one.

"I wouldn't do that. Take that. Not unless you gave it."

She just watches me.

I touch her hair and when she doesn't squirm away, I take her face in my hands and kiss her. It's our first real kiss. I'm starved for it and I can't stop kissing her. My fingers tangle in her hair so when I finally draw back, she's breathless like I've stolen the breath from her. Her eyes are so deep a violet they're almost black and she's so fucking beautiful.

I wipe a tear from her cheek, and she watches me closely as I crouch down, my hands on her knees.

"I want you, but I won't take what you don't give, do you understand? I won't hurt you," I tell her.

She's silent.

"Do you believe me?" As I ask, I wonder if I believe me. Because I will hurt her, won't I? Even if I'm telling the truth, I will end up hurting her.

She nods. I'm not sure if it's because she believes me or if she's trying to appease me.

"Hades knew he'd condemn her when he gave her the fruit," I say. Did Persephone know she'd be damned if she ate it? That she'd be bound to him? Maybe that's the important question. The one I don't know the answer to. "Open your legs for me, Persephone."

"Hayden—"

I shake my head. "Hades." I hear myself, how I sound. My voice low, hoarse. "When it's us, like this, you call me Hades."

It's who we are. Hades the monster. Persephone the innocent

The abduction of Persephone.

The rape?

No. Not that. Never that.

"Hades." She tilts her head, studying me. I wonder what she sees.

She opens her legs just a little and I shift my gaze to look down at her little pink pussy, the pretty lips parted, and all I want right now is to kneel before her and look at her, smell her, touch her, taste her. I want to worship her.

I shift my gaze back to hers. "Wider." My voice is raw at the scent and sight of her.

She obeys and I'm harder for it.

I think she's the most beautiful thing in the world. Like this. Like she is right now. Naked and open for me.

I don't speak. I have nothing to say. I just need this. Need her eyes on me. Her body beneath mine. Her heat around me.

She grips my shoulders when I pull her forward, opening her wider. Her nipples turn into hard points, every muscle taut, the pink lips of her pussy obediently open as if waiting just for me.

Persephone.

My Persephone.

I bow my head, inhaling her scent. "You're beautiful." I kiss her belly, kiss her breast, her mouth.

With her hands on me, she turns my face to hers. "I lied."

I wait.

"You do scare me."

I reach up, wipe a tear. I don't know what to say. So instead, I guide her to lie on her back as I kneel between her open legs and push them up, bending her knees so I can see all of her.

I'm hard. So fucking hard. I'm going to fuck her. I'm going to bury my dick deep inside her and mark her, but I have to take care. I need to be careful with her.

I bring my mouth to her, lick her clit, circling it, sliding my tongue over the length of her to her asshole, circling that too.

"Hades," she gasps.

"Persephone," I reply, my voice hoarse. I come back to her clit, take it into my mouth.

"Oh, god."

I grip her cheeks and pull them wide. I eat her pussy like it's a meal, like I'm a condemned man and it's my final meal. Maybe I am condemned. Maybe I always was with her because she tastes even better than I remember. Fuck, fuck me, because I've wanted this for so long. I've wanted her for so fucking long. Only her. Every other woman has been a poor substitute for her.

Sliding my thumb to her asshole, I suck her clit hard. I want her to come. I need her to come. Now. Right now. On my tongue.

"Hades!" Her hands are fists in my hair and her thighs lock around my head. When I push my thumb into that tight little hole, she comes so hard, she's bucking with it. Her pussy is so wet, it's dripping. I eat her up, devour her and if I don't get inside her soon, I'm going to blow in my pants.

When her body goes limp, I draw back, look at her. She blinks her sleepy eyes and watches me as I straighten, strip off the rest of my clothes and stand over her. I give her a minute to process what's coming. Process how many inches she'll take.

She draws back a little, panicked when she meets my eyes again.

"I don't think I can—"

"Birth control," I say.

"What?"

"Birth control. Are you protected?"

"What?" Her eyes are on my cock.

I lean down, cup her face. "Focus. Birth control. I don't have a condom and I need to fuck you. Right now. Do I need to fuck your ass?"

"My...what?" She shakes her head. "I'm on the pill. I..."

"That's good." I nudge her knees wide and place one of

mine between them. I fist my cock. "Keep your legs spread wide. I want to see your wet little cunt."

I smear precum with my thumb and wipe it across her mouth.

She licks her lips but I'm not sure it's conscious. Seeing her do it makes me harder.

I rub the length of my dick through her wet folds, watching her face as I do, as I stimulate her still sensitive clit.

"You're wet for me. That's good. It'll be easier for you," I tell her, taking one leg and bending it backward, opening her wide and bringing my cock to her entrance.

"Hades, I…I'm not ready."

"Sweetheart." I stretch her tight pussy with the head of my cock. "You'll never be ready to take me."

"You're too big!" She tries to squirm away.

I grab her wrists, spread her arms to either side and push in a little farther.

"It's going to hurt," she says.

"Yes, it is. And I'm sorry about that." I kiss her mouth and taste those sweet lips, thinking I could kiss her forever. "But then it's going to feel so fucking good, too." I weave my fingers with hers, releasing her other hand to cup the top of her head. She brings that hand to my shoulder, her nails already digging into my back.

I slide deeper into her and she's so fucking tight.

"Relax," I tell her, kissing her again. "I'm going to make you come again. Relax and open. It'll be easier."

She closes her eyes, nods, tries to free her hand from mine.

I shift her other arm to my back.

"Open your eyes, sweetheart."

She shakes her head.

"Open them. Look at me."

She does and she whimpers when I move a little, feeling her barrier. Virgin. Like she was saving herself for me all along.

My Persephone. My doomed bride.

"Hurt me, Persephone. Hurt me like I'm going to hurt you. Dig your nails into me and bleed me."

She draws her nails down my back, the pain makes me harder and I let out a moan.

"Good. Good girl. Whatever you do, don't stop looking at me, okay?" I ask her and she nods. We're so close right now, we're so fucking close and I know I'm going to hurt her now. I have to.

And I lied a minute ago. Some part of me wants to.

When I draw back, she braces herself, fingernails embedded in my back, and when I thrust, she cries out. I feel the rush of blood, warm and wet. *Fuck* I'm inside her, I'm all the way inside her and for a minute, I can't think, can't do anything but feel.

Feel her.

Her.

Her tight cunt squeezes my dick, blood wet and warm and staining me.

"You're mine," I say, drawing back and thrusting deep. "You were always mine. Always."

I fuck her hard, I can't hold back. I feel her move beneath me and hear her whimpers. When I come, I come so fucking hard, I can't see straight. All I can do is feel and know that I'm filling her up. Marking her. Staining her.

10

PERSEPHONE

I can't move when he stills. I'm still trapped beneath him, his elbows on either side of my face caging me in, one giant hand cupping the top of my head.

He looks at me, and I watch his green-gold eyes refocus on mine. He touches my cheek, kisses my forehead.

His words ring in my ears.

"You're mine. You were always mine. Always."

He's right. He and I, there's something between us, a strange, almost unnatural bond. Whatever it is, it keeps drawing us together for better or worse.

Mostly worse.

He slides out of me, a wet warmth spilling onto my thighs. Even that hurts. I'm sore, raw. He's too big.

"All right?" he asks, shifting more of his weight off me. I didn't realize I was struggling to breathe until I can do so freely again. "Persephone?"

I blink. He's waiting for an answer. What the fuck is wrong with me that I can't seem to answer?

He grins, slides down my body. "You need to come

again." And as he says it, he ducks his face down and he has my clit in his mouth again. Fuck. Oh my god. Fuck.

"Hades." I'm bloody. A mess. I grip the hair on his head. "Don't."

He takes hold of my wrists and tugs my hands off without taking his mouth from my clit. It takes me all of three seconds to come again, to come like I did before.

But even as I'm coning, I feel the loss of him inside me. It's the strangest thing but I want him inside me and on top of me, his weight smothering me.

I want it now, while I'm raw and coming on his tongue. This feeling, it's intense pleasure and unbearable pain together, the pain inside me, inside my heart, my belly.

The pleasure.

Fuck, the absolute ecstasy.

I close my eyes and give myself over to it because I can't do anything else. He won't allow it.

I let myself go and just let him hold me. I lose myself in orgasm. I'm so far gone, I don't even realize he's back on top of me again, wiping my face. He's wiping tears from my eyes because I'm crying, and I don't even know it.

"It won't always hurt," he says.

But it will. Doesn't he know? With us, it will always hurt.

He gets up off the bed, going into the bathroom. I hear water run. He's filling the tub.

There's no way I'm getting into another ice bath.

Before I can get out of the bed, though, he's back. He's holding a damp washcloth. I shift my gaze to the stained sheets, my stained thighs.

"Stay, Persephone."

He doesn't give me a choice as he's already on the bed, one big hand pushing me to lie back down as he sets the damp cloth between my legs.

I wince, looking down and watching how gentle he is now.

"I'm going to stain you."

His words again. But it was me who stained him.

His stain, though, it will go deeper than blood on the sheets.

"Are you all right?" he asks again after he's cleaned between my legs.

I nod, wince when I try to sit up but push through the pain. Where is my voice? Why can't I speak?

A moment later, he stands and, before I can protest, he lifts me into his arms.

"I don't want an ice bath," I start, animated now at the prospect. I push against his chest but he's immovable, bigger and stronger than I remember him being five years ago. "Please, Hades!"

"You're not getting an ice bath. Stop struggling."

Inside the bathroom, he tests the water then gently lowers me into the almost full tub.

"Okay?" he asks.

I nod. It's warm and I'm shivering with cold.

"Good. I'll be right back."

But when he turns, I gasp.

He stops instantly as if he didn't realize it himself.

I can't speak. I can't form words.

He turns his head a little, just enough to see me.

And all I can do is take in the crisscrossed scars there. The divots of missing skin deep and old.

"My father was an asshole," he says when I finally meet his eyes.

Without another word, he walks out of the room and I'm left with that vision of his back. I remember our first meeting, the bruised jaw.

His father did that to him?

I hear the bedroom door open and close and wonder what he's doing. I draw my knees up, hug them in the warm water. I let my mind wander to what just happened. How it happened.

For a moment, I wonder if I'd said I wasn't on the pill if he would have fucked me in the ass. I quickly push the thought aside. It's both arousing and scary as hell to think of him having me like that. I haven't seen many men naked, but I'm not a complete novice even if I am a virgin. None have been close to as big as Hayden Montgomery.

I hear him again and I realize what he's doing. He's building a fire in the bedroom fireplace.

He's back in the bathroom a moment later. He washes his hands, eyes on me in the mirror as he does. He then walks to the bathtub. When I drag my gaze from the monster hanging between his legs up to his face, I realize he means to get in with me.

"Hayden, I—"

But he's behind me and pulling me to him, cradling me between his legs.

"Why are you still a virgin?" he asks, holding me to him until I stop fighting to pull away.

"You're not wasting any time."

"You were engaged to Jonas. Why didn't you fuck? He didn't expect you to fuck?"

Does he feel me stiffen at the mention of his stepbrother?

"Why did you do it?" he asks, and I don't follow this new question.

"Do what?"

"Accept his proposal? You knew what he was. You had to know after Halloween."

I did. Or I should have. "I didn't marry him." It's a stupid defense.

"But you were going to."

"Look, I don't want to talk about him, okay? Off limits. What we're doing, this crazy thing," I shake my head. "It's physical. That's all. You don't get anything else."

"That's not all and you know it."

"Hayden, please—"

"And I'll get everything I want. But fine. For now. What do you want to talk about?"

I turn to look back at him. "Why did you do that to me today? With your brother. You knew he was coming. You knew he'd find us."

"Because you insisted."

"You know I wouldn't have if I'd known."

"Then next time, trust me."

Trust him?

"Let's move to a different topic. You don't want to talk about Jonas, I don't want to talk about Ares."

"Fine. Where have you been these last five years?"

He grins, lifts me like I weigh nothing and turns me around. The tub is big enough for two, but water still splashes out onto the floor. He looks at my face and the way he looks at me, it's different than anyone else. Like he's seeing inside me.

"I told you I'd hurt you," he says.

I don't want to talk about the sex, not until I've had time to process. "So, you're not going to answer that question either?"

"Here and there. Nowhere special."

"I saw you, you know?"

"Saw me?"

"At Nora's funeral."

At the mention of her name, a sadness clouds his eyes. A sadness I know he's trying to hide. It's the same sadness I saw that first day I met him out on the street with the broken doll.

But then his jaw tightens, and he shuts down. I feel it like someone opened a window and let in a sudden chill.

"Did you," he says. It's a comment, not a question.

"Why were you hiding?" I ask.

"I wasn't hiding."

"You were."

Time stretches as silence grows heavy in the room. "Nora was good," he says. "She shouldn't have died like that."

I look down, suddenly feeling like I'm intruding, like I shouldn't see him like this.

I nod my head. "I still miss her."

Silence.

"We had this crazy idea we'd be best friends forever. That we'd live here like this forever. We were young and pretty naïve."

Silence still.

I chance a glance up to find his eyes locked on me. The hardness inside them has me leaning away from him. I wonder if he knows more about her suicide than he lets on, but he can't. He can't know that. I only learned the truth a few months ago myself.

"We used to tell each other everything. I thought so, at least," I add. If she'd told me, I wonder if it would have made a difference. If I could have helped her.

"You never really know someone, not what's really inside their head."

I think about what he says and look down into the water. "Nora and me, I thought we were different." It's quiet for a long moment and when I look back up at him, he's still studying me. "But I was wrong."

"I was living in the building my grandfather left me," he says, changing the subject.

"I knew he left it to you, but I thought it was uninhabitable."

"It was condemned. But I had no place to go."

"You were right here all those years?"

"Most of the time."

"I never saw you."

"It's not a part of town you'd have any business in."

"Why?"

"Why what?"

"Why did you leave home? Because of...your back?"

"That was before. When I was a kid. I still have the belt he used."

I reach out, touch his face.

He takes my hand. "Don't feel sorry for me, Persephone. I gave as good as I got."

"You were a child."

"I knew my grandfather was leaving me the building but that wasn't all. He was changing his will. He was going to cut my father out. Leave everything to Ares and me. I overheard him arguing with my dad that Halloween night."

"What? Why?"

"I don't know the reason. I just know he was pissed with my father. But then he died in that fire before he could change anything. I guess the building he'd already arranged for, but the rest still went to my dad and he cut me off financially. I had a little money and a lot of hate. I lived off of both. I built my own empire. I turned the building around. Bought another. Then another."

"I don't understand. He was your father."

"He took a belt to us, Ares and me. He was a drunk for most of our childhood. Until he met Carry, strangely enough. I guess he loved her more than he loved either of us."

"I'm sorry."

"Don't be. I am who I am today partly because of how I grew up and I'm not unhappy."

"Are you happy, though?"

He stops, like the question catches him off guard. "I think it's naïve to expect to be happy as an adult, Persephone."

"I don't believe that."

He shrugs a shoulder.

"Do you still have a lot of hate?" I ask him.

He studies me, grins. He stands and water glides off him. He truly does look like a Greek God standing over me and it makes my insides quiver.

"I don't allow hate to rule me. I take justice into my own hands and punish those who deserve to be punished. I simply level the scales."

"Do I deserve to be punished?"

He steps out of the tub and grabs a towel, wrapping it around his hips. He stands there, eyes narrowed, looking at me so intently it makes the hair on the back of my neck stand on end.

"She loved him, too, you know," he says instead of answering my question. "Persephone loved Hades."

I'm taken back to our first meeting at the club. When he'd told me why Hades had taken Persephone and I'd told him Hades had loved her.

He holds out his hand, palm up, and I look at it and wonder at the dichotomy of this. He is my enemy. He will trample me because I will be caught underfoot.

Hades loved Persephone. And he's right. She loved him, too.

But his love, it condemned her. It could only take. It could only ever make her dark. She wasn't the same even in the time she spent in the light.

Because once you let darkness love you, it won't ever let you go.

And you won't want it to.

11

HAYDEN

She places her hand inside mine and I help her out of the tub. I wrap a towel around her, dry her. Back in the bedroom, she opens a dresser drawer and steps into a pair of black satin panties, then pulls an oversized sweater over her head.

Her hair is damp. She goes into the bathroom and returns a moment later with it piled on top of her head in a bun.

I pull on a pair of sweats I'd brought with me. I don't bother with a shirt.

"You brought an overnight bag?" she asks, eyeing the duffel on her bed.

"It's here or the club. I told you I don't want anything getting in the way of you and me in bed."

"So, you're moving in?"

I cock my head to the side. "Unless you're moving into the club. I thought you'd want to be close to Lizzie."

"Well, that was...considerate. Thank you."

I look at her, see how she looks at me. She doesn't quite trust me, but I think she wants to. She's still naïve.

Out of her league, bastard.

I take the bottle of sleeping pills I'd found and hold them up to her. "If I see you taking these or any other drug like this, you're going to answer to me."

She reaches for the bottle, but I hold it out of reach.

"They're not drugs. They're prescription sleeping pills," she says.

"Prescribed to Irina."

"I just didn't have time to go to the doctor."

"I don't care." I walk into the bathroom and she follows.

"What are you doing?" she asks when I take the cap off.

"Getting rid of them." I dump the remaining pills into the toilet.

"They're not mine!"

I flush the toilet and turn to her. "Then you won't mind."

"I really just couldn't sleep. You said so yourself, I looked a wreck."

"You're overwhelmed but that's over."

"How is it over?"

"Your father's in a facility. Irina is gone. The house is sorted. You have a job."

"All for the low, low price of my body."

I grin, wrap an arm around the back of her neck and pull her to me. "Don't forget your soul."

She looks at me like I'm crazy and maybe I am.

I let her go and walk out into the bedroom. I check the fire, make sure the screen is in place then move to the door. "Is there food in the house? Storm's too bad to go out."

"I think so."

"Let's go downstairs."

I follow her down the hall. "Where's your sister?"

"Sleeping over at a friend's house."

I turn on lights as we go, looking into the empty rooms

until we get into the kitchen. It's a very large kitchen with Portuguese tile floors, a long, thick wooden counter, high-end stainless-steel appliances and a breakfast bar.

I open the refrigerator to see what she has. Not much but it'll do. "Get me a whiskey and I'll make you dinner."

She disappears into what I know is the study and returns a few minutes later with a bottle of whiskey. She pours me a glass and takes a seat, tucking her legs underneath her.

I whisk eggs, add herbs and begin to make scrambled eggs.

"I never imagined you as a cook."

I drink my whiskey, leaning against the counter and watching her.

"It's just eggs."

"Still."

I study her, the fact that she was a virgin still baffling, especially considering she was engaged to Jonas. But that in itself is baffling.

"Why did you agree to marry Jonas? I mean, after that night."

That night.

Halloween night five years ago.

She knows the night I mean, too. I don't have to spell it out. Instead, I sip my drink and wait for her to answer.

"I don't remember much of the party," she says. "I've never felt so out of control and I'd only had one drink. I know that."

"My stepbrother—your one-time fiancé—drugged you. You still refuse to believe that?"

"I remember when you came. I don't think I've ever felt so grateful. So relieved."

I look through two cupboards before I find dishes and

plate the scrambled eggs. I put one in front of her and stand across from her to eat mine.

"Eat. Every bite," I tell her, handing her a fork. "You realize what he would have done to you if I hadn't shown up?"

She nods without looking at me.

"And yet, you accepted his proposal of marriage? Ares may be right. You have questionable taste and sense."

"He was different after Nora's death. At least I thought he was."

"You protected him. The morning after, you protected him."

She looks up at me. "I wasn't protecting him. I was protecting myself."

"From a would-be rapist you then agree to marry?"

She puts her fork down, weaves her fingers into her hair and closes her eyes. "I made a mistake, okay? Can you please just drop it?"

I narrow my eyes and study her. "What aren't you telling me?"

She looks quickly away. "Nothing. And besides..." she shifts her gaze back to mine. "I have another question."

"You ask but never answer."

"What we...What happened afterward, when you brought me home...I don't know if it was real."

I arch my eyebrows.

"I mean, did we..."

I chew a forkful of eggs. "I cleaned up after you puked. I then put you to bed."

"I was naked when I woke up."

"Because the rain soaked you. You were sixteen and I was twenty, Persephone. I didn't touch you."

Liar.

"The other night, you said you'd *been in my panties*."

"I wouldn't fuck an almost unconscious girl. Never mind a minor." I finish my plate and reach for the bottle of whisky. "What about what Jonas did? Wasn't that enough for you?"

She pushes the eggs around.

"Eat," I tell her.

She does and once she's finished, I collect our dishes and put them in the sink.

"Your back, Hayden."

I don't move. I let her take it in. Take in the consequence of hate.

When I turn around her eyes are still wide. I walk around the counter, standing so close to her I can smell her, a faint vanilla and something else, something soft and sensual at once. I pick up my whiskey and finish it.

"Your father did that to you. He was beating you while we were right here. Just steps away."

"You grew up in an ivory castle, sweetheart."

"Did he beat Jonas too?"

I feel my eyes narrow when I hear the way she asks it. Feel a hot rage bubble up inside me.

"Jonas. Always Jonas for you, isn't it?" I grip her jaw and I know from the look on her face, from the sound she makes that I'm hurting her, but I don't care. "You'd better get over that fast. You're mine and I don't want to hear his name from your mouth again. Understand that, Persephone."

She tugs free of my grip and slides off the chair. "I'm not anyone's, Hayden. *You* understand *that*."

12

PERSEPHONE

It's dark when I open my eyes. I'm alone. I wonder where he slept. If he slept.

The fire has died down to a glow, but the room feels warmer than it has in a long time.

I sit up, pick up my phone and check the time. Three o'clock.

Getting up, I pull on the sweater from earlier.

Outside, I hear snowplows already at work. I hug my arms to myself and walk out of my bedroom to look for him.

The house is quiet as I go down the stairs. It's dark down here too and for a moment, I wonder if he's gone. But a glance out the front window tells me his Range Rover is still parked outside. When I turn back into the house, I see the light underneath the study door.

I walk quietly toward it, the carpet-less floor cold on my bare feet. I put my hand on the doorknob but before I turn it, I hear him.

"I want to know the link between Benedetti and Abbot, and I figure you're the man to call."

Benedetti? The name is vaguely familiar.

He's silent, and I assume the person he's on the phone with is speaking.

"Then call in a fucking favor." Silence. "Yeah, I'll owe you one, brother."

Brother? Ares. No way he'd be talking to Jonas.

I turn the doorknob, open the door.

Hayden looks completely unfazed at my entrance, not at all like I expect. It's certainly not the look of a man caught red-handed where he shouldn't be, sitting behind my father's desk with my father's papers spread out before him.

His gaze sweeps over me. "I'll talk to you later," he says into the phone and sets it on the desk.

"What the hell do you think you're doing?" I ask. I walk inside, close the door behind me and approach the desk to get a look at the sheets he has strewn about.

He sits back, picks up his glass of whiskey.

"Couldn't sleep?" he asks casually.

I study the first sheet, pick up another. Financial reports from both my father's campaign and Abbot Enterprises. "I asked you a question," I say.

He raises his eyebrows.

"Why are you in here? In my father's private study? Looking through his private things?"

"The company will be mine in a few days' time. All these *private things* will be mine."

"I haven't signed anything yet."

"You will."

"Who do you want information on?"

He finishes his drink, stands.

I swallow because he's still shirtless and his sweats are hanging so low on his hips, I can see the trail of dark hair disappearing inside and the memory of what we did, of him inside me, makes my belly flutter. I feel myself flush with heat as I look at him there.

"A man named Dominic Benedetti. A business associate of your father's."

It's huge. How can it be so big?

"Eyes up here, sweetheart."

My gaze snaps up to his and I'm embarrassed at his smirk. He knew exactly what had distracted me.

"What?" I ask.

"Italian mafia. Ring a bell?"

"Mafia?"

"He made some very generous donations to your father's campaign a few months back."

"That doesn't make sense."

"A local mob boss donating to your father's campaign doesn't make sense?"

I remember overhearing my father a few days before the accident. Remember him arguing heatedly with someone.

"Persephone?"

I shake my head. "No. Of course not. I mean...my father didn't deal with crooks."

"No? Even though the proof is in the papers you're holding?"

"I already told you he wouldn't do that."

He reaches to take the papers from me. "Well, if you don't know about it, I guess that's one thing he did right not involving his children in his dirtier dealings."

"He didn't have dirty dealings," I say, tugging the pages back.

"No, of course he didn't. Everything was on the up-and-up. He was a nice man, isn't that what you told me?"

"Don't talk about him in the past tense."

He walks around the desk and I find myself backing up a step. This time, he takes my wrist and forces the pages from me. He puts them on the desk and slides his thumb into my palm.

"You shouldn't be in here," I manage.

"I hope you weren't eavesdropping. You can understand I wouldn't like that."

"You're in my house. In my father's study."

"My house. My study. Don't do it again."

"Are you threatening me?"

"I'm telling you how it is and how it will be going forward."

"Informing me of my new reality. I'm very aware, thank you."

"I'm not sure you are. But you will be, when we're done," he says.

He pulls me to him, switching his grip so he has both of my wrists at my back in one of his hands as he weaves the other into my hair.

"Stop."

I tug to get free, but he doesn't give.

He leans his face down, and for a moment, I think he's going to kiss me, and I think I might bite him if he does.

But he doesn't kiss me. Instead, he takes a deep, purposeful breath in, brushing his cheek against mine. The rough hair on his jaw sends a shiver along my spine.

"I like my smell on you."

With a sharp tug, I'm pressed up to him, his other hand flat against my back and I feel him, feel his hardness at my belly.

"And I like being inside you."

"Let go."

"I smell you, too, Persephone," he whispers, not letting me go but sliding his hand down to my ass and squeezing it. "I smell how wet you are."

"I'm not," it's a lie and it fades quickly when he slips two fingers into the crotch of my panties. "I hate you."

"You and I both know that's not true. Now," he says, turning me sharply and, with one swipe of his arm, clearing the desk before he pushes me down over it. He pins me with a hand splayed out at my lower back and all I can do is grip the edges of the desk. I crane my neck to look back, to watch him as he pushes my panties down and, with his other hand cups a cheek and opens me.

The way he has his hand on me forces my back to arch, pushing my ass up. He drags his gaze to mine and grins.

"Let me go," I try, wriggling to get free.

"You're dripping, sweetheart," he says in that rumble, that rattle against his chest.

I look away, unable to hold his gaze. And when he slides his fingers along my folds, I hear my own gasp. But it's when he trails one wet finger up to my asshole that I'm undone.

"You liked my finger in your ass earlier."

"I didn't."

"You came." I can hear his grin.

He pushes in and I whimper, tensing every muscle and I don't move, don't breathe. I can't.

"Your asshole is even tighter than your cunt."

I can't speak. My hands are flat on the desk and I'm staring at the wall. I can feel the evidence of my arousal streak down my inner thigh as he pushes his finger in and out and in and out.

"Mmmm." It's that rattle again and then something

warm and wet is on me, on my thigh. I look back to find it's his tongue. He's licking that smear of moisture up to its source.

"Please." Please what? What am I asking for? *Begging* for?

He's moved his hand from my lower back, but he doesn't need to keep me pinned, not when he's hooked his finger in my ass. I crane my neck to look at him, find him watching me. I see him drop his sweats.

I draw a sharp breath in and close my eyes when he begins his slow stretch of my pussy, his thick cock sliding into the wet passage, pushing through any resistance and when he slides his other hand between my legs and takes my clit between two fingers, I come.

It's pathetic. He hasn't even begun to fuck me yet, not like I know he will. I'm coming and I can't hide the fact. I know he feels me as my walls squeeze around both his finger and his cock. When he begins to move, when he begins to fuck me, really fuck me, he's rough and hard and I come again.

His breath is ragged, and I open my eyes and turn to watch him. He's looking down at himself as he fucks me and seeing him like this, it sends me into another abyss of pleasure, one more orgasm when I think I can't take anymore.

When my knees buckle, he holds me up, thickening inside me as he thrusts one final time and I watch him come. Watch him fill me up and all I can manage is an exhale. His name on my breath.

"Hades."

It's so soft I don't even think he hears it and I know as I take his seed that I am finished. That I was always ever finished with him.

Hades.

He was my savior once.

Twice.

Now he's become my tormentor.

And I don't ever want him to let me go.

13

PERSEPHONE

I wake to someone humming softly.

Blinking against the bright light, I open my eyes and see a woman I don't recognize opening the curtains.

I rub my eyes, opening them again, but she's still right there.

She turns to me as I sit up, being reminded instantly of how my night ended. Well, how my morning began.

I tug the blanket up as I realize I'm naked.

"Good morning, Miss," the woman says.

"Who are you?" I ask, looking on the other side of the bed, finding it empty. The only evidence that Hayden slept here the dent in the pillow.

"My name is Anna. Mr. Montgomery sent me." As she says this, she pours coffee from a silver carafe and brings it to me.

"I'm sorry, who sent you?" I ask, taking the coffee as there's nowhere for her to put it since the majority of my furniture is gone.

"I work for Mr. Montgomery. Would you like breakfast brought up or will you dine downstairs?"

"What?" I give a shake of my head, blink but find her still standing here and the coffee in my hands still steaming.

"Breakfast—"

"No, that's not...I'm sorry, but what are you doing here?" We let our staff go weeks ago.

"Oh, anything you need." She checks her watch. "You are expected at Mr. Montgomery's office soon. He chose some clothes for you."

"Pardon?" He chose clothes for me? I look at the dress hanging on the closet door, the matching pumps. "Unbelievable."

"The car will be here in an hour," she says, checking her watch.

"What time is it?" I turn to pick up my phone but almost spill the coffee as I reach for it on the floor.

"Quarter past ten in the morning."

"That late." I push the blanket off to get up but remember my state of undress and stop.

She politely busies herself picking up my discarded clothes. I grab Hayden's shirt which is still on the foot of the bed, putting it on. I smell him on it and hate that I'm inclined to inhale deeply.

"Listen, Anna." She turns to me. "I don't know why Hayden—Mr. Montgomery—sent you, but I don't need a housekeeper." *Lie.* I can't exactly manage this house on my own. "I appreciate your help, but you can tell him I don't need you."

"I'm sure you two can discuss it when you see him this morning. Shall I bring breakfast up? Cook has prepared something warm."

"Cook?"

She nods.

I just stare at her as she picks up the coffee tray. "No. Thank you."

"I'll be downstairs then."

There's a cook too?

When Anna leaves, I walk into the bathroom and switch on the shower, looking at my reflection in the mirror as the water warms up. The bags under my eyes seem to have lessened. I guess the seven hours of sleep I must have gotten after that session in the study did the trick. I can't remember the last time I slept so well and so long.

And I can't remember how I got to bed.

I shake my head, tell myself that I hate Hayden, and step into the shower. I shampoo and condition, being gentle as I wash between my legs. I'm tender and it's no surprise. The man is a giant.

When I'm finished, I wrap a towel around my hair and one around *my person*. I roll my eyes remembering the language of the contract. I bypass the dress and pumps and opt for a pair of jeans, an oversized sweater, and a pair of boots that won't have me breaking my neck as I trudge around town in the snow.

I pull my wet hair into a bun at the top of my head, drop my phone into my purse and walk out of the bedroom, rifling through my bag for the keys to my Jeep as I go.

Anna is still humming when I get downstairs, but I don't stop to tell her I'm leaving. Instead, I grab my coat and walk out the door well ahead of the car Hayden is apparently sending for me.

The driveway's been plowed and I'm guessing I have Hayden to thank for that. The Jeep handles snow well so a few minutes later, I'm on my way to the club.

I dial Lizzie, but the phone goes directly to voice mail. I leave her a message anyway. I ask when she'll be home, also telling her not to be surprised by our new maid and cook because I have a feeling they're not going to up and leave on my word. Hayden's people only jump on his command.

With the roads as they are, it takes me twenty minutes longer than yesterday to get to the club. When I walk in, I see Peter.

He looks as thrilled to see me as I am to see him. He opens his mouth and I just hold up a hand.

"If you'll just let him know I'm here," I say, heading him off, even taking off my coat and handing it to him.

He smiles, looking relieved, and gestures for me to take a seat on the cognac colored Chesterfield. The fire crackles in the fireplace and the smell of the cinnamon rolls a waiter carries into the dining room makes my stomach rumble.

I'm looking for where I can get some coffee when an irate looking Hayden stalks through the door, dark eyes pinning me to the spot.

He opens his mouth, looks me over and must change his mind because instead of saying a word, he shakes his head, takes me by the elbow and walks me through the restaurant to the hidden elevator doors.

"You don't have to be so rough," I tell him as I try to tug free.

"I think you need rough." Is his reply as he watches the numbers on the screen above the doors.

"Not everything is about sex, you know."

"I didn't say a word about sex."

"Your dirty mind twisted my meaning."

"Right." He hustles me into the elevator and releases me, punching in his code for floor thirteen, I guess.

"What is wrong with you?" I ask.

"Why didn't you wait for the driver?"

"Because I can drive myself. Believe it or not, I got along perfectly well before you walked back into my life."

"*Perfectly well* is questionable."

The doors slide open and he gestures for me to enter his office. He follows close behind.

"I don't know who you think you are, but we need to get some things straight," I say.

He leans against his desk, folds his arms across his chest and studies me, eyes sliding over me momentarily before returning to my face.

"Smug doesn't become you," I say as I take in his smirk.

"What was wrong with the dress I chose? I thought you'd want to at least give the appearance of being a professional."

"What was wrong with it is that you chose it for me. You don't dictate what I wear. And by the way, four-inch heels in this snow is a sure way for me to break my neck. Although maybe that's what you want. It'd probably make things easier for you."

"That's the farthest thing from what I want," he says, more serious than I expect. "I'm surprised you don't know that yet."

"Hah!"

"And if you'd have waited for my driver, he'd have driven you door to door. Minimizes the risk."

"And then you'd have more of me to look at. Isn't that how you'd put it during our first meeting?"

He grins. "That is always a bonus. I do like looking at you, Persephone. I'd like to look at you now on your knees swallowing my dick."

My jaw drops open.

Ignore him. He's just fucking with you.

"Have you sucked cock before, or will I have to teach you how?"

I stalk up to him, hands fisted at my sides, my head about to explode. What I want to do is slap that irritating smirk off his face but I'm smarter than that so instead, I poke a finger at his chest.

"I will never—never—kneel for you."

He laughs outright, tugging me close as the elevator dings behind me. This close, I smell aftershave and remember it lingering on my sheets, on his shirt that I'd put on this morning.

I feel the heat coming off him and no matter how desperately I want to want to pull away, energy pulses, radiates off him and it's like a lasso. I can't get away even as electricity like a live wire singes my skin.

"Never say never, sweetheart," he whispers against my ear before spinning me around as the elevator doors slide open and a man I don't know walks inside.

"Ethan," Hayden says, pulling me to his side as the man approaches.

"Hayden." The man extends his hand to shake Hayden's. "Morning." He looks at me, checks his watch. "Am I late?"

"You're right on time. Ms. Abbot was early. Anxious to get things done."

I glare at Hayden.

He smirks. Again.

One day, I am going to wipe that arrogance off his face. One happy day.

"This is Persephone Abbot," Hayden says.

"Percy," I correct, extending my hand to shake his.

"*Persephone*," Hayden continues. "This is Ethan Smith,

the attorney who is handling the takeover of Abbot Enterprises."

It takes all I have to school my features, to put on a blank face. "Did you know my father, Mr. Smith?"

"Ethan, please."

"Ethan."

"I'd met him once. I heard what happened to him. How is he doing?"

My heart twists. "He'll be fine. Better every day," I lie. I don't know why. More for myself than anyone else, I guess.

"I'm glad to hear it."

"Should we get to business?" Hayden asks, finally releasing my arm.

The moment he walks away from me, I feel a chill. Like there's a sudden drop in temperature. It's such a strange sensation and not the first time I've felt it around him.

He pushes a button on his phone and orders coffee to be brought up.

"Are there any cinnamon rolls?" I ask, squeezing the muscles of my stomach to quiet the rumble.

He smiles approvingly. "And cinnamon rolls."

When he hangs up, he gestures to the sitting area where I perch on the sofa, a chesterfield that matches the one downstairs. The leather is worn and comfortable. I sat on it yesterday too, but I'd been so distracted, so over-tired, I barely remember the day.

My mind revisits last night, though. Hayden finding me asleep. Hayden trying to wake me up. Did he really think I was trying to hurt myself? He got so angry once he knew I was all right.

The thought takes me back to Nora and I wonder if those were the pills she'd used. I wonder if that's what got him so upset.

But he was right. It was stupid to take so many of them. I was just desperate for sleep.

"Persephone?" Hayden asks, eyebrows arched.

I look at him, then at Ethan who is pointing to something on the contract he's laid out.

"I'm sorry, I missed that." I seem to have missed the entire conversation.

"The amount you and Hayden agreed upon for the shares. If you'll initial here?"

I look down at the number, confused. We hadn't agreed on anything. We hadn't discussed it at all. I know from my conversation with my father's attorney the amount I can expect, considering the position I'm in, but the number I see in front of me is double that.

I shift my gaze to Hayden, then read the number again.

"I..." I'm not a numbers person. I never have been. But even I know that's too much. "Should I have my lawyer here?" I ask Hayden, realizing how stupid it must sound asking the man who is ready to take over our company by any means necessary, if I need a lawyer.

"If you'd like, you can call him now," Hayden says. "That number is fair, though."

"More than fair," Ethan adds. "Technically, their worth is much lo—"

"That's not necessary, Ethan," Hayden cuts him off. "I'm not taking advantage of you, Persephone."

I look at him, remembering how he was last night. For as harsh as he is, he's also tender. Gentle. Almost caring. My eyes warm with tears and sometimes I hate being a woman. I cry at everything good or bad, happy or sad.

I break eye contact and stand, clearing my throat. "I'll just make the call." I don't have to look at him to know that was wrong. The amount is generous. I know it. But still, he is taking my family's company. That's what I need to remember.

I pick up my purse, dig for my phone inside it. I move away from the seating area and dial my father's attorney. He answers quickly, it's his private line. He and my father are friends. They have been since graduating Yale together. He's had dinner at my house countless times and is more like an uncle to me than an attorney.

I start to explain what's happened, but he stops me. "I have a copy of the paperwork here. Montgomery sent it earlier today. I'd prefer to be there with you, but honestly, it's more than we could have expected."

"And I have no options." I'm not sure why I'm asking.

"I'm afraid not, Percy."

"Thank you." I hang up and when I turn around, I find the men discussing something as they drink coffee. A plate stacked high with cinnamon rolls sits on the table, a butter dish beside it, but I've lost my appetite.

When I return, they stop their conversation.

I pick up the pen and initial beside the number. I don't look at Hayden as Ethan explains a few more things and finally we're at the last page and I sign. I just sign.

Hayden turns the contract around as I set the pen down, I'm not sure what I feel. Defeat. Loss. I don't know. But this is final.

He signs his name and a moment later, the men stand.

"It was nice to meet you, Percy," Ethan says. "If you need anything else," he adds, handing me a card, "don't hesitate."

"Thank you."

I watch Hayden walk Ethan to the elevator and when he's gone, Hayden turns to me.

"All right?"

I force a deep breath in before I stand to face him. "Not really, no."

"I was generous."

"You still took what rightfully belongs to my family."

"Just control of it. Not much will change in the day to day."

"Still." I busy myself looking for the keys to the Jeep. "I'm leaving. I guess you'll be back later to take more of what doesn't belong to you?"

I think if he got angry, it'd be better. If he looked at me like I was an adversary. Not the way he's looking at me now. Like I'm something to be pitied.

"Don't," I tell him, my voice catching in my throat.

"Don't what?"

"Don't pretend to care. Don't pretend like you give a single fuck. You're leveling the scales, taking justice into your own hands. Justice for what, I have no idea, but I know you feel you're owed and there's no point in saying more. You have what you want. Abbot Enterprises. The Abbot family home."

I see his jaw tense.

"And you have me. Well, my body at least. I hope you'll be very happy." I step past him meaning to get to the elevator, knowing I won't. Knowing he won't let me.

And just like that, his hand clasps around my arm stopping me in my tracks.

"Your father put you here, in my path. Not me. Don't presume to know my motives."

"They're very clear, Hayden. Take. Take everything from my family. From me."

His eyes narrow dangerously, and I draw a deep breath in.

"I wish you'd tell me what it is he did, then at least I'd

know. And maybe I'd understand why you hate him so much. Why you hate us so much."

"I don't hate *you*."

"No? But you get even. And I'm collateral damage." I exhale a sharp breath, shake my head and tilt it. "Tell me something, are you there yet? Are the scales balanced yet?"

"Don't do this."

"Why not? Why does it matter?"

"I don't hate *you*, Persephone."

"That little detail doesn't matter either. I'm still here. I'm the one signing away my father's company. I'm the one who pays. Tell me, is it enough yet? Have I paid enough for our sins?"

"His sins. *His*."

"Like I said, it doesn't matter."

"I'm warning you. Stand down, Persephone."

"Stand down. Roll over and betray my own father. Yours may have been shitty to you, but mine wasn't. Mine was—*is* —good."

His eye twitches. "He isn't." His nostrils flare as he forces a breath in and I can see him reining himself in, trying to check his anger.

"I guess we'll have to agree to disagree."

He grips the hair at the back of my head, snapping the clip holding it in place. He's so close, the tips of our noses touch. And like this, this close, his eyes are on fire. Ablaze with fury.

"You want to know if it's enough?"

I swallow, nod, because I'm too stubborn to stand down. To heed his warning.

"We're just getting started," he whispers, twisting my hair, making me wince.

My hands are flat against his chest and we look at each other like this. Facing off before the battle.

But the thing is, he's already won. We both know it.

Now it's a matter of enjoying the spoils of war.

Me.

He shifts his grip so his hands come to my shoulders, settling like two weights there.

"Kneel," he commands.

"No."

"I said kneel."

"I will bite your dick off if you put it near my mouth."

His glare is that of a predator who's cornered its prey. "I have no doubt, but it's not your mouth I'm interested in right now."

Something in his eyes makes my heart beat faster and sends heat to my core because even like this, even as enemies, I'm turned on. This is what he does to me.

He spins me around and leans in close behind me. I feel him at my back. Feel the heat of his breath on my neck when he repeats that one word. "Kneel."

He doesn't wait for me to comply. I guess he knows I won't. Instead, he forces me down and even though I know it's pointless, I resist. He kneels behind me and shifts one hand to my throat and the other down to undo my jeans. When he slides his hand into my panties to cup my sex, I want to want to pull away.

But when he touches me, it's like I'm lost, like I'm not myself. I come apart at his touch and it scares me like nothing else does.

He rubs my clit and releases my throat when he does. No need to hold me in place. I'm panting. I can't get enough.

"You hate yourself for wanting this. Wanting me." His

breath tickles my ear and it's as if he's read my mind because he's certainly reading my body.

"I hate you," I say, sucking in an audible breath when he pinches my clit.

He reaches for the butter dish beside the now cold cinnamon rolls.

"You wish you hated me." He drags my jeans and panties down and pushes me forward so I'm on my hands and knees. He then shoves my knees as far apart as he can with my jeans pushed down and settles himself between them.

He spreads me open and I look back at him. Look at him looking at me and fuck. Seeing him like this. Seeing us like this. What it does to me, it makes me heady and it's something I can't reconcile.

He shifts his gaze to meet mine and scoops a thick glob of butter with his fingers while placing his other hand between my shoulder blades and pushing.

"Down on your elbows. Ass up."

I do as he says only because physically, I'm no match. At least that's what I tell myself.

"What are you doing?"

He keeps his gaze on mine as he smears that butter on my asshole. When I understand what he means to do, how he plans to fuck me, a panic sets in and I'm back up on hands and knees, crawling away.

Or trying to.

He keeps me in position with one hand clamped around my hip as he laughs, pushing a thick finger into my asshole.

"Oh god!"

"What am I doing?" he asks, sliding that finger in and out, the butter making the passage slippery.

"Hayden, please—"

"Hades," he corrects.

He pulls his finger out to collect more butter. Shifting his hand to push me back down to my elbows, he grips his thick cock with the other and rubs butter all over it. As afraid as I am, I'm equally aroused.

"What am I doing?" he asks again.

I just stare back at him.

"I'm bringing you down a notch."

14

HAYDEN

I'm not sure what I prefer. A woman on her knees her mouth filled with my cock, or a woman on her knees about to take my dick in her pussy or her ass.

I guess the common theme here is a woman on her knees.

And Persephone on her knees like this, fuck, if I'm not careful I'll blow in my fist just looking at her.

"Don't worry," I say, scooping up the last of the butter and finger-fucking her tight little hole. "I've lubricated you inside and out. You just try to relax and enjoy the ride." I pull my fingers out and bring the head of my cock to her tight hole.

"No, no, no! You'll rip me in two! Please!" Her eyes go wide as I grip her hips with both hands, using my thumbs to spread her ass cheeks wider. I close my eyes and enjoy that initial squeeze.

"Fuuuuck," I open my eyes and look at her. "You'll be the death of me." I pump slowly, taking centimeter by centimeter. I don't want to hurt her. I want her ready when I fuck her. I want to watch her swallow her pride as she comes multiple times with my dick up her tight ass.

"It hurts!"

I slide one hand down to her clit and when I take it into my hand, she catches her breath. For a moment, she's fighting it, fighting me, but I feel when her body relaxes, when she arches her back just a little.

"Do you hate me now?" I ask when she closes her eyes and I take an inch. Her asshole is tight and warm and slippery with the butter lubricant. "Tell me," I say, pumping slowly, looking down at her as she stretches to take my length, my girth.

When she doesn't reply, I smack her ass.

She gasps and her eyes fly open.

"I asked you a question."

"I..." she starts but I'm rubbing her clit again. I'm about half-way in and fuck, I'm going to come hard.

"Cat got your tongue?"

Her answer is a whimper as her mouth opens and her eyes close.

I grin, rub her swollen nub and watch her face because she's so fucking beautiful when she comes. When her walls begin to pulse around my cock, I claim more of her, her moans making me harder, her asshole opening to me like a greedy little thing that wants more. More. More.

I'm happy to oblige.

When I'm fully seated, I stop, taking a moment to enjoy the tremors of aftershock as she pants and tries to force my hand from her clit.

"I'm all the way in. All the way inside your tight little hole. Are you ready to get your ass fucked, sweetheart?"

"I can't...It's too much—"

"You can and you will. You'll take my cum too. I'm going to fill you up with my cum."

And when I pull out and thrust back in, she lets out a loud moan, and arches her back. The words she's saying are nonsensical. The only one I recognize is my own name.

Hades.

The name she gave me a breath on her tongue.

Her life's breath.

God.

Fuck.

This woman. Fuck. Fuck me. I'm screwed.

Because I know what this is.

And as her walls throb again, I thrust deep inside her and still there. It's like just then, in that moment, time is suspended. Stopping just for us and we're both coming. She's moaning my name, her cheek on the floor, eyes closed, one hand fisted, the other clawing at the carpet as I fill her up. As I empty inside her and I claim this other part of her. And all the while I know the truth, even if she doesn't.

She owns a part of me. She always has.

No. That's not it.

Persephone owns my fucking soul.

15

PERSEPHONE

How is it like this with him? How is everything different with him?

He's gentle after. He lifts me up and cradles me on his lap like I'm his most precious possession.

I lay my head against his warm chest and close my eyes. I listen to his heartbeat and let myself snuggle into the safety of his arms.

And like last night, I want to cry.

I don't understand this confusion of emotion. This chaos inside my head. My heart.

He's right. I don't hate him. And it's not just that that scares me. It's that the opposite is true. It's always been true. Maybe since that first day out on the curb when I was a kid.

And I know I'm fucked. I am well and truly fucked.

That's exactly why I can't do this. Why I can't let him hold me. Why I can't let him be gentle. Tender, even.

I can't take comfort in his arms, or against his chest. I can't feel protected. Safe.

I can't.

I push away, look up at him.

He seems surprised but doesn't speak. He studies me instead and I have to be careful because I think maybe I'm wrong. Maybe he's not human.

He can't just read my mind. I think he can see inside my soul.

"I don't want Anna," I blurt out.

"What?" He's clearly taken aback.

"I don't want a cook."

My throat feels full, like the emotion is going to choke me. Like it's going to cut off my oxygen and kill me.

I push away, try to stand, stumbling as I do with my jeans around my ankles.

He's already got his pants up. I guess he took care of that after fucking me.

I bend to pull my jeans up while he gets to his feet. He disappears into a room I didn't realize was there—another one of those doors flush with the wall like the elevator. I hear water running and a few moments later, he returns, drying his hands.

"Let me clean you," he says.

I still feel him inside me, his cum inside me. And this insane, masochistic part of me, it wants that part of him.

Wants any part of him.

I shake my head, rub my face. "Where's my coat?" I ask, snatching my purse from the couch.

"Persephone—"

"I need to go." I swipe my hand over my eyes, hoping he thinks it's just an itch. Not the tears I need to hide.

"What's going on?" he asks.

I take a deep breath in, my gaze falling on the empty butter dish. I try not to think about what he did with that butter.

"Persephone?"

I think about other things instead. Bad things.

Nora.

No, not that. That's too sad.

Jonas?

Bad, yes. But not that either. That will only steal my strength.

My father.

Yes.

My father.

I conjure up the image of him lying in his hospital bed. I think about the man who ran him over and drove away. I think about how maybe it wasn't an accident. How that's always been in the back of my mind.

I think about my betrayal today, signing that contract and giving Hayden control of Abbot Enterprises while my father lies helpless in a hospital bed. I think about being cornered by Hayden and I steel my spine because I have to.

I force a grin that must make me look insane and try to swallow that lump in my throat. Try to ignore the twisting in my belly. The constricting of my heart.

"Well, you did it. You brought me down a notch. Congratulations." Tears. Fucking tears. I hate them. "I'm going to go see my father now."

I remember then that my coat is downstairs. I took it off when I came in here. God, how I'd come in here. Cavalier. A warrior!

A fucking idiot.

"Don't worry," I hear my voice quaver. "I'll be home later for whatever humiliations you have planned for me tonight." I make my way to the elevator and look at the keypad. Fuck, I can't even get out of here. "Let me out," I say, staring straight ahead because I can't look at him.

"Mind telling me what the hell just happened?" he asks.

I push buttons, it's ridiculous I know, but I'm desperate.

He captures my fingers, closes his big hand around them.

"Persephone."

I can't do this. "Let me out."

"Talk to me."

"Let me the fuck out!"

He holds me, presses his body to mine. His arm wraps around me, hugging me to him but I can't lean into him. I can't rest my cheek against his chest. I can't. Not if I want to survive this. Survive him.

Too late.

"Stay," he says.

I open my mouth and I know he hears it. Hears me crying. "I paid my time for now. You can't require more."

"Stay with me," a whisper, and then silence. Just his breath at my ear, just my tears sliding down my face.

"Let me go." Because if you don't, I'm going to lose it. I'm going to lose it here and now and I can't do that. "Please, Hades."

Keeping my hand in his, he stretches his arm to punch in the code on the pad by the elevator.

I thank God that the doors slide open instantly. I don't look back when I step inside. I don't look at my reflection, either. I don't meet his eyes in the mirror. I keep my gaze down, very aware of his eyes on me.

And when the doors slide closed, I let my shoulders slump and rest my forehead against the mirrored wall, finally meeting my reflection. What I see scares me. Because what I see is a woman broken.

"I'm going to stain you, Persephone."

Is this what he means by that? That he'll break me in order to own me. A body is not a soul, doesn't he know that?

But with Hayden, it's different. Different than it was with Jonas even when we were engaged.

Jonas never had any claim on me.

Hayden? He can and will steal my soul.

A few moments later, the elevator doors open again, and I hear the sound of men talking, smell cigars and whiskey. Isn't it early for such indulgences?

Before turning, I find my sunglasses in my bag and slip them on my face. Without bothering to ask for my coat, I walk out, shivering in the cold morning air.

I find my Jeep, get in then fumble with the key to get the engine started.

And when I finally drive away, it's not to the facility where my father is housed. It's back home, well, to the back entrance of the house where I trudge through melting snow and make my way to the chapel between our properties. Make my way into that dreary place and hug my arms to myself as I sit in a broken pew, making myself look at the wrecked altar. At the broken Christ half-hanging on his cross from the wall.

I don't know why I come here. Why I call for God here of all places. It's not like he ever answers. Not for me. Not for Nora. Not when we needed him. And certainly not now.

16

PERSEPHONE

The shadows have grown long before I pull the Jeep onto the driveaway. I'm surprised when I do to see the truck from Sotheby's consignment parked outside.

I can't deal with this right now.

Climbing out of the Jeep, I walk up the front steps of the house, open the door. I hear Anna right away. Am I surprised she's still here? Not really.

"Hello?" I call out, appreciating the warmth of the house. The broken walls of the chapel don't offer much protection.

They've lit the fireplace in the entryway. It's a huge one. I haven't seen it lit in a very long time. It was always too much of a bother for my father, so he only did it when we had company, which was less and less often in the last years.

If I think back now, I see the signs of what's come. Signs of our decline. If I'd paid closer attention, would I have known earlier? Would I have been able to help? To make a difference?

But my father was larger than life to me. I could rely on

him. Lean all my weight into him. I never even imagined a life without him. And it never occurred to me we might one day lose everything.

"Anna?" I walk toward the sound of a man laughing.

What I find, though, isn't what I expect.

"What's going on?" I ask, stepping into the dining room to see them place the final pieces of furniture back exactly where they belong.

The two men from yesterday and Anna look up at me. The men appear confused, but Anna smiles. "Mr. Montgomery arranged for the delivery, Miss. If anything isn't in the right place, we can rearrange it."

"I think I remembered how you'd set it up," one of the men says.

I walk out of the dining room and into the living room. Same thing there. All the furniture back in place.

"I don't understand," I say, although I'm not sure to whom.

"If you'll just sign here," the shorter man with the clipboard says to me. "We'll get out of your hair."

"But why did you bring it back?"

He looks puzzled. "Not a question we normally get." He smiles awkwardly, eyes his colleague.

"I didn't..." I swallow my pride. "I can't pay for it." If they think they'll get their money back, they're mistaken.

"I just do the deliveries, Ms. Abbot. If you'll sign?"

I take the pen and sign and a few moments later, they're gone, and I'm left looking at Anna.

"Oh, your sister came by to pick up some clothes. She said she's spending a few more nights with her friend. She wanted me to let you know."

"She did? When?"

"About an hour ago. And Mr. Montgomery's asked that

you be ready by half past seven. He asked that you wear the red gown."

I dig for my phone in my purse and switch it back on. I'd switched it off when Hayden wouldn't stop calling me.

I have thirteen missed calls from him.

Ignoring them, I try to dial Lizzie, but her phone goes right to voicemail, so I disconnect.

"Would you like something to eat?" Anna asks.

I shake my head, turn to walk away while my brain works to make sense of this. I should just ask Hayden. He's the one who arranged for the return of our things. Did he buy our furniture back? Although, I guess like the house it's his furniture now.

I go upstairs, checking the time on my phone when a message comes through.

"You disappear again, and we have a problem."

Hayden.

And he's pissed.

Good.

I tuck the phone into my pocket, and I wonder if Anna reported my return to him. I guess so.

I go up to my room and sit on the edge of the bed. I call Celia and apologize for not coming. I ask her how dad is— the same—and promise to visit tomorrow. I then strip off my clothes and run a bath, locking the bathroom door and soaking until the water cools, all the while thinking about what happened. Why it felt like it did—not like he said was his intent at all. Not him taking me down a notch.

Was it the same for him?

"Don't be stupid," I tell myself out loud and climb out of the tub to get ready for tonight.

I did, after all, promise to be available for further humiliations.

17

HAYDEN

I carry Persephone's coat as I walk through the house to look into the now furnished rooms. Everything back in place like I remember it.

Anna is talking, giving me a rundown of events, but her voice is like a buzzing in my ear and I don't really care.

"Is she upstairs?" I ask, cutting Anna off as I glance up the long, curving staircase. She'd better be.

"Yes, sir," she says.

I nod and head up, opening her bedroom door. She's sitting at the vanity that's been replaced and wordlessly meets my gaze in the mirror.

I toss her coat onto the bed and take a look around the room. "Everything where you want it?"

She puts down the tube of lipstick and half-turns. She's wearing the dress I told her to wear, which surprises me. The red is stunning on her, setting off her creamy skin and dark hair.

"Why did you buy back the furniture?"

"Isn't 'thank you' more appropriate?"

"I didn't ask you to do it. And besides, it's not for me. It's your house. Your furniture. I'm just your tenant."

I don't know what the fuck is up with her. I thought the afternoon on her own would clear her head, but if she wants to play it this way, fine. I'll engage.

"I thought it was a fitting reward after this morning."

Her eyes narrow. "Like a 'thank-you-for-the-fuck'?"

"Exactly. Speaking of, how's your ass?"

"Fuck you."

I chuckle. "Brought your coat back. You were in a state to leave without it."

"Aren't all the women you fuck *in a state*?"

"I'm glad to see you're starting to appreciate the honor of your position."

She snorts.

"Speaking of positions, having you on your knees with your ass in the air may be my favorite for you."

Without bothering to look at me, she flips me off and I grin, check the time. "I need to shower and change."

She shrugs a shoulder like she could care less, her attention to applying lipstick.

I walk into the bathroom and strip off my things, showering quickly. My clothes have been moved into the closet. Anna is a competent housekeeper. I put on my tux and am adjusting the bowtie when I walk back into the bedroom.

"Where did you go?" I ask.

"Nowhere."

"Not to your father."

"No, not there."

"Then where?"

She lifts her gaze to meet mine. "None of your business."

"Everything about you is my business. But fine."

I pick up my phone which I'd left on the dresser and

type in a text to Peter: *Get a tracker installed on Ms. Abbot's Jeep. It's at the house. I want it done tonight.*

I get an instant reply confirming he'll take care of it. This is the kind of service money buys.

I tuck my phone into my pocket, take the tuxedo jacket off the hanger and put it on. I go to Persephone, place my hands on her shoulders and squeeze.

"Red is your color."

She drops a compact into her clutch and I step back for her to stand. She's wearing four-inch heels, but the top of her head just barely comes to my chin. I take a moment to look her over.

"Turn," I tell her.

She grits her teeth and turns. The dress hugs her curves, accentuating her tiny waist, the flare of her hips and her round ass.

She faces me again. "Satisfied?"

"More than."

I touch the lock of hair allowed to escape her twist, tuck it behind her ear, take in the dark kohl that makes her eyes look huge, the deep crimson lipstick I want to kiss off, to smear across her face.

Stain her.

I wrap my hand around the nape of her slender neck. She's so much smaller than me and I don't know if it's that or something else that makes me feel so protective of her.

"What happened this morning?" I ask.

"You were there. I'm sure you remember the details."

"What upset you?"

"You mean apart from signing over controlling shares of Abbot Enterprises and having my ass fucked?"

"I thought you enjoyed the ass fucking. You came. More than once."

"You said yourself you were bringing me down a notch. You got what you wanted."

"You don't have to fight me."

"Yes, I do."

"I'll take care of you. You know that."

"I know no such thing. And really, this is just strange. What do you want, Hayden? You want to see our family destroyed, yet you'll *take care* of me? Do you just want me in your debt? Oh wait, no. You want me on my knees."

"You asked me earlier if you deserved to be punished. You do not. But you are caught up in this."

"Because of who I am."

"Yes."

"Tell me what you think he did."

"Not what I think. What I know." I check my watch, grit my teeth as the evening draws nearer. I'm not looking forward to this. "We need to go." I take her elbow.

"Wait." She pulls free and picks up her clutch. I open the door. She walks out and down the stairs ahead of me.

Shane is waiting at the door.

"What is the auction for?" she asks as I lay her coat over her shoulders.

I put my own coat on and signal to Shane who opens the door.

Persephone shudders at the sudden icy chill.

I wrap an arm around her, and we walk to the car, climbing into the backseat. I glance at my house in the darkness, a hulking, broken thing left to rot. I wonder if Nora haunts it. I hope not. I hope she's at peace.

"A fund raiser for Senator Hughes," I say.

"Senator Hughes? He was going to run against my father. He's corrupt, Hayden. You support him?"

I turn to her, give her a grin. "Politics are complicated."

"No, they aren't. You either have morals or you don't. They're actually quite simple."

"Is that so? And on which side did your father fall?"

"I can't go. I won't support my father's rival."

"Your father's out of the race, sweetheart."

"Don't be a jerk."

"Besides, you'll get to see Jonas again. Won't that be nice?"

"What?" her face drains of color. It surprises me.

"My father will be there too. It'll be a fucking family reunion."

"Hayden," she starts, putting her hand on my arm. "I don't want to go. I can't."

"Can't and won't are two different things. You're going."

"Please."

"Don't worry, sweetheart, daddy will never find out."

"It's not...I just...."

"You just what?"

She studies me for a long moment, then shakes her head. "Please don't make me. I'm asking."

"Why?"

"Just...please."

I study her, more curious than ever. "Tell me and I'll think about it."

"I can't do that."

"Then you're going. It's very simple."

I'm surprised when she shifts her gaze out the window, dropping the argument. I half expect her to pick it up again, but she remains quiet until we pull into the parking lot at the event center.

Two hundred-fifty guests. A five-course meal. Ten-thousand dollars a plate.

We pull to a stop and I open my door, stepping out. I

take in a deep breath of fresh, icy air and extend my hand to help Persephone out.

She places her small, clammy hand in mine. I think about how surprised my father will be to see me tonight. How surprised Jonas will be to see Persephone on my arm.

My father made a donation to the Hughes campaign, but I doubled it. I guess he thought I wouldn't see it coming. But I see everything. And I forget nothing.

"Hayden," Persephone says, finally stepping out of the car. Her face is paler as she looks beyond me at the interior buzzing with donors. "It'll be awkward."

"I could give a fuck about awkward. Let's go."

PERSEPHONE

My ears are ringing when we walk into the luxurious event space. Someone plays the piano in the background as formally dressed waiters carry trays of champagne in crystal flutes.

I don't want to lean into Hayden's hand which is resting on the bare skin of my lower back, but he will be the only thing standing between me and Jonas tonight.

"You're shivering," Hayden says.

"It's cold." We left our coats at the coat check.

A waiter passes with a tray of champagne and I reach out to take one. Hayden watches me swallow the contents.

"Did you eat this afternoon?"

"Why are you so concerned with my diet?"

"Because I don't want you passing out."

"I won't pass out." I place my empty glass back on the tray and take a full one.

"Take it easy on the champagne."

"Hayden Montgomery! I don't believe it," a woman says.

We both turn to watch her approach. I'd guess her to be in her late thirties. A man follows close behind and the difference in how they look at Hayden is night and day. "Color me surprised when I saw your name on the guest list," she says flirtatiously, and I decide instantly that I don't like her.

"Monica," Hayden says, letting her touch her cheeks to his as if they're Europeans greeting each other. "A pleasant surprise, I hope."

"You're always a pleasant surprise, darling."

I can't help my snort and she turns to me, eyes not quite as warm as they were when she looked at Hayden.

"This is Persephone," Hayden says, fingers caressing the naked part of my back.

Monica smiles because she has to.

The man she's with clears his throat. "You'd think they'd offer whiskey," he says, taking a flute of champagne off a passing waiter's tray.

"Frank," Hayden says, his smile more of a sneer. "Good to see you out and about."

"Is it?" he asks, shifting his gaze to me, openly looking me over but not greeting me.

Monica leans in close to Hayden. "Your father's holding court in the blue room," she whispers.

Hayden stiffens beside me. "Is he?"

"I thought you'd want to know."

"Thank you." He turns to me. "Shall we?"

"Nice to meet you," I say out of habit as we walk away. "That was gross. She looks at you like it's her birthday and you're her cake."

He smiles, his attention straight ahead as he guides me through the room. "Don't worry, sweetheart, I only have eyes for you."

"Oh, I'm not worried. I just don't want you limiting your options." I give him a smirk when he glances my way.

"You've perked up."

I set my empty champagne on a passing waiter's tray and pick up a new one.

Hayden eyes me warily.

"Dinner isn't for half an hour at least. Anna said you didn't eat this morning and I'm guessing you didn't take yourself out to lunch when you disappeared so take it easy. I'm not saying it again."

"You don't dictate what I eat or drink." To make my point, I swallow a gulp. I'll need this to face Jonas.

His eyes narrow and he opens his mouth to say something but we both hear his father at the same time. I don't know what he feels at the sound, but panic grips me.

"I need to use the lady's room," I say, slipping away before he can respond.

Sweat collects under my arms and beads across my forehead. Sound seems to bounce off the walls of the hall as too many people talk at once, the noise a constant buzzing in my ear. I can't make out a single word as I weave through throngs of people and make my way toward the bathrooms which are tucked away at the end of a hall.

The moment I'm inside, I lock the door behind me and lean against it.

My heart is pounding, and I've broken into a full sweat. Anxiety knots stomach and the champagne I swallowed leaves a bitter taste in my mouth.

I haven't seen Jonas since the night after I broke off our engagement. Hayden is right. Jonas is not a good guy. I should have known it after that Halloween night. But when Nora died, he was so broken up, so upset and it seemed I was the only one who could comfort him.

He left for university soon after her death and I didn't see him for four years. And when he came home, he seemed different than he'd been. Like he'd changed. He even looked different. Gone was the devil-may-care attitude that made people want to be around him. There was something darker about him. Something infinitely sadder and it drew me.

Jonas thought it best we keep the fact that we were dating a secret. He thought it might be strange for our families. I went along with it assuming it was because my father and his father weren't on good terms, only telling my father after we got engaged. I remember he'd been livid.

But then, after the hit-and-run, I was left in charge of Abbot Enterprises. I found something that made me see things differently. That made me understand why Jonas wanted to keep our relationship a secret. And I know my father had never intended for me to find it. That's when I'd understood his reaction to our announcement.

I broke off our engagement that same night.

Jonas had become angry to the point of violence. I'd never seen him like that before. It was like a switch had been flipped and to this day, I think the only reason it wasn't worse was because I told him I knew what he'd done.

He tried to call the next night. The one after that. Every night for a month. Left apologies on voicemail. Sent flowers. Begged me to give him another chance. To let him explain.

When I didn't reply, the messages got ugly until I finally threatened to go to the police.

"I can't do this," I say out loud. I step away from the door and force a deep breath in. I set my clutch on the counter, turn on the tap and wet a towel with cold water, patting it along my forehead and the back of my neck to cool myself. My face has gone a sickly white and I'm dizzy.

I sit on the velvet couch until the dizziness passes. There's a knock on the door.

"Just a minute," I call out.

I get up, force a deep breath in. I'll slip away. Tell Hayden I didn't feel well. Tell him he was right about the champagne. Anything to get out of this. Get out of having to see Jonas again.

The knock comes again, and I steel my spine. Picking up my clutch, I open the door and a woman gives me an annoyed glance before slipping past me into the lady's room.

I quickly glance around for Hayden but when I don't see him, I make my way to the exit. I pass the coat check and remember that Hayden has our claim tickets so, hugging my arms to myself, I'm about to step out into the icy night when a voice stops me dead in my tracks.

"Well, well."

A chill runs down my suddenly rigid spine.

"You're leaving early," he says. "Without even a hello."

I still don't turn and for the number of people in here, it may as well be just the two of us.

Jonas Montgomery steps in front of me. I look up at him, at his bright blue eyes. Eyes that lie. That hide the real man inside.

He's wearing a tuxedo like Hayden and runs his fingers through his dirty blond hair pushing it off his forehead.

The all-American boy. A boy all the girls look twice at.

They wouldn't if they knew him. Really knew him. They'd see the shadow of his soul leeching into his handsome face, his bright eyes.

"Are you taking turns with the Montgomery men?" he asks, swallowing the last of his drink and setting the glass aside. I see from the way he moves that he's already had too much.

"You're drunk," I say.

"Am I?"

I sidestep to get around him but he blocks my path.

"Get out of my way, Jonas."

"No. Not until you talk to me."

"I'm not talking to you."

"On his order?" he snorts. Hate fills his eyes as they skim over me.

He splays his hand across my belly and walks me backward until we're in an alcove just beside the exit doors.

"Is dad next? You always did behave like a whore around him. Or is he too old for you? Maybe Ares? Hell, maybe you can take Ares and Hayden together. A threesome. One up your tight ass and one in your big mouth. Can you even tell them apart?"

"If he sees you with me, he'll kill you."

"He's busy."

"What do you want?"

"You don't return my fucking calls. You need to return my calls."

"I don't *need* to do anything. Leave me alone."

He looks me over then leans close. "You look good. Sucking my bastard brother's dick agrees with you."

"Get away from me. I'm warning you."

He laughs in my face and I wonder if he's stoned too when I see how his pupils are dilated.

"You're *warning* me?" He rubs the corner of his mouth with his thumb. "Warning me about what?"

"I can still go to the police."

"You're not going to do that."

He's right. I'm not. I can't.

I straighten, steeling my spine. Jonas Montgomery is a bully. Always has been.

"Get away from me."

"Don't be like that, baby," he says more gently, changing tactics.

"I'm not your baby."

He leans in closer and I can smell his stale breath. "You won't see me. You won't let me talk to you. How can I explain when you won't let me talk to you? I told you I was sorry. You just made me so angry that night." He leans his weight into his hand which is still pressed to my belly. "Don't you see how much I care about you?"

"If you really cared about me, you'd respect my wishes," I try, knowing Jonas doesn't care about anyone. I don't know if he has the capacity to even if he believes he does. He's sick. Twisted.

I push at his hand, but he shifts it higher, his gaze sliding to my breast that he's almost cupping. When he returns his eyes to mine, there's a meanness inside them, a cruelty I remember from the last night I saw him.

A cruelty that scares me.

"I don't want to have to hurt you again," he warns, and I force his words to give me strength, not steal it away. Not like then.

I can fight. I will. Even if he's stronger than me, people will hear. He can't hurt me, not here.

He brings his mouth to my ear, his cheek to my cheek and I squeeze my eyes shut.

"But I will."

"Oh, I know you will. But remember one thing." I set my hands on his shoulders, he grins. But he's got the wrong idea. I force a cold smile and whisper my next words. "I know what you did."

His blue eyes turn to ice, his body going rigid with rage.

With all the force I can muster, I bring my knee up hard

because I want to smash his balls so hard, he can't ever fuck again.

But he's ready for me. Men like him must always be ready when a woman fights.

He catches my knee between his thighs and grips my neck hard.

"You're a whore, you know that?" he sneers and squeezes his hand around my throat before I can make a sound.

I'm on tiptoe, hands desperately trying to pry his arm off, but I'm no match. I never was. I can't even scream. He's cut off my oxygen. All these people here, all the people milling around drinking their champagne just a few feet from us and no one to help me.

Jonas leans in close, his breath wet against my cheek. "Does my brother know?"

"Get...off."

"Did you tell him?"

I try to shake my head, to mouth the word 'no'.

"No one would believe you anyway. No one."

Just as my vision starts to fade, I hear him. I hear Hayden. And an instant later, Jonas' hand is gone from my neck and I suck in oxygen.

My knees buckle as I watch Hayden loom over his step-brother, his hand around Jonas' throat lifting Jonas off his feet.

"Did she tell me what?" he asks Jonas just before slamming him against the wall.

I scream as Jonas' head bounces off and I grab Hayden's arm when he draws it back to punch him.

"Stop! Hayden stop!"

"Did she tell me what?" Hayden asks again as I hang off his arm.

"Sloppy seconds, brother?" Jonas taunts.

"I'm not your brother, asshole."

Jonas is flippant even though he must know that physically, he's no match. "No, you're the bastard. Thanks for reminding me."

I see the rage collecting in Hayden's eyes and I think he's going to kill him. I really think he's going to kill Jonas.

"He's drunk, Hayden." I try to tug at his arm, to get him away. "And he's not worth it."

But it's like he doesn't hear me, and I realize how quiet it's gotten. How a crowd has gathered around us when only moments ago when Jonas would have choked me, when I needed help, no one came.

"Walk away, Persephone," Hayden tells me, never taking his eyes off Jonas.

I shake my head, tears burning my eyes. "You'll kill him."

"I said walk away," he tells me. "Now."

I cling, hugging his arm to me. "Walk away with me, Hades."

Jonas snorts. "Persephone and Hades. You think you're some mythical couple? A god? You're nothing. Nothing but a bastard. And you know what? You can have the whore. Fucking her is like fucking a block of ice."

Rage vibrates off Hayden and he gives his arm a powerful shake, sending me flying. I slam against the wall, my breath a whoosh of air forced from my lungs, my head colliding hard. My vision goes black momentarily. At least I think it's momentary.

When I open my eyes, I'm on the floor and for a second, I think I'm seeing double but then I realize it's Ares and he's between Hayden and Jonas and he's saying something to Hayden, but I can't make out words. All I hear is a ringing in my ears.

I wince when I touch the back of my head and my fingers come away wet. Wet with blood.

When I look up Hayden is standing over me. A crowd has gathered and they're all looking down at me.

Jeremiah Montgomery is there then, and, in my mind, I see Hayden's scarred back again. He did that to him. He hurt him like that.

He pushes through the circle of people, takes in the scene as my hearing returns and it's so loud, it hurts.

In the confusion, Jonas walks away without a backward glance and Hayden crouches down in front of me. He touches my cheek and he's saying something, but I can't make out the words. It doesn't matter though because he lifts me up in his arms and there are so many people watching.

He hands me over to Ares. I know because of their dimples. Hayden's is on his right cheek, Ares' on his left.

He's talking, saying something.

Hayden takes off his jacket, covers me with it. It's warm and I smell him, and I close my eyes. A moment later, I'm outside and he's putting me into a car and we're driving.

"You okay?" he asks.

I blink, look up at him. "You're not Hayden."

"No, I'm not."

"My head hurts." And as I say it, I feel myself slide down the seat and into his hard shoulder and no matter how I try, I can't keep my eyes from closing.

19

HAYDEN

"You're causing a scene, son."

I look to the spot where she was. Her clutch is lying on the floor and there's a smear of red where her head hit the wall.

Fuck.

Fuck. Fuck. Fuck.

I bend to pick up her bag before turning to face my father.

"You think I give a fuck what people think?" Even as I say it, people disperse behind him, their whispered murmurs the buzz of vultures. Of bottom-feeders.

"No, I don't think you do."

I look at my father. I remember how I'd looked at him growing up. When he'd been bigger than me and had no qualms about using his size to intimidate me and worse.

I see him as he is now. Older, hair whiter, shoulders not quite as broad, hands not quite as threatening.

I remember the night of the fire. That Halloween that everything changed. Clear as day, I remember the argument I overheard between my father and grandfather, my father telling him he had no right. My grandfather, a formidable man, telling my father it was his own fault for bringing *that filth* into his home.

He was talking about Nora. It was the one area my grandfather and I disagreed. He hated her. He hated her from the very beginning even when she was just a little girl.

Then came the mention of me and Ares. My grandfather telling my father that he was cut out. That when he died, my brother and I would inherit everything.

My father had lost his shit, had threatened him. They'd argued a little longer, and when my grandfather dismissed him, my father walked out. I hid in the shadows and although I know he saw me, he kept walking.

I walked out too after that. Out to that chapel where I found the three of them, Jonas, Nora and Persephone.

"You took your brother's fiancée? You can fuck any woman you want, and you take her?"

"Ex-fiancée. She left him months ago."

"As you can see, there's still love between them. You have no right to her."

"Love between them?" I snort. "Knowing you like I do I can actually see how you'd think that."

"You've always been a cocky asshole, you know that? You beating women now too?" my father asks, gesturing to the bloody spot on the wall.

I narrow my eyes and feel my body tense. My hands fist. I force myself to breathe, to keep control.

"Like you beat children?" I ask through gritted teeth. "Is that what you and grandfather were fighting about the night of the fire? The night he died?"

My father falters but only momentarily. But that moment, it's what I need.

"He was changing his will. He was leaving it all to me and Ares," I say.

"Did you have your ear to the door?"

"I didn't need to. You were both screaming."

"If you knew him, you wouldn't saint him."

"What the hell does that mean?"

His eyes narrow and he opens his mouth just as a gong sounds, signaling the call to dinner and the senator's speech.

"Maybe one day I'll tell you. Hell, you deserve to know the kind of man he was."

"You mean now that he's not here to defend himself against your lies?"

My father's eye twitches. He lifts his head a little higher, looking down his nose at me. "You should go. You don't belong here."

Why does that sting? "I wasn't planning on staying, but I have something for you first."

I reach into my pocket, taking out the envelope, the reason I came. I relax a little at the sight of it and slap it against my father's chest.

"Choke on this, old man." I lean toward him. "You're finished."

He looks down at it, his face falling a little when I pull my hand away and the envelope drops to the floor, the senator's name clear on it. I'm sure he can guess what's inside.

"Enjoy your evening," I say, and I walk out before he can speak another word.

20

HAYDEN

I take a cab to the club. It's a busy night, but entertainment on weekends always draws a big crowd.

Peter greets me at the door and takes my coat and Persephone's which was still at coat check.

"My brother?"

"Upstairs. Doctor Allen is up there too."

I nod, make my way to the elevator. A few men call out my name, but I don't stop, punching in my code instead so the elevator comes directly down wherever it is. I get in and start my ascent to the thirteenth floor.

I'd imagined tonight going differently. I'd thought I'd enjoy it. Enjoy seeing their faces as we approached the table, taking our seats. I thought I'd savor the moment Senator Hughes thanked his biggest donors and mentioned his plans for the city, the revitalizing of neighborhoods, the building of hotels.

And mostly, I'd enjoy the fact that my father's name wouldn't be mentioned once.

But instead, I walk into my office to find Ares pouring

himself a whiskey. He pours a second for me when he sees me.

"Where is she?"

"Your room."

I nod, sip my drink and study the closed door between my office and living quarters. The thirteenth floor is my domain. I live and work here.

"How is she?" I ask Ares who I can feel is studying me from the bar as I lean against my desk. I have to drag my gaze from the door to him.

"She'll be fine. Doctor's talking to her now."

"Is she hurt?"

He shakes his head. "I don't think so, but she'll have a bump on her head."

"Fuck."

"It's not like you hit her."

"No, but I'm the reason she hit her head against that wall."

"Why in hell do you let that little prick get to you?"

"He had his hands on her." I swallow my drink, feel it burn its way down my throat before moving to the bar to pick up the bottle and pour another.

"They have history. I'm sure he doesn't love the fact that his brother—whom he hates—is fucking his ex-fiancée."

"That's the thing."

"What's the thing?" Ares asks.

"She was a virgin."

He raises his eyebrows, sips his drink. "They're all virgins once."

"I mean with me. So, he never touched her. But they were engaged. I don't get it."

"Maybe Jonas is more old-fashioned than we think."

I shake my head. "She's weird about him."

"You're her ex-fiancée's brother. That's what's weird."

But I remember what she said to him that I overheard. *I know what you did.* I want to change the subject. "Find out anything on the mafia connection?"

"Benedetti and Abbot were going into business together."

"What?"

"Benedetti approached him about permits for some new properties in the city a couple of years ago. Abbot turned him down, because you know, holier than thou Quincy Abbot."

"Hypocrite." I swallow more of my whiskey.

"Well, looks like about a year ago, Abbot had a change of heart."

"A year?"

Ares nods. "About the time you began the dismantling of Abbot Enterprises, I believe."

It is. "And Benedetti got the permits?"

"More than that. They partnered. But that's not public knowledge. There was a sizeable donation made to Abbot's re-election campaign. I believe you mentioned it the other night. Benedetti bought him."

"So, what happened? Why the hit-and-run? Seems pretty counterintuitive to kill or attempt to kill the senator you've got in your pocket."

"You're assuming it was Benedetti and you know what they say about assuming." Ares finishes his drink just as the door between the office and my private rooms opens and Dr. Allen walks out.

"Dr. Allen. Thank you for coming," I say, shaking his hand.

"Of course, Hayden."

"How is she?"

"Sleeping. She'll be fine. Just a bump on her head. I don't believe she has a concussion, but it may be good for you to keep an eye on her tonight. I'll come back in the morning."

"Thank you."

When he leaves, I head through the office and into my living room. Ares follows and I open the bedroom door to see her sleeping on my bed.

"I hurt her."

"It was an accident." He puts his hand on my shoulder. "I'm going to go."

I turn to him. "Where does Benedetti stand now with the building?"

"Construction was halted after the accident."

"You and I both know it wasn't an accident."

"It's not a mob hit, though. Makes no sense that it would be. At least not a Benedetti hit."

"I need one more favor, Ares."

"You're going to owe me big at this rate."

"Get me a meeting with Benedetti."

He seems surprised. "You sure you want to be involved with him?"

"I already am. I control Abbot Enterprises."

Ares chuckles. "How does she feel about that?"

"Don't worry about her."

"I'll arrange it. Hope you know what you're doing." With that he leaves, and I walk into the bedroom.

PERSEPHONE

"*You and I both know it wasn't an accident.*"

I hear them, but I'm not sure it isn't a dream.

Benedetti. That name again. What had Hayden said? Mafia. Why would they make a donation to my dad's campaign? Why had he accepted it?

No, it's a mistake. It has to be.

I hear water running and when I roll onto my side his scent is all around me, like I'm wrapped up in his arms.

Then I remember how he slammed me into the wall with one of those arms.

It was an accident, I know. I was trying to pry him from Jonas before he killed him because if he ever found out what Jonas did, he would kill him.

A door closes and again, I'm not sure if I'm dreaming but I feel myself drift off. I don't fight it. It's pitch black. It must be the middle of the night.

The next time I blink my eyes open, it's not as dark. I see the nightstand, the glass of water.

Unfamiliar.

But then I remember. I'm at the club. Ares brought me to

Hayden's club. I didn't know there was a whole apartment behind one of the doors of his office, but I know I'm in Hayden's bedroom. In his bed. And I remember there was a doctor.

I move and the blanket shifts and I find that I'm naked but for my panties. Who undressed me?

I pull myself to a seat, hold the blanket to my chest until the wave of dizziness passes.

Although it's still dark in the room, there's a sliver of deep orange light penetrating the slats of the wooden blinds covering the windows.

Ice clinks in a glass and I shudder, remembering that night in my father's room. Remembering Hayden sitting there in the dark waiting for me.

He's here now, too. I feel him.

And as my eyes adjust, I make out his form.

Déjà vu.

He's sitting in an armchair drinking his whiskey and his eyes are locked on me. Watching me. He's always watching.

I remain still and we stare at each other for a minute. I wonder how long he was standing there when Jonas had me cornered. Wonder how much he heard.

Wordlessly he rises. He's still wearing his tuxedo shirt, unbuttoned to the middle of his chest. The bowtie is gone, and when he takes a clumsy step toward the bed, I look down and see that he's barefoot.

He comes to stand beside the bed, sips his whiskey then holds it out to me.

I shake my head.

"Do you have anything with him?" he asks.

"What?"

"Jonas. Do you have anything with him?"

I think he's drunk. He's slurring his words.

"What time is it?"

He leans down. "Tell me."

I shake my head. "No. Nothing. Why would you even ask that?"

He straightens, nods his head and finishes his drink.

"What time is it?" I ask again.

"Morning."

"I've been out all night?"

He nods.

I absently go to scratch the back of my head and wince when I feel the bump there.

"I did that," Hayden says.

"It was an accident, Hayden." He doesn't comment. He looks tired, weary. "Did you sleep? Have you been up all night?"

"You're going to get hurt again," he says, not answering me. He walks away, toward the dresser where I see the nearly empty bottle of whiskey. Where I watch him pour clumsily, splashing some on the dresser. He turns to sit back down on the armchair.

"Have you been drinking all night?"

He sips from his glass, eyes on me. "You said something. You said you know what he did. What did Jonas do?"

I shift my gaze, hoping he can't read me in the darkness. "I'm not sure what you're talking about."

"The important question is what were you and Jonas talking about?"

"Nothing. I don't know. He was drunk or stoned or both. He was making no sense."

"What did he do, Persephone? You have something on him."

"I'm not sure what you mean."

It's silent for a long moment. "Were you going to leave with him?"

"Leave with him? No. Never."

"But you were going to leave."

I lean back against his headboard and hug the blanket a little closer. I feel strangely safe here. Warm and protected.

"Answer me," Hayden says, drawing me back into the present.

"I was looking for you to tell you. You were right, the champagne had gotten to me."

"Don't lie to me, Persephone."

I study him, but there are too many shadows to read his eyes. "I didn't want to see him. I thought it would be awkward and I was right."

"What I witnessed wasn't awkward, it was two people who share a secret. A big one."

"No, it wasn't. He and I share nothing. I told him to get away from me, to leave me alone and when he wouldn't, I tried to knee him in the balls to make him, but he was faster than me and he attacked. That's when you came upon us. And thank goodness you did."

He sets his whiskey aside and stands up. "I would have killed him if he'd hurt you."

He gets to the bed and pulls the blanket away, exposing most of me. I instinctively cover my breasts and watch him look me over before he meets my eyes again.

"But it wasn't him who hurt you. It was me."

"I'm fine. It was an accident."

My mind drifts, remembering other voices from earlier. *"You and I both know it wasn't an accident."*

I rub my forehead, trying to make sense of the words as they fade again.

Hayden extends his arm, draws the corner of my panties

down a little, then looks at me again. "You're mine. You know that, don't you?"

I get up onto my knees, put my hands on his shoulders. I kiss his cheek, his mouth. I taste whiskey on his lips and feel the rough stubble along his jaw and all the while he remains like a statue, unblinking. Watching me.

I slide my hand down over the expanse of exposed chest to undo the remaining buttons, pulling his shirt open. I open his belt next, then the zipper on his slacks. But when I slip my hand inside to cup him, he grabs hold of my wrist.

"You said 'I know what you did'. What did he do?"

I feel the smooth skin of his thick, hard cock. I keep my eyes locked on his and move my fingers, even though he has my wrist. With my other hand, I push his pants down.

"You heard wrong," I lie.

I kiss him again and he weaves his big hand into my hair, cupping my skull and releasing my wrist.

He kisses me hard, claiming my mouth with his, then draws me backward, studying me for a long moment before pushing my head downward, down to him.

I lick my lips and open my mouth and he guides himself into me. He closes his eyes and lets out a long moan and I'm wet hearing him, seeing him like this. I taste him, taste his salty, masculine taste as he glides into my mouth and out and in and out until he pulls me off and draws me back up to kiss me again and I wonder if he can taste himself on my lips.

He pushes me backward on the bed tearing the flimsy lace of my panties as he hurries to rid me of them and a moment later, he's between my legs and he's pushing into me with a grunt. His hands are on the bed on either side of my head and his eyes are intense and dark and this is more than sex. The way he's looking at me, it's so much more.

"I know what I heard." He thrusts hard as if he'll fuck the truth out of me.

I bite my lip, taste blood as I wrap my hands around his biceps, loving his strength, his power.

"What is it?" he asks, thrusting again. "What did he do?"

"Nothing. There's nothing."

His next thrust forces the breath from my lungs.

"You're lying to me."

"I'm not." I shake my head, find it hard to focus as I try to pull him to me.

He studies me, and I know he doesn't believe me, but he changes course. "You're mine, not his, not anyone's, you understand that?" he asks as he takes my wrists and leans over me, forcing my legs wider, stretching my arms across the bed. "Do you understand?" He stresses each word with a thrust that hurts and feels so good at once.

I nod. I try to. I'm breathless. I need to come. I need to come with him.

He grips my hair and tugs. His eyes have gone black.

"Mine. Say it."

"You're hurting—"

"Say it!"

"Yours."

He moans and I feel him thickening inside me.

"Yours," I repeat, gripping his shoulders to brace myself for this final phase of fucking. Of his claiming. His staining me.

"Mine. Only mine."

I nod, I'm close. I'm so close. He said once he was giving me what I always wanted, and he was right. This is what I've always wanted. Even if this thing, whatever it is, has the power to destroy us both.

"Say it again," he commands, thrusts coming shorter, faster, more frantic.

"Yours. Only ever yours," I manage as an orgasm shatters my world and all I feel is him, all I see is the blur of him, and all I hear is the curse he mutters as he throbs inside me, coming, coming, filling me up and he's more beast than man, I think, and we're coming together and so close, so close and only when the orgasm begins to fade do I realize I'm still muttering those words.

Telling him I'm his. Only his. Only ever his.

She sleeps again after. She just closes her eyes and falls asleep like it's the most natural thing to be in my bed.

Or maybe that's the blow to her head, asshole.

My phone buzzes on the nightstand. I move without disturbing her and pick it up to see it's Ares. I click into the message.

Ares: I'm downstairs.

Me: To what do I owe this honor?

Ares: Benedetti called me before I had a chance to call him. He heard control of Abbot Enterprises has changed hands. He'll be at the club within the hour.

Me: Doesn't waste any time.

Ares: Anxious to get your joint project going again, I guess. Get your ass out of bed.

I glance at Persephone who is still sleeping soundly.

Me: Be right down.

I set the phone down and extricate my arm from beneath her head. She mutters something and rolls onto her side but is quiet again and as much as I'd like to stay here with her, I force myself to go into the bathroom to shower.

When I walk back out of the bathroom ten minutes later, she's sitting up on the bed looking soft from sleep.

"You should go back to sleep," I tell her.

She holds up my phone. "You got a text."

I take it from her, read the message that's still on the locked screen.

Ares: Correction. Benedetti will be here in thirty minutes.

"I don't appreciate you snooping."

"I wasn't snooping. It woke me up and I thought it was mine. I grabbed it out of habit. Why is Benedetti coming here? And by here I assume Ares means the club?"

"Business. How's your head?"

"Fine. What do you mean business? What business?"

I cup the back of her head, feeling the bump. I don't miss her wince and guilt twists my gut. "Lie back down, Persephone. Get some more sleep."

I walk past her to the closet.

She's behind me a moment later pulling her arms through last night's discarded tuxedo shirt.

I look her over and my dick's hard looking at her like this, naked but for my shirt which is about ten sizes too big for her.

"You're going to make me late," I say with a grin, letting my towel drop, curling a hand around her waist.

She looks down at my erection then up at me. "You're trying to distract me."

"Maybe I am." I kiss her, slide my hand between her legs. "Sore?"

"Stop." She tries to turn her head, to push my hand away.

"Because I'll need to fuck you again when I'm back."

"We need to talk about Benedetti."

"Later. Get back into bed and wait for me. Call down for breakfast. Dr. Allen should be here soon to check on you." I turn to get dressed.

"I'm not getting back into bed. I want to know what he wants. You said he's with the mafia. What *business* do you have with the mafia?"

"Your father's business." I button up my slacks, tuck my phone into my pocket and pull on a clean shirt as I turn back to her. "And he's not *with* the mafia. He *is* the mafia."

"Well, Abbot Enterprises won't have anything to do with him. I need my clothes." She looks around my closet like her things might be here.

"No, you don't," I tell her, taking her by the arm and walking her into the bedroom. "Get back into bed. You won't be going anywhere near Benedetti."

"I'm not kidding," she says, turning to face me again. "My father wouldn't want to deal with him."

"Your father was already dealing with him. There was a contract and you saw the financials yourself."

"I need to know why he would. If he was blackmailing him—"

"Sweetheart." I take her face in my hands. "This is the fucking mafia we're talking about. Do you think Dominic Benedetti is just going to tell you if he was blackmailing your father? Do you think he's going to tell you anything about his business at all?"

"Dad wouldn't deal with the mob."

"Let me take care of this. Take care of you."

"Whatever you think, he wasn't corrupt."

I feel that familiar burning in my gut at her proclamation. "I've told you before, you didn't know your father as well as you think you did." I pull the covers back and gesture for her to get into the bed.

"Stop talking about him in the past tense."

I take a long breath in. "Be reasonable, Persephone—"

"And this isn't something you can decide. It's my family's name—"

"My patience is wearing thin."

"My father's company," she continues like she hasn't heard me. "I can't let you—"

"*I* control Abbot Enterprises. The only reason it's still called Abbot Enterprises is because you asked me not to change the name."

"Don't do me any favors."

I bite back my response. "Bed, Persephone."

"No, Hades."

"Don't push me."

"I have every right to be there."

"And I'm telling you you're not going to be. Period. Get in the fucking bed. You hit your head hard last night."

"And whose fault is that?"

I stop, grit my teeth. Her words are like a slap to my face. She's right, though. The fault was mine. All mine.

She spins on her heel. "Where are my clothes?"

I follow her, take her arm because we're not done. "You're not thinking clearly. I'll make sure you get some clothes, but right now, I need you to do as you're told."

Her eyebrows rise high on her forehead and she glances down at where I'm holding her. "You need me to *do as I'm told*?"

Fuck.

My phone buzzes in my pocket.

"Just get in the fucking bed. I need to go."

"Fuck you."

"Fuck me? All right, that's about enough." I lift her and set her on the bed. She tries instantly to slip away, but I hold her against the headboard and bring my face to hers. "I'm not letting you near Benedetti. No fucking way. You're staying here and that's final."

She has both hands around my arm and is trying to push me off.

Keeping her against the headboard, I open the nightstand drawer and take out a set of handcuffs.

"This isn't exactly how I would normally use these," I start, cuffing one of her wrists. "But you leave me no choice."

"What the hell are you doing?"

She watches, fighting against me as I cuff her to the bed.

"You can't do this!"

I put the key to unlock them into my pocket and straighten. "I just did, sweetheart."

She slips off the bed, tugging at her wrist and before I can walk away, she brings her free hand to my face, digging her nails into my cheek.

"Take this thing off, you bastard!"

"Christ." I catch her wrist and pull her hand away, but not before she's broken skin. "You want me to get rough? Is that it?"

"I want you to let me go! I have every right to be at that meeting and you know it. I won't let you destroy our business. Our name."

"If you'd just listen, you'd know I'm only protecting you."

"Maybe the one I need protecting from is you!"

My phone rings this time. I have no doubt it's Ares wondering where the hell I am. I'm about to reach into my pocket to grab it when, in that moment of distraction, Persephone's free hand wraps around my neck and she rams her knee up into my balls.

"Fuck!" I double over as an almost electric pain shoots through me.

Shock registers on her face and with a gasp, she scoots backward on the bed, says something but I don't hear her and when I look at her again, her eyes have gone huge as she waits for my reaction.

I swallow back the pain, straighten to my full height. Move in on her as she backs as far as she can from me, plastering herself to the headboard. I splay the flat of my hand across her chest, seeing how it spans almost the whole of it.

Her hand closes over my forearm and I ease my thumb and forefinger away from her throat.

"You'll answer for that," I say, my voice low and deep. I ignore my phone which is ringing again. Ares needs to calm the fuck down. "We're not playing a fucking game here. You are so far out of your league you don't even see playing field. We're doing this my way. Hell, we're doing everything my way. You signed a contract. Two in fact. I own you. Get clear on that. Get clear fast." I turn to walk away.

"And if I don't give you what you want, you'll take it by force whether it's the company or me? Is that what you mean?"

I stop dead in my tracks, the words, their implication, the accusation in her tone, this second time she's made it, hitting me like a brick.

"Isn't that what you're doing?" she adds.

I turn back to face her. "Are you finished?"

"Look at me. I'm cuffed to your bed. You're stronger than me. Might makes right, isn't that the saying? Isn't that what men like you believe?"

"Men like me?" I almost laugh but it's an ugly thing because her words cut sharp. "If you knew what your own father was capable of—" I cut myself off, shake my head.

"You don't know anything about my father! Look at us. Look at me." She makes a point of trying to lift her cuffed wrist. "You're no different than Jonas!"

Something in my expression must change because she winces, staring back at me like she's wondering what the fuck she just said.

"Is that what he did? Force you?"

She doesn't answer. Doesn't blink. Doesn't even breathe.

My phone rings. I need to go.

"We'll continue this discussion when I'm back but just so we're clear, I *do not* force women. In fact, all I've done is try to take care of you since I've been back. You'll stay here. You'll eat breakfast. You'll wait for me. You will not leave this room, understood?"

"I'm cuffed to the bed so yeah, I understand. Asshole."

I walk out of the bedroom and through the living room into my office. I take a moment to go into the bathroom there and splash water on my face because what the fuck just happened? I look up at my reflection, see the little crescent shapes where her fingernails broke skin.

I think about everything, I think about why I'm doing this. Why she's here now. I think about last night, what I overheard Jonas ask her. I think about her comment. I think about my stepbrother with his hands on her.

And I think about paying him a visit.

Because I want to know exactly what it is he's afraid she told me.

23

HAYDEN

I step off the elevator to find Peter anxiously waiting for me. I notice the bead of sweat on his forehead as I greet him, taking in the members already seated and having breakfast at tables in the restaurant.

His eyes grow wide when he sees the damage on my face.

"It's nothing," I say before he can say anything. "Where are they?"

"Your brother and," he clears his throat, "his guest are in the boardroom." He's clearly very uncomfortable.

"What time did his guest arrive?"

"About ten minutes ago. His wife is with him. And there are quite a few men." Again, he clears his throat and signals to the two standing by the entrance of the restaurant.

"Relax, Peter." I reach into my pocket and take out the key to the cuffs. I hold them out for Peter. "In about twenty minutes, get breakfast sent up to Persephone. She's cuffed to the bed so she may be...upset. Uncuff her. See what clothes she wants sent over and get someone out to her house to get them but she's not to leave my rooms."

"Yes, sir."

"In fact, keep her shoes down here just in case she gets any ideas."

He nods.

"Coffee's been sent into the meeting?"

"Yes, sir."

"Thank you."

I walk to the boardroom doors, nod to Benedetti's man standing just outside it.

He reaches to open the door for me, and I step inside, meeting my brother's gaze across the room. No one is seated yet.

Ares has his hands in his pockets, his suit jacket open, watching the scene before him.

Three more men, Benedetti soldiers I presume, stand along the perimeter of the room, one of them looking me over before shifting his gaze away.

I recognize Dominic Benedetti from the papers. He's bigger in person though, every bit head of the family.

He's standing in the middle of the room talking to the woman, his wife, I guess, who has her back to me.

When I walk in, he lifts his gaze momentarily from her to me before wrapping a possessive hand around the back of her neck and turning her toward the door.

I see the bump then. She's pregnant. Maybe four or five months along.

He whispers something to her, and she nods, looks up to meet my gaze but doesn't smile.

She's striking and the two of them together are interesting to see. I think this may be a side of Dominic Benedetti not many witness.

"I'm not scared of that man," she says loud enough for me to hear.

"I know you're not," Dominic says. "But you will keep the extra guards, Gia. You try to send them away again and we have a problem."

She exhales, purses her lips. "You know I can handle myself."

"No one is questioning that," he says, and when he splays his hand over her softly rounded belly, I shift my gaze away, the moment a very private one. "I won't take a chance with either of you. This isn't up for discussion." He straightens, nods to one of his men who steps forward.

"Mrs. Benedetti," the guard says, gesturing to the door.

She glances at me again and I get a feeling she can handle herself just fine. She turns back to her husband and brushes something off his shoulder before touching his cheek.

She leans in to whisper something I don't hear. Whatever it is has him smiling. A moment later, she's gone with the soldier and Benedetti turns to me, then looks at Ares, then back at me.

"Hayden Montgomery," he says, extending his hand. "Ares didn't tell me you were identical twins. Good to meet you."

I shake his hand. "Good to meet you. Let's sit down."

I take my place at the head of the oval table. Ares and Dominic sit on either side. Two soldiers remain in the room and we wait to begin until the server has poured coffee and left.

I notice Dominic looking at the scratches on my face, but he doesn't comment.

"I hear you've taken control of Abbot Enterprises."

I nod. "News travels fast."

"I don't want to waste time, especially after Abbot's *acci-*

dent. Are you aware of the contract between Abbot and myself?"

"You were helping to fund the newest hotel Abbot was building in the city."

"Not *helping* to fund. All financing was and is provided by me. Abbot didn't have the resources to build at the time we came to the agreement."

"He needed money and you needed permits."

He smiles but it's a wholly different smile than the one he showed his wife. "The end result will profit both Abbot Enterprises and me."

"Persephone Abbot took over control of the company after her father's accident. Why didn't you proceed with her as you would had the accident not occurred?"

"Two reasons. First, because we hit several permit issues that without Quincy's pull, I've been unable to resolve and second because I made a promise to Quincy. He didn't want his family involved in our dealings."

"More than one dealing?"

Again, he just smiles. "I liked Quincy. Seemed like a decent man."

"So everyone keeps telling me."

He doesn't reply and I wonder if he hears the disdain in my voice.

Ares clears his throat and we both turn to him. "You mentioned the *accident.*"

Dominic nods. "We all know the hit-and-run wasn't an accident. And that's the more important reason I'm here. It's the reason I have extra protection for my family. We have a common enemy."

I feel my eyes narrow.

"Jeremiah Montgomery," Dominic says.

"Dear ole dad," Ares says.

"If this has to do with Hughes, he's no longer in my father's pocket," I say.

"No, he's in yours," Dominic replies.

"And now that I have a stake in Abbot Enterprises, I'll make sure we have whatever permits we need to proceed."

"There's no love lost between you and your father, is there?" he says it like he already knows. "In fact, you're doing everything in your power to destroy him. Why?"

I force a grin. "Family business. I'm sure you understand."

He cocks his head to the side and narrows his eyes. "The sting is a little different when family betrays us, isn't it?"

"As you know," I reply, because I know a little something about Benedetti family history too. About how he got to where he is with two older brothers who were ahead of him in the ascent to the throne.

"You will honor the contract Abbot and I agreed upon, including the transfer of the hotel to me one year after its completion," he says it like it's not a question, but I answer anyway because I'm not afraid of him.

"I'm not in the same position as Abbot. I have the capital and wouldn't need to sell."

"But you need an ally. More than you realize."

"I can handle my father."

"I'm sure you can but do you really think he's the only player in this? This hotel goes up and I own the city. My enemies will have to find new holes to call home."

"Are you telling me my father is backed by another mafia family?"

He nods. "One who will do anything he needs to do to destroy me. Destroy my wife."

"I'm not up on my mob trivia. Who are we talking about?"

"Angus Scava."

Ares whistles and I see him lean back in his chair. I scratch my forehead, go through the details I know about Scava, which aren't many. He isn't as powerful as Benedetti, that's the most important, but I've heard his name more and more of late.

"What does he have with you? Or your wife?"

"Family business. I'm sure you understand."

I nod. They are, after all, my own words.

"How did our father get involved with Scava?" Ares asks.

"He needed Quincy Abbot to keep quiet about something. That detail I don't know, but he used Abbot's arrangement with me to blackmail him into keeping his mouth shut about what it is he knows. Or knew. Once people get wind a senator is working with a mob boss, well, they assume corruption."

"But isn't it corrupt?"

He grins. "Much like you, I'm in business to make money. You'll do what you need to do to get what you want, won't you? Don't you? Does that make you corrupt?"

I think of Persephone upstairs in my room. Handcuffed to my bed. Corrupt doesn't begin to cover what I'm doing to her.

"If you know who is responsible for the hit-and-run, you'd better tell me."

"I have my ideas."

"You think Scava ordered it?" Ares asks.

"I didn't say that. And I have a feeling if it was Scava the man would be dead, not in a coma no matter the little chance he has to wake."

"Why would Scava work with my father? I understand my father going to a man like him if he needed something like the hit-and-run, because you are suggesting it was my father, but I don't see what Scava would get out of it."

"Your father had Hughes in his pocket. It's as hard for Angus Scava to get the permits he needs as it is for me."

"And now that I'm the man with Hughes in my pocket, my father has lost his value."

Dominic nods. "Don't underestimate the fact that you and anything precious to you also becomes a target. I can offer my protection, since we're partners."

"We're not partners, and I can take care of what's mine."

"As you wish." He checks his watch then looks at me again, his gaze level and cool and I'm reminded of his reputation. His ruthlessness.

"I want to get home to my wife and family," he says, standing. "I can count on you to continue our business?"

I stand too. "The contract is airtight." I already had my lawyer look into it, and I can't get out of it even if I want to.

He smiles, extends his hand. "That secret your father is hiding, I'm very curious."

I study him, try to read him. But he gives nothing away. "As am I."

We drop our hands and Dominic turns to my brother. "Ares. I'll see you next week."

"See you then."

We watch Dominic Benedetti exit with his entourage of soldiers and only when he's gone do I turn to my brother.

"What business do you have with him?" I ask Ares.

"Nothing you'd be interested in. What happened to your face?"

"Nothing. Be careful, brother. Dominic Benedetti is a dangerous man."

"I can say the same to you."

I sit back down. "You think father's behind the hit-and-run?"

"I don't know. He's a bastard but that seems a step too far even for him."

"I'll pay him a visit later. Right now, I have to get upstairs."

"How is she?"

"A handful."

"You've always liked a handful, brother."

24

PERSEPHONE

When Hayden finally returns, I'm sitting in his office behind his desk. He steps off the elevator and pauses, raising one eyebrow before his face breaks into a smile. I notice he's carrying my boots.

"You look good there," he says, setting the boots down and coming around the desk. "But get out." He takes my arm and lifts me up.

I look up at him, again feeling at a disadvantage barefoot because he's so much taller than me.

"Doctor says you're fine," he says. "I'm glad to hear that."

"I have a hard head."

"That's for sure."

"You cuffed me to the bed."

"You left me no choice."

"Don't do it again."

"Don't be unreasonable again."

I exhale an audible breath. "How was the meeting?" I sit down and pick up the boots to put them on. Peter had someone bring over several sweaters and jeans but when I asked him about shoes, he told me he forgot. My guess is it was Hayden's way of making sure I did as I was told and stayed put.

Hayden presses some keys on the keyboard, his attention to the monitor. "Were you snooping?"

"Couldn't break into your computer or I would have."

He smiles like it's what he expected.

"Are you going to tell me about the meeting?"

He takes a few moments, the keys clicking as he types something before he sits back in his chair and faces me.

"We have to finish our earlier discussion first."

I try to keep my expression blank. I'm not sure I succeed.

"Come here, Persephone," he says, pushing his chair back a little.

I get up, go to him, take his hand when he extends it.

He shifts his attention to that hand, caresses it with his thumb. He looks at me and tugs me to him, drawing me down to sit on his lap, my legs between his.

Being this close to him does something to me. Always has. My heart beats a little faster, and it takes all I have not to curl up into him.

For a long moment, he studies my face and the look in his green-gold eyes, it's different than earlier. No longer hard or angry. Softer, like how he just caressed my hand.

He slides one hand up to cup the back of my head, gentle where the bump is. He doesn't speak but draws me down and puts his lips to my forehead and I close my eyes at the contact. At the tenderness of it.

When he pulls back, he looks at me, eyes just inches from mine.

"I didn't mean it," I say. "You're not like him. You're nothing like him."

Jonas. I don't need to say his name.

He nods. He's studying me so intently it's hard to hold his gaze.

"What did he do to you?"

I touch a button on his shirt, steeling myself before returning my gaze to his.

"Nothing. He didn't do anything to me. He just didn't take it well when I broke off our engagement."

"What does that mean *didn't take it well*?"

I shake my head, shrug a shoulder. "He wasn't happy, that's all."

"You said something earlier."

"I told you, it wasn't—"

"Did he force you, Persephone?"

I swallow, feel myself weaken, feel my skin go clammy. I shake my head and I hear myself talk but it's like I'm on autopilot. "I was a virgin. How would I be a virgin if he forced me?"

"There are other ways."

"He didn't rape me."

"You don't need to protect him."

"I'm not protecting him."

"Are you lying to me?"

"Nothing I've told you is a lie. Not one word."

"And the things you're leaving out?"

I look away, beyond him and out the window at the dark fall day.

"It's going to storm again," I say, looking back at him.

He watches me with narrowed eyes but this secret he can't draw from me.

"You don't have to be afraid of him anymore. I'll kill him before I let him touch you again."

"I know you will. And that's why you can't go near him, Hayden."

"Tell me what he did."

"Leave it alone."

"Persephone—"

"I said leave it alone."

"What are you hiding?"

"Nothing."

"But you're afraid of him."

"I'm not...it's not—"

"You're mine. I protect what's mine."

I need to change the subject. We can't talk about Jonas. Ever. "Only temporarily yours."

His eyes narrow. "There's that word again." He takes my face in his hands and pulls me so close that my nose is almost touching his. "It doesn't have to be temporary."

"You mean I can be your permanent whore?" I hear my own voice and I hate myself for saying it.

His hold on me tightens. "Is that what you think you are to me?"

"We have a contract that says as much."

He clenches his jaw, eyes hardening. "Is that what you want? Me to stick to the letter of the contract?"

"It's not...I—"

"Is that what you want?" He squeezes his fingers a little, just a little. Just enough.

"It's probably easier." It twists my heart to say it.

"Easier?"

"In the long run." Fuck. Fuck. Fuck. This is wrong. But I'm not doing it to protect Jonas. I'm protecting Hayden. He just can't know it, no matter the cost, because this truth would damage him. It might destroy him. And so, I go on lying even though I feel sick for it. "So no one gets the wrong idea." Does he hear the tremor in my voice?

He snorts, nods. "Of course." He pushes me off his lap

and down to the floor so I'm kneeling between his open legs and instantly, everything shifts.

"Then I'll have you on your knees," he says, pulling my hair into a ponytail and leaning down to kiss my mouth. "So you don't get the wrong idea."

He leans down to undo my jeans and slips his hand inside, into my panties to cup my sex. He draws back and looks at me as he rubs, and my mouth falls open because when he touches me, I forget everything else. Everything but him and as I watch him, I think how beautiful he is, and I hate myself for what I'm doing. For lying to him.

"You like this?" he asks.

When I don't answer, he tugs on my hair.

"I asked you a question. I want to be clear you're not getting the wrong idea."

"I didn't mean—"

"Do you like my hands on your pussy?" he asks, his tone harsh. "If you're my whore, I want to know."

That word makes me flinch. "Hades—"

"Say it. Tell me." He tugs harder.

"Yes."

"Do better than that. Tell me what you like."

"Why are you doing this?"

He draws his hand out of my panties and brings his fingers to my mouth, wipes them across my lips, my face, then opens his belt, undoes his pants and fists his cock with the hand that's still wet with me.

I watch him stroke himself, long and slow, precum beading the smooth head of his hard cock.

He rises to his feet and I look up at him, feeling the slight pressure on my skull as he keeps my face tilted upward.

"You're not getting the wrong idea, are you, Persephone?"

"What?"

"Don't stop looking at me," he says as he guides his cock into my mouth. "I want to watch you take me when I fuck your face."

He moves me over him, taking his time, and I do as he says, I keep my eyes on his as he pushes in deeper and deeper. I push against his thighs, but he doesn't stop and it's getting harder to keep my eyes on his as he begins to move faster, deeper, cutting off my oxygen as he penetrates my throat.

I shove against his thighs, try to turn my head to get some air.

"You have to learn how to suck my cock if you're my whore," he says, tugging hard once. "That's what you said, isn't it? That you're my whore?"

"Hades," I choke out.

"Take it," he commands, thrusting. "Take it, Persephone."

I push against him as his grip tightens and with his other hand, he grabs hold of the edge of the desk and leans over me and I don't hear him when he speaks, I don't hear his words as he fucks my face and there's nothing gentle about this fucking. Nothing tender in his touch.

Tears blur my vision as he nears the end, his cock growing impossibly thicker as I feel that jerk, that twitch before he stills. He makes a sound from deep inside his chest and I feel him empty down my throat, reflex working to swallow all he's giving me and just when I think I'm going to pass out from lack of oxygen, he pulls out, dropping into his seat. He hugs me to him, my face pressed to his lap.

I listen to his shortened breath and I wipe my tears as I

let him hold me like this. Because I need this, need to pretend I'm not what I said I was. Need to pretend I'm more. Just for a few minutes. I need to feel his strength, his dominance. I need to feel him hold me.

But then he abruptly pushes the chair back, releasing me so I drop to my hands.

I look up at him.

He watches me as he stands, looming over me with a look on his face that's cruel. That's not my Hades, the man who stayed up to watch me sleep last night. To make sure I was okay.

He tucks himself back into his pants, eyes cold and unreadable.

"Get cleaned up and get out. My driver will take you to see your father and then you'll go home where you'll stay until I need your services again."

He walks away, and I watch him go, watch him walk to the elevator and punch in the code. When the doors open, he turns to me, holding them open. He raises his eyebrows.

I get to my feet, zip up my jeans. I'm unsteady as I walk around his desk and pick up my clutch from last night. I get to the elevator and stop.

"Hayden, I didn't—"

"I have a busy day."

I swallow back my hurt and when he reaches up, I think he's going to hug me or something, but he just wipes his thumb over the corner of my mouth, cleaning off what I couldn't swallow.

That single act humiliates and hurts more than his words.

I bow my head, unable to look at him. Not wanting him to see me like this. Because it's my own fault. I deserve this. You reap what you sow, and I sowed distrust.

25

HAYDEN

I knew today would be a shitty day before it started. This day always is. What just happened with Persephone makes it shittier, but that's my fault. I guess I'd somehow gotten my hopes up with her.

Anyway, how did I expect this to go? She's not in my bed by choice. She's there because she has to be. And maybe she was right to remind me of it. Because maybe I was the one getting the wrong fucking idea.

A glance at the shopping bag in the passenger seat of the SUV has my mind shifting gears to Nora. I start the engine and pull out of my parking spot.

There was no suicide note, but the coroner still ruled her death a suicide. She'd swallowed enough sleeping pills to put a horse out and just to be sure, she'd slit her wrists. I wonder if the pills had started their work or if she felt any pain.

The last time I'd seen her was that Halloween, just days before she did it. That night was a line of demarcation in all our lives.

Nora and I weren't blood. My father adopted her when she

was nine. I loved her, though. Right away. I had an idea what she'd come from. I'd woken her up from nightmares that seemed to stalk her nightly and every time, she'd just smile and hug me and refuse to tell me a word of what haunted her.

The memory tightens my chest. My dad may have been shitty to me but I'm sure it was nothing to what she'd been through. Not if I remember the terror in her eyes on those nights.

When Persephone moved in next door, they instantly became friends.

I wonder if Persephone remembers today is Nora's birthday.

As I approach the building that houses my father's office, I force thoughts of Nora out of my mind. There's time to think about her. To remember her. Right now, though, I need to talk to my father.

I park and climb out, looking up at the high-rise in the posh neighborhood. It's one of his own buildings and he's mortgaged to his eyeballs, a fact he doesn't know I know. I wonder if he could sell the plot of land the Montgomery ruin stands on, he would.

His hands are tied, though.

That house has been the seat of the Montgomery family for generations. If he tries to sell it, he loses it and, as first-born, it becomes mine. But if he holds onto it, when he dies, he can leave it to whichever of us he wants. I'm guessing that'll be Jonas who isn't even a Montgomery by blood.

I'm sure my grandfather will flip in his grave when that day comes.

I enter the building, half-expecting to be turned away. I wouldn't be surprised if my father banned me from entering the premises. I push the button to call the elevator and take off my gloves as I wait for it to descend. In a few minutes, I'm riding up to the twenty-second floor.

There, the receptionist greets me, quickly hiding her surprise at seeing me there. I smile and bypass her to walk through the office, aware of the silence that descends as people recognize me, the whispers that follow in my wake.

My father's secretary is on her feet and around the desk before I get to his door. The receptionist must have notified her.

"Hayden. What a surprise. How are you?" she asks awkwardly.

"Maryanne, good to see you," I say. "No need to announce me."

She follows me as I make my way to the door, puts her hand on my arm to stop me.

"I'm afraid you can't go in there just now. He's in a meeting."

I smile, remove her hand. "I'll let him know you tried to stop me," I say as I open the door to find my father sitting behind his desk and Jonas leaning his weight against the floor-to-ceiling window.

"What the..." my father starts, then stops as soon as he sees me.

"I'm sorry, Mr. Montgomery, I tried to tell him you were in a meeting, sir."

"Dad," I greet, walking inside.

"Should I call security, sir?" Maryanne asks.

"Maryanne, I thought we were friends," I say, my tone mocking as I move to close the door in her face.

"What the hell are you doing here?" Jonas asks.

My father is leaning back against his seat watching me.

Two birds, one stone, I think to myself. I take a seat.

"Had an interesting meeting with Dominic Benedetti today."

Jonas snorts. He works for dad. He has since he came of age and dad's been grooming him to take over the family business. Or what will be left of it when I'm through.

"You working with the mob now?" Jonas asks.

"You'd know more about that than I would," I say to him, keeping my eyes on my father. "When did you get involved with Angus Scava?"

"That's privileged information. You chose not to be a part of the family business, remember, son? You lost your privilege," my father answers. "And now that you stole controlling shares of Abbot Enterprises from poor Quincy's daughter, we're competitors."

"Poor Quincy?" I have to chuckle. "You two were friends?"

"Why are you here?" he asks.

"I want to know your business with Scava."

"Like I said, that's privileged. Unless you're here to discuss the sale of the property Abbot stole out from under me, we have no business."

"Did you have anything to do with Abbot's hit-and-run?"

There's a flicker, the smallest twitch at the corner of his eye. If I didn't know my father so well, I wouldn't notice. I doubt most people would.

"What the hell are you talking about?" he answers, a millisecond too late. "That was an accident. A tragic accident."

"He was your enemy."

"He was my competitor. There's a difference."

"But him being out of the picture would have worked out fine for you and your partner, Angus Scava."

"It would have but you stepped into Abbot's shoes, didn't you? Maybe *you* were driving the car that hit him."

"Not my M.O. As you know, I like for my enemies to see me coming." I give him a wide grin.

My father glares.

Jonas walks toward us, leans against the desk and folds his arms across his chest. "How's Percy? You knock some sense into her?"

I get to my feet and step to him. "If I learn you laid a finger on her—"

"We were engaged," he interrupts. "I laid more than a finger on her."

I grit my teeth. He's egging me on. It's not true. I know that for a fact. "If you ever hurt her, I will kill you, do you understand me?"

"Are you threatening me? I thought we were better than that. Letting pussy get in the way of our brotherly love and all."

I take him by the collar because I can't not. "Be careful, Jonas, be very fucking careful."

"Today was your sister's birthday," my father says, interrupting. "Let's honor that by not killing each other, shall we?"

Jonas' expression changes, the fight goes out of him. It's like his whole body seems to cave in on itself.

"Don't tell me you miss her," I say.

He looks at me. "Some of us are human. With feelings."

"Fuck you."

"Fuck you."

The door opens then, and two security guards enter.

My father is on his feet. "Let's not cause a scene here too, son."

"Yeah, *son*," Jonas mocks.

One of the guards puts a hand to my shoulder. I shrug it off.

"Stay away from Persephone," I tell Jonas once more before turning to my father. "Have you signed off on my bid yet?" I put in an offer to buy a part of the company. It would save him, but it would give me control.

"Fuck your bid," he says.

I grin but it's forced. "You're almost out of money."

"You've got bad information."

"I don't think so. I'll give you twenty-four hours."

"Sir, come with us," the guard says.

"I'm on my way out," I tell him, turning to the two men and pushing through them.

"Follow him. Make sure he leaves the building," I hear Jonas tell them as I make my way back out of the offices.

PERSEPHONE

I pick up the bottle of vodka and I pour myself another generous glass. Half the bottle is gone because no matter how hard I try I can't stop going over what happened with Hayden this morning. How he dismissed me afterward.

I feel humiliated and used and I know it's my own fault. I asked for it, but I couldn't think of any other way to distract him.

On top of that, today is October 31st. Nora's birthday.

I was sixteen when she died and back then, it was hard to get to the cemetery with having to rely on my stepmom or dad for a ride so every year on this night, once everyone had gone to bed, I'd sneak out to the chapel ruin to spend a few minutes talking to her, letting her know I hadn't forgotten her. The last couple of years I wasn't sneaking anymore, but I still only went after everyone was in bed.

My dad always got weird when I brought up Nora. Grew quiet. I know better since the accident why that was.

Drinking the rest of the vodka, I stand up. I turn around to take the painting off the wall and set it on the floor.

Behind it is my father's safe. I have the combination. Our lawyer gave it to me in a sealed envelope after dad's accident and I'm the only one who knows it.

I enter the numbers which I've memorized, my heart heavy as Hayden's words come back to me.

"If you knew what your own father was capable of—"

The door feels heavier than usual and I stumble backward once before finally getting it open. Inside are files containing deeds and original copies of contracts, etc. Exactly what you'd expect. After the accident, when I first opened it, I found a second compartment inside the safe. A hidden one.

Lifting the folders out, I reach back and slip my hand into that compartment now. I feel the velvet wrapping. I pull it out and set the folders back in place.

Looking down at what I know is a book beneath the velvet, I brush away a speck of dust.

I look at it for a long minute, remember the last time I saw it. It was also the first time. I haven't been able to look at it since.

It was two days after the hit-and-run. When we were just glad he was alive, even if he was unconscious. Dad had left me in charge of Abbot Enterprises. I wonder if he ever considered that something might happen to him and that I'd be the one to find this. I don't think so. I think he would have destroyed it if he'd given it a thought.

I set the book down on the desk, close the safe door and hang the painting back up. Hayden's words echo in my mind. *"If you knew what your own father was capable of—"*

"You're wrong. So wrong," I say out loud and sit down.

I pick up my glass and swallow back the contents before unwrapping the velvet. I should stop with the vodka but tonight, I need it.

I don't touch the book at first. It's mine. I'd lent it to Nora years ago. I think we were maybe thirteen or fourteen and she'd never returned it. Or maybe she just hadn't had a chance to.

But somehow, it's here. Somehow my father had it hidden away in his safe.

The book opens easily to the page where she'd tucked the photo and I wonder again why my father had it. Why he was hiding it. And I know I shouldn't look. I should burn it. Destroy any evidence for everyone's sake. But here I am, my heart in my throat, taking out the small photograph.

Did dad confront either of them, I wonder? How long had he known?

I look at Nora's face. I think this is the last photo of her before she died. There's no date, but we'd gone to get our hair cut together and she'd chopped hers off. I'd been so surprised, but now it makes sense. Like she was preparing. It was only weeks before that Halloween when everything changed.

Nora is looking into the camera. She's smiling her smile and even through the picture, I see how sad it is.

And him, he's not smiling. Not at all.

He's looking at her. I wonder if he realized she was taking the photo from the angle. I can't imagine he'd have gone along with it.

They're both naked and the way he has his arm across her chest, hand closed over her breast, the way he's looking at her, it makes me feel a little sick.

I think about my father seeing this. Why would he keep it? And how did he get it?

I turn it over, look at the two words written there. I recognize her handwriting.

I can't.

That's it. Two words.

Pouring myself another vodka, I drain the glass just as my cell phone rings, startling me so I gasp like I've just been caught doing something I shouldn't be doing. I look at the screen. The number is blocked. I check the time. A few minutes to midnight.

It could be Lizzie.

I swipe the green bar to answer, not wanting to put the phone to my ear for some reason. I push the button for speaker and say hello. I have to repeat myself when there's no reply.

An exhale of breath and a man's voice, one unfamiliar to me, comes on. "You're late. Better get to the chapel before your boyfriend does."

Before I can even register the message, the caller disconnects.

I sit there for a long minute looking at it, then shift my gaze back to the book where I'm holding the page open. The photograph partially hidden beneath my fingers.

"You're late. Better get to the chapel before your boyfriend does."

I shift my attention back to the phone unsure if that just happened or if it was the vodka and my imagination. But either way, I need to get to the chapel.

I fold the velvet over it and shove it into a drawer, suddenly in a hurry to get to the church.

Taking my phone with me, I hastily walk through the quiet, dark house. Hadn't I turned on any lights earlier? I go through the kitchen, slipping on my coat and opening the door as I zip it up. Freezing rain falls, the start of another storm, the slushy remains of the snow mud beneath my boots now.

Lightning in the distance brightens my path as I make my way to the chapel. I glance over at the ruin of the Montgomery house, dark and even more foreboding since the fire. I don't know why Jeremiah Montgomery didn't repair it. Why he's left it to rot.

I hug my arms to myself as I walk quickly to the church, taking my phone out of my pocket to use the flashlight as the night goes black between those electrical flashes.

I'm almost there though. I can smell it, over the smell of rain. It's like incense still lingers in the air from when the chapel was in use. I wonder how long ago that was.

When I get closer, I notice something odd. Out of place. It makes me stop.

It's not pitch-black inside.

I look around, suddenly afraid. The night is so dark, someone could be hiding, couldn't they?

The caller.

But why?

How did he know when I come out here? That I would come here at all? And why did he want me to come?

A wet wind blows, animating me again and I hurry toward the broken entrance and push the door open. The creak is eerie, and I see the source of the dim light. It's the altar candles. They've been lit and they flicker with my entrance and it makes me remember that night. Our last Halloween.

A shudder runs along my spine colder than the outside air.

For a moment, I'm a child again. A scared little girl who believes in ghosts.

Nora and I became best friends almost as soon as I moved into my father's house, but she had a darker side. We were ten that first Halloween and I remember coming out here with her. She'd thought it would be fun to be here on that particular night and since it was her birthday, I couldn't refuse. We did it every year after that and those nights, she was so energized, almost manic. When we were thirteen, I remember Jonas had joined us. He was with us a lot after that.

That was the first year they began to don their black cloaks. Nora had said Jonas had gotten them for her birthday.

He and Nora had been there when I arrived. They were wearing their black cloaks with hoods up and they'd lit the candles. At the center of the altar was a Ouija board. I remember how scared I'd been that night. How I'd run home when the cross hanging over the altar had broken with an unearthly noise. How the two of them had looked standing underneath it in their black cloaks, hoods up, covering their heads and shadowing their faces.

My mind wanders to the last Halloween the three of us were here. It was only days before she'd do it. I remember how Nora had been. How Jonas had been. I can't think about what he might have done, what she might have made him do, if Hayden hadn't come.

I shake my head, force myself into the present. I steel myself. Because someone wants me here. Why?

I scan the interior. I'm alone. But it doesn't make me any less afraid though.

I climb two of the steps, my eyes on the altar. I try not to see the stain on the stone. Because this is where she did it. Where Nora died. I swear I can feel her here tonight and I shudder.

But when I'm at the top of the sixth step, I see it.

I see what's between the two burning candles. A dark red envelope stark on the ancient slab.

I walk inside and the moment I do, something crashes behind me. I jump, spinning around, and watch as the broken door hits the stone again, clattering closed.

It's just the door. It's always done that.

Taking a shuddering breath, I face the altar again and walk with heavy steps toward it. My heart races and in my periphery, I see the evidence of Nora's suicide seeped into the stone, the red black now, a part of the stone forever like she's part of it forever. Part of this place.

I take another deep, shaky breath in and look at the envelope and I recognize her handwriting right away. I swallow, wrap my arms around myself because even with my coat, I'm freezing.

I make myself read the single letter she wrote in her dramatic script at the center.

It's the letter Q.

"If you knew what your own father was capable of—"

My hand trembles as I reach for it. I pick it up, turn it over. It was sealed once and ripped when it opened.

I reach inside to take out the three pieces of paper there.

Two I recognize. A torn check. My father's name and our address on the top left-hand corner. It's made out to Nora Montgomery.

My stomach turns.

"If you knew what your own father was capable of—"

Against the warnings repeating in my mind, I open the folded, yellowed sheet of paper and I read the few words.

Dear Q,
I can't lie to you anymore. It's not yours. And I can't accept your money because I can't get rid of it. I'm sorry. I love him.

Nora

"What are you doing out here?"

I gasp spinning and backing into the altar, the envelope falling to the church floor.

Hayden stands looking at me, eyes dark, hair wet, clothes disheveled.

"I saw the light. I followed you," he says.

The light? My cell phone.

He looks me over, looks at the burning candles, the papers in my hand, the envelope by my feet and it's like all the vodka I drank is just hitting me now.

It's not yours...I can't get rid of it.

No. It's not what I think. It can't be. I would have known, wouldn't I?

"If you knew what your own father was capable of—"

"What did he do?" I ask so quietly I'm not sure he hears me.

He steps closer, eyes intent on me but not hard. Not like earlier. This is the other Hayden. This is my Hades.

"What did he do?" I ask again, my face wet with tears.

His gaze shifts momentarily to what I'm holding and when thunder claps too near the church, I stumble backward, startled.

"Have you been drinking, Persephone?"

"What did he do?" I demand.

I know, though. I don't need it spoken out loud, do I? Spoken words have power.

It's not yours...

The implication of those words. No. It can't be true.

"Why are you out here? It's freezing." He goes to touch me, but I move just out of reach.

"You know, don't you?" I say. "You've known all along. That's what this is about." We all have secrets.

He reaches me this time, touching my hair, my face, cupping it in his warm hands. "You're wet. Freezing. Let's go inside."

He shifts his gaze to the papers again, takes them from me, bends to pick up the envelope. He scans the letter and when he looks at me, I see his confusion.

I look at the altar. See the years-old blood. "He was sleeping with her?" My voice breaks as I hear those words aloud. "Was my dad..."

I knew, didn't I? I saw how he looked at her. If I'm honest, I knew.

"Hayden?"

He's watching me when I turn to him, everything blurry from tears.

Lightning strikes, electrifying the sky.

"Let's go to the house," he says.

I shake my head, push against him when he tries to move me. "Tell me."

"We'll talk at the house."

I turn to the altar. I reach out my hand and I touch the blood along the edge of it. I don't know what I expect but I only feel cold stone.

"Persephone."

"She was pregnant, wasn't she?" I remember my stepmom gleefully spreading what I'd then thought a rumor. I remember the rage with which my father told her to shut her mouth. I'd never heard him talk to her like that before. I'd never heard him raise his voice ever. And I'd never seen him slam his fist so hard into the dining room table that it dented.

I'd also never heard him cry but he did the night of her

funeral. In his office. He sobbed. It was three in the morning. I'd come downstairs because I couldn't sleep, and I'd heard him.

"Persephone."

I turn to Hayden. I don't know if he's even blinked, he's watching me so closely.

"Do you remember that Halloween?" I ask.

His reply, after a long pause, is a nod.

"It wasn't Jonas who drugged me." I look away, look at the altar, things starting to fall into place. "It was Nora who gave me the drink. The only drink I had that night."

I sit down on one of the remaining pews, suddenly feeling the weight of it all, the vodka only blurring the very edges of each vivid memory.

"Nora who made sure I drank it."

I watch rain pour in from the empty window frame.

"I'm right, aren't I? She was pregnant?" I ask, looking up to find his eyes still on me. "I wasn't sure it was true. I thought it was my stepmom being ugly."

This letter explains why dad kept the photo. Why he hid it.

I love him.

Not my father. She didn't love my father. But I think he loved her.

I'm going to be sick.

A gust of wind blows in through the empty windows and the candles go out, leaving us stranded in the dark. Lightning shatters that darkness and I see it again, the three of us that last Halloween when it stormed like it is tonight.

Jonas, Nora and me. Me on the altar. Me with my skirt pushed up to my waist.

Nora holding me down. Nora telling him to do it.

To rape me?

She was playing a game. A sick game.

"We're going back to the house," Hayden says and before I can protest, before I can say a word, he lifts me in his arms and we're moving fast through the heavy rain as lightning strikes again and I cling to him, holding tight, remembering. Remembering that night.

The thunderstorm had been as wild as this one. He'd carried me home then too. Just like now.

And in my room, he'd stripped off my wet clothes and laid me on my bed and I still remember looking up at him, how he'd looked so big, so dark, his hair soaked, clothes soaked.

I remember his beautiful face when I'd opened my legs to him.

I remember the hunger in his dark eyes when he'd knelt beside the bed and looked at me and then, finally, touched me. I remember how soft his tongue had felt when he'd kissed me there.

It was our first kiss.

His mouth on my sex.

Then his tongue on me. Inside me. Me bucking, fisting handfuls of his hair as I came.

His lips glistened after and I remember how he'd left. Wordless. There, then gone, like a ghost. Like he hadn't been there at all.

My memories of that night had been fragmented, scattered. I'd been unable to collect the events together. Unwilling to face her betrayal. Unable to face Hayden. Because he lied too. After.

"Do it again," I say, realizing we're inside and he's laying me on my bed. "Kiss me again, like that night. Kiss me there."

He looms over me, like he had then, and then he's stripping off my clothes and I'm naked and I open my legs for him, and history repeats as his eyes darken with a familiar hunger as he looks at me.

"Put your mouth on me," I beg. "I need you to put your mouth on me."

He meets my eyes and crouches between my legs and I watch him, watch him watching me and when he closes his mouth over my sex, I close my eyes and arch my back and I feel him. I only feel him. His hands on my thighs, his mouth on my sex, his tongue licking me, lips closing around my clit to suck and I come fast, my hips jerking as I grip handfuls of hair and for a moment, I don't think about any of it. Not Nora. Not Jonas. Not my father. Not anything but Hades. Not anything but his mouth on me.

And when he rises moments later and I open my eyes, his hands are on either side of my head trapping me as he pushes into me and I'm filled with him, his cock inside me, his body on top of mine, his eyes watching me and I think he knows too now. He knows what they did. He must.

But it doesn't matter. Not right now.

Nothing matters but this, him inside me, and when I feel him come, I hear the sounds he makes when he doesn't utter a word, and I watch him and I take those final, punishing thrusts as he empties inside me and I think how fucked up everything is. How fucked up everything but this is.

HAYDEN

I stay inside her for a long time afterward just looking at her. She watches me, too, and I think about her in all of this and I can't think about what I read in that letter. What it means. I just look at her and she's so fucking beautiful and I think I'll never get close enough to her.

"I didn't mean what I said earlier," she says. "At your office."

"I know."

Silence descends again.

"Why did you go to the chapel and not the cemetery?" I ask.

Her gaze drifts past me to the papers from inside that blood-red envelope that have fallen off the bed and onto the floor.

"I don't know. I always go to the chapel. Every year since she..." She furrows her brow, quiet again, then returns her gaze to mine. "Nora gave me the drink that night. Told me to finish it. It wasn't Jonas."

She said that earlier too. At the chapel.

"You don't remember right," I tell her. "You were drugged."

She shakes her head, rubs her face with both hands. "She told him to do it, Hayden. When he hesitated. When you found us."

"No." I feel the lump in my throat.

"It's true."

"She told him to rape you?"

Her forehead wrinkles. "I don't know."

"Think!"

"Blood on the stone. Virgin blood on the altar. Mine."

Blood on the stone. Except in the end, it was Nora's.

"She's dead." I get up out of the bed. "In the ground. You're not going to do this to her." I don't look at the envelope or its contents on the floor as I head into the bathroom to shower.

"You saw the letter."

I stop at the door between the two rooms but only momentarily. I walk into the bathroom and close the door behind me but before I'm even in the shower, the door opens, and Persephone is inside.

I switch on the shower.

"I think he loved her," she says.

My jaw tightens and my hands fist. "You don't want to do this," I warn without looking at her.

"I think they both did."

At that, I spin around, put my hand on her chest and walk her backward to the wall.

Her hands wrap around my forearm but I'm not hurting her, just keeping her there. Warning her.

"Your father raped my sister. Even if she didn't say no, she was fifteen."

"I don't know what he did. I hope he wakes up so I can

ask him. But you read her letter. You know there was someone else. Someone she loved."

I swallow, grit my teeth. I let her go, turning, running my hand through my hair still wet with rain. I spin to face her. "Who?"

She cowers back and I wonder what I look like. How crazed I must appear.

"Tell me who." She's mute. "There's no one else. No one!" I snap. Fuck. "Get in the shower."

Obediently, she walks into the shower and I follow. She stands beneath the flow looking at me, studying me. Pitying me?

I watch her. My brain is going a thousand miles a minute. I pour shower gel into my hands and lather them up. I scrub her shoulders, her arms, her breasts then turn her, and I wash her back. I slide my hand between her legs to clean her then set both forearms against the wall on either side of her face.

She turns her head, shifts her gaze so our eyes meet.

We stay like this for a minute. I want to be sure she hears what I say.

"You are not my enemy, Persephone. I'm warning you to keep it that way."

I mean what I'm saying. I don't want to hurt her. I don't want her hurt even if there's no ending I see where she will walk away unscathed.

You know there was someone else. Someone she loved.

I shake my head, dislodge the thought as I switch off the water and step out, grabbing a towel for myself without looking back as I wrap it around my hips and walk back into the bedroom. There, I go into the closet to find the clothes I'd brought neatly folded and put on a pair of jeans.

A phone rings inside and I try to remember where my

cell phone is. I'd left it in the SUV. This must be Perse-phone's.

I pull a sweater over my head as I walk back into the bedroom to watch Persephone dig into the pocket of her coat to retrieve the phone.

It starts to ring again, and she looks at it, her face a little paler.

"Who is it?" I ask, coming up behind her.

She glances at me as I read the screen. Unknown caller.

I take the phone from her hands and swipe the green bar to answer.

"Hello."

A girl sniffles on the other end of the line. Persephone is watching me, eyes wide.

"Who is this?" I ask.

"Is...Where's Percy?"

"Who is this?" I repeat.

"Where's my sister?" the voice breaks.

It's Lizzie.

I put the call on speaker. "Persephone's here. You're on speaker phone."

"Percy?" Lizzie asks meekly.

"Lizzie!" Persephone grabs the phone and puts it to her ear. "Lizzie, are you okay? Where are you?"

Silence as she listens to her sister.

"Stay there. Lock the door and stay there and I'll be there as soon as I can. I'm leaving right now." It's quiet again, and Persephone nods. "Yes, okay. It's okay. I'm coming. Just don't open the door for anyone but me." She disconnects and turns to me. "I have to go."

She looks around wildly, then picks up her coat and begins to put it on.

I grab her arm to stop her. "What's going on?"

"My sister's in trouble. She's at a hotel. I have to go, Hayden. She's scared."

"Put some clothes on," I tell her, taking the coat. "What hotel?"

She tells me the name of the place and the town, which is almost a two-hour drive. She looks at the wet clothes discarded on the floor.

I walk her into the closet, choose the first sweater and jeans I see, and she's dressed in a few minutes. We're about to walk out when she stops.

"Wait. I need...she doesn't have clothes."

I process but don't ask the obvious question.

She goes back into her closet to retrieve some things and while she does, I pick up the red envelope and the papers that were inside it and shove them all into my pocket.

"My phone's in the SUV. I'll send some men—"

She shakes her head. "She'll think they're with him."

"I'll just make sure they watch the room."

She nods, distracted as I lead her out the door and down the stairs. "I should have checked on her. Pushed her to come home or at least tell me where she was."

We're in the Range Rover a minute later and I'm driving to the hotel. I push a button to call Peter who answers on the second ring. He's available 24/7. It's why I pay him the amount I do.

I tell him to get some men out to the property, a motel along Highway 87. I can imagine the kind of place knowing the area.

"Make sure they just keep an eye on her room. Thirty-three, that's right. No one goes in." I disconnect the call and glance at Persephone who is staring straight ahead. "She'll be fine."

"I didn't get the phone number. I should have gotten the number."

"She wasn't calling from her cell phone?"

She shakes her head.

"Did she tell you anything?"

"That she made a mistake." She looks at me. "She sounded terrified."

I nod, push on the accelerator. "My men will be there within the hour. We'll be there in less than two. Don't worry."

She leans back in her chair. "I hate Halloween. I hate it."

"It's not Halloween anymore." It's past midnight now. Technicality.

My mind wanders to the contents of that envelope which I stuffed into my pocket as Persephone picked up clothes for her sister. They're burning a hole there now.

You know there was someone else. Someone she loved.

No. I can't think about that right now. "Do you always take candles out there?" I ask, remembering the thick altar candles which looked brand new.

She turns to me. "Sometimes. But I didn't tonight."

"What do you mean? Who then?"

"Someone called me, Hayden. A man. It was a little before midnight. They knew I would go out there."

"What?"

"I don't know. I...I'd been drinking." She pushes her hand into her hair. "It's all so much now. Too much."

"What man?"

"I don't know. He called and said I was late. And he said," she turns to me. "He said I'd better get down there before my boyfriend does."

"Another mystery man." She doesn't comment. "He called you on your cell phone?"

She nods.

"Give it to me."

"There was no caller ID."

"Give it to me."

She reaches into her coat pocket and hands me her cell phone.

Keeping one hand on the steering wheel, I take it.

"What's your password?"

"8789."

I punch it in and scroll through her calls. I see more than one without a caller ID in missed calls and the one she answered a few minutes before midnight.

"You didn't recognize the caller's voice?"

"No."

"Any idea who it could be?"

"Someone who knew about my visits."

I look straight ahead absently reading the sign we pass. "Who knows you go out there?"

"No one. Lizzie maybe, but no one else. My dad."

I'm thinking. Who would want her to have that letter?

"My father was sleeping with her," she says quietly. "That's why you're doing this."

I keep my gaze straight head, grip the steering wheel harder than I need to. I nod.

"How long?"

"I don't know."

"How did you find out?"

"Autopsy revealed she was fourteen weeks pregnant. I investigated."

"He was broken up over her death."

"Don't talk to me about how he felt. I don't care how he felt."

"You don't know—"

"She was fifteen," I bark. "That's all I need to know."

"I was going to say you don't know the whole story."

"And you do?"

She exhales, shifts her gaze to her lap.

"You were close with her. You never suspected she was pregnant? Suicidal?"

She shifts her gaze out the side window. "You said once that you don't know people. That you never really know someone, not what's really inside their head." She returns her gaze to mine. "You were right because I didn't know. I didn't know anything about any of it."

The way she says that is strange, but before I can ask what she means, she continues.

"She was sad, I knew that. Even when she tried to pretend she wasn't. Especially at the end."

It's silent for a long minute.

"But the baby wasn't my father's. She said it herself. He was trying to help her."

"He was trying to cover up his mistake. Whether or not the baby was his doesn't change the fact that he raped a fifteen-year-old girl."

She winces at my use of that word and I see that letter again like it's tattooed into my brain.

Dear Q,

I can't lie to you anymore. It's not yours. And I can't accept your money because I can't get rid of it. I'm sorry. I love him.

Nora

"You have to admit there was someone else. You can't deny it, not after seeing that letter," she says.

"Who is he then? This man she loved?" I turn to her to see the back of her head because she keeps her gaze out the window and it's silent again and I realize something. "You know."

She looks at me but just then her phone rings and she shifts her gaze to it.

"Answer. Put it on speaker."

She does as she's told. "Hello?"

"There's a car outside, Percy. There are men inside it. I think they're back."

As if on cue, my phone buzzes with a text from Peter telling me our men are in place.

"It's all right." I say. "They're my men."

"Percy?"

"That's Hayden Montgomery. It's okay, he's coming with me. He's helping us."

Silence, then: "Can you stay on the phone with me until you get here? I don't want to hang up."

Persephone nods. "Yes. Yes, we won't hang up."

28

PERSEPHONE

Hayden's attention remains fixed on the road, his hands tight on the steering wheel. He's processing what he's just learned. Trying to make sense of it. I know. I did the same thing when I first found out.

I tell Lizzie about my visit to dad. I talk to keep her distracted as much as to keep from being questioned by Hayden, telling her about the facility, telling her I think it'll be good for him. Both the doctors and the facility are top-notch.

"They'd cut his hair and he looked good," I tell her. I want to say he looked better but that may be me wanting to see something that isn't there because the doctor was very clear that there was no change and not to expect one.

"Will you take me to visit him tomorrow?" she asks.

"Yes. We'll go together. He'll like that."

It's silent for a while but we don't hang up. Instead, we fill the space with talk about nothing.

"We're just getting off the exit," Hayden says a little while later.

I sit up taller, taking in the broken streetlamps, the flashing light of an all-night diner, the arrow pointing into the glaringly bright, empty place.

"It's two blocks away," Hayden says.

The hotel is more of a run-down motel that looks like it hasn't been renovated since the seventies and I cringe at the thought that my baby sister is alone and scared here in one of these decrepit rooms.

"Is that you?" she asks as Hayden pulls into the parking spot next to one of two other cars there.

"It's us. You can open the door."

Two men climb out of that other car and Hayden kills the engine. I slide out of the passenger side and carry the bundle of clothes to the room and when I see Lizzie's frightened face peer out from around the half-open door, I breathe a sigh of relief.

I look back to Hayden, who is watching me as one of the men talks, I guess filling him in.

Lizzie opens the door a little wider, remaining mostly behind it, and I enter.

"Percy!" she hugs me so tight it hurts.

I hug her back, feel the scratchy, threadbare towel she's wrapped around herself. I pull back when she finally lets me, and I look at her.

Her eyes are puffy from crying but her makeup is gone, and I know Lizzie. She hasn't even left her bedroom without a pound of makeup on in over a year. Her curly hair which she normally straightens hangs in ringlets around her shoulders and on her arm, I see the purplish bruises in the shape of a hand and one more high on her cheekbone.

I take her face in my hands. "Did they hurt you?"

Her breathing is shallow, and she wraps her arms around herself, shivering. I realize how cold it is in here.

"Get dressed. Let's get out of here."

She drops the towel and I'm relieved when I see she's still wearing her panties and bra. She pulls on the sweater and yoga pants, which are a little big on her, but they'll do. She bends down to put on the sneakers.

"I forgot socks," I say.

She shakes her head as she straightens. "It's okay." She looks up at me. She's just over five feet tall so I have a few inches on her. "And they didn't hurt me like that."

I nod, relieved.

There's a knock on the door and Hayden pushes it open. He looks Lizzie over then runs his gaze around the room before turning his full attention to her again.

I see her swallow when he does and I think about how he looks, how big he is, how intimidating.

"What happened?" he asks.

She looks at me. "It's okay," I tell her. "This is Hayden Montgomery. You've met him before, I think."

She nods, then turns to me. "Can we please go home?"

"Not until you tell me what happened," Hayden says.

Lizzie looks like she's just barely keeping it together.

I touch Hayden's arm. "We can talk at home." When he doesn't move, I step between him and her and take his hands. "She's scared."

He drags his gaze from her to me then back. "One question. Who am I looking for?"

Now Lizzie does start to sob, and I wrap my arm around her and walk around Hayden to the SUV. I open the back door and help her in, then close it and go back to Hayden who is standing outside the motel room talking to one of his men who just lit a cigarette.

"Can we go home?"

"No. You'll stay at the club. Both of you."

29

HAYDEN

When we get to the club, Persephone and Lizzie disappear into one of the guest rooms. They emerge half an hour later and take a seat on the couch in my office. Lizzie's hair is wet, so I assume she just showered.

I'm sitting behind my desk. I look Lizzie over. She seems younger than fifteen and looks at me like she doesn't quite trust me. I don't remember the last time I saw her, but it's been years.

I walk around the desk and sit in the armchair across from the couch.

"Can we do this tomorrow?" Persephone asks.

"No." I look at Lizzie who looks back at me.

"Hayden—"

"No, it's okay. I'd rather get it over with," Lizzie says.

"I'm glad you feel that way. Who were you with?"

"I told my sister already that I left with Marigold. We just went on a little road trip."

"And Marigold is?"

"Her friend. She lives nearby," Persephone answers for her.

"And where is Marigold now?"

"Back home," Lizzie answers.

"You *left* with Marigold. So, it was just the two of you?"

She looks sheepish, glances at her sister, then back at me. "Yes."

"Try again."

"I don't think she'd lie," Persephone interjects.

"Room was paid for in cash and registered to Joe Blow," I say. "Try again," I tell Lizzie.

Persephone looks at her sister, surprised.

"We left together and met Matt," Lizzie says.

"Matt?" I raise my eyebrows.

"A...friend of Marigold's. From school. He drove us to Manhattan. We were just going to hang out for a couple of nights. Get away from things here. He had a deal on a hotel, and it sounded like fun."

"What's Matt's last name and how old is he?" I ask.

"Johnson and I don't know how old he is."

"What would you guess? Your age?"

She shakes her head. "Older."

"How much older?"

She quickly glances at her sister then back to me. "I don't know. Maybe twenty."

"And where were Matt and Marigold when you were at that motel?"

She hesitates, her attention suddenly entirely taken up by a fingernail.

"I asked you a question."

"Lizzie, he just wants to help."

Lizzie takes a breath in before answering. "We'd gone to a club. Matt and Marigold hooked up and I didn't want to be in the way, so I stuck around after they left. Met someone there."

"How did you get into a club?" Persephone asks. "You're fifteen."

"Matt has a friend in New York who makes fake IDs."

"Matt sounds like a winner. You'll stay away from him and this Marigold," I say.

"You can't tell me what to do."

"I just did. This 'someone' you met, name?"

Her expression changes, darkens. "He said his name was Mike."

"Matt, Mike, quite the night—"

"Hayden," Persephone gives me a look.

"What's Mike's last name?"

"I never got it."

"How old would you say Mike is?"

"Early twenties."

"Lizzie!" Persephone exclaims.

"And Mike took you to the fancy hotel where we picked you up?"

She pulls her hands into her lap and drags the sleeves of the sweater down into her palms. She nods. "He got quiet in the car. Different than he was inside the club. I knew something was wrong when we left, but I didn't know what to do. When we got to the motel, they were waiting." Her expression changes as her eyes redden.

"Who was waiting?" Persephone asks.

Lizzie wipes her tears. "Two men. Older. Scarier. They spoke in Italian, I think. I couldn't understand them. One handed Mike a wad of cash and Mike didn't say a word. He didn't even look at me. He just got back in his car and left and the man who gave him the money, he took my purse and my phone, and I barely had time to scream before they dragged me into the room and...started." Her voice breaks off at the end.

"Can we not do this now?" Persephone asks.

"We have to do it," I tell her, then turn to her sister. "Started what?"

She caves into herself a little and she won't look at either of us.

I lean forward, try to get her to look at me. "Did they hurt you, Lizzie?"

"No," Persephone answers as Lizzie shakes her head.

I lean back in my seat.

"Not like that," Lizzie adds.

"Where are your clothes?" I ask.

"They took them. And my purse and phone."

"What did they do?"

She looks away, wipes her eyes with the heels of her hands. "They took pictures." She hugs her knees into her chest and hides her face.

I meet Persephone's eyes.

"I didn't want to but when I said no, the one who paid Mike hit me. The other one, the photographer, he stopped him when he tried to hit me again. His name was Angelo, I know that. He called the photographer that. And I was scared. I thought...I thought they could kill me if they wanted to. Or something else."

"You're sure it was Italian they spoke?"

"Pretty sure." She nods. "I think the one with the camera didn't speak English."

"What did they say they would do with the photos?"

She shrugs a shoulder. "They didn't."

"Did you hear anything else? Any last names?"

"Just Angelo. When they were done, they told me to go into the bathroom to put on my underthings, but they didn't give me back the rest of my clothes. They told me not to come out until they said and that's when I saw the headlights of a car shine into the room. I went into the bathroom and locked the door. It was stupid, I knew they could break into it if they wanted, but they didn't come in."

"Did you hear the man who came in?"

"He spoke in Italian too, but he sounded different. I think he was American but knew Italian and I could tell he was in charge."

"How?"

"I don't know. I just did. And then a few minutes later, they were gone. I waited until I was sure and then I came out and called you. They'd taken my clothes so I couldn't leave. I didn't even have shoes. They had my purse and phone and I didn't know what to do. I was so scared."

She turns her face into Persephone's chest and Persephone hugs her.

I stand. "I'll find Matt Johnson where?"

30

HAYDEN

Matt Johnson's grease covered overalls stick out from beneath the engine of the crappy car he's working on. The garage doors are wide open. It's a sunny day even if it is cold. In the shop next door, I see a girl blowing pink bubble gum and watching us.

I have three men with me. One just lit up a cigarette and is leaning against our car parked across the street. Another walks into the shop where the girl is. Shane is with me.

"Turn that shit off," I tell Shane and a moment later, he unplugs the radio playing the crap music Matt Johnson listens to.

"Hey, what the fuck?" Matt starts, his tone already grating on my nerves.

I watch him roll himself out from under the car. He stops before he's fully out, hands still on the fender, taking me in.

"You look older than twenty," I say.

"Who the fuck are you?"

"Get out from under there." I kick his boot.

"I asked you who you are."

He pulls himself to stand and I step toward him. I've got about half a foot and thirty pounds on him. He loses his bravado, leans against the car and brings his attention to wiping his hands on a dirty towel. I can see him scanning the road though.

"Don't make me chase you," I tell him.

He looks up at me and like the idiot I expect him to be, he drops the towel and sprints. Or tries to.

I shoot my arm out and slam it against his throat, stopping him before he gets two feet from me. He drops backward, the car breaking his fall. The girl who's chewing the bubble gum picks up the phone, her mouth dropping open.

I'm not worried about her though. My man will make sure no one is called until I'm done here.

Matt's trying to catch his breath, both hands around his throat.

"I expected Lizzie Abbot to have slightly better taste in friends."

At the mention of her name, his eyes go huge.

I crouch down, grateful for the garage smell covering up Matt's special scent.

"I don't know any Lizzie Abbot, man."

"No? How old are you exactly?"

"Twenty-six."

"And you hang around with high school kids?"

He looks around nervously.

"Easy money, I guess, selling them weed and arranging for fake IDs."

"Look, I don't know what you're talking about or where you get your *facts*," he actually uses air quotes. "But you got the wrong guy."

"Quite frankly," I continue, ignoring his outburst. "I don't care what the fuck you do, but I do want to know who you work for."

"Man, I work for myself. And old man Harvey here at the garage."

"I don't care about the garage. Who's your supplier?"

He looks around again, then at my shoes and suit. "You're not a cop?"

Dumbass. "No, I'm not. Supplier?"

I think he's going to tell me and am pleased at how easy this will be, but then the idiot speaks. "I have no supplier. I don't know what you're talking about."

I stand up, nod to Shane. "Jog his memory, will you?"

"Sure thing," he says, as I push the button to close the garage door.

"Wait, wait man. What the fuck!" I hear the first punch thrown, then the second while I check the time. Matt whimpers like a little girl. One more punch and I turn around to find him cowering.

"You broke my nose!"

I nod for Shane to stop, pick up the greasy towel and toss it to Matt.

He holds it up to his bleeding nose.

"You'll want to get that set pretty fast or you'll be even uglier," I tell him as I crouch down to get in his face. "Supplier. Who is it?"

"I can't—"

I grip him by the throat and haul him up to slam him against the hood of the car. It knocks the wind out of him, leaving him panting.

"Who the fuck is your supplier."

"Italians. I don't know who. I just know the one I buy the

product from. Rudy. I don't even fucking know if that's his real name."

"Rudy. Last name?"

"Like I said, I don't even know if that's a real first name!"

"Did Rudy pay for your trip to New York City? Your hotel?"

He looks around again, from me to Shane and back. I have my answer, but I want to hear it from him.

"It was a bonus."

"Right. And he told you who to bring?"

He nods. "Look, I don't know her. Lizzie Abbot. Me and Mari, we have a good thing."

"You know they're fifteen, right? Statutory rape. Do those words mean anything to you?"

"No way she's fifteen. They're both older."

"Did Rudy pay you to bring them to the city?"

"Yeah. Gave me the car to use and even got us a nice hotel."

"And who does Rudy work for?"

"I don't know. He's my only contact."

I grip his collar and haul him to me. He puts both his hands up in defense. "There's a name I've heard. I'm not sure if that's it."

"And?"

"It's a weird fucking name. Anger or something. Angus."

I pause. "Last name."

"Scava."

Mother fucker.

I turn, walk to the garage door and push the button to open it. I look back at Matt.

"If I hear you've even breathed near Lizzie Abbot, I will break more than your nose, understand?"

"Yeah, man, yeah. I don't sell to her. It's Mari. Mari likes the stuff."

"I don't give a shit. Don't go near her again."

I walk out to my waiting car, my men following. "Let's go see Benedetti."

31

PERSEPHONE

Lizzie is in her room packing clothes and schoolbooks when I slip into the study to find the book still in the drawer I'd hastily shoved it into. I open it to where the photograph is stuck between the pages and I think I understand it all now. After seeing the letter Nora left, things fall into place. Make sense.

"Ready," Lizzie says from behind me, startling me.

I turn, closing my palm over the photo and tucking it into my coat pocket. "Okay. Let's go."

I'm surprised she didn't put up more resistance about having to stay at the club, but I think she's scared. I think what happened shook her up.

She hasn't bothered to put on makeup or straighten her hair and is wearing an oversized top and baggy sweats.

"Hey," I start, wrapping my arm around her shoulders. "It's going to be okay. You're safe now."

"Why is he helping us?" she asks me.

I bite my lip.

"Because you're sleeping with him?"

"Lizzie—"

She shakes her head. "I'm not judging you, Percy. I know you're doing what you think you have to do. Material things aren't worth it, though. The house. The business. It's not worth it."

"It's more complicated than that."

"You like him. That's how it's complicated?"

I open my mouth to answer, but she shrugs a shoulder. "At least he's not a complete creep like his brother but I wouldn't trust him. You know how much dad hated them."

"I trust that Hayden doesn't want to see either of us get hurt. And I need his help right now. Can you trust me at least?"

"Just don't be surprised if he turns out to be a jerk."

"Let's go see dad."

A driver takes us to the hospital. Hayden wants a guard with us, which, given what happened with Lizzie, I'm not opposed to. Although I need to take care of something that he can't know about.

Celia is waiting for us at the hospital and, after a big hug, she takes us into dad's room, telling the guard he has to wait out in the hallway because of the number of visitors allowed inside. I'm not sure if she just made that up or it's true but I'm grateful.

Lizzie goes right to dad to take his hand and start talking to him and Celia slips me her car keys.

"I just need an hour, Celia."

"It's fine. Keep it as long as you need it."

"What do you need an hour for?" Lizzie asks.

"I need to take care of something. Can you stay here with dad until I'm back?"

She squints her eyes. "What are you taking care of?"

"Can you just do this for me?"

She considers. "Sure."

"Thanks."

Celia unlocks a door that leads to a back corridor and I slip out, walking quickly to the stairs and taking them down and out to the parking lot. I locate Celia's car and within a few minutes I'm heading to Jonas' apartment in the city.

Traffic is light but it's the middle of the morning so it should be. I park Celia's car and head to the front doors where the doorman greets me warmly.

"Percy! What a nice surprise."

I smile and say hello. "I'm here to see Jonas," I say. "I took a chance he'd be in."

"He didn't mention anything but I'm sure he'll be pleased," he says, obviously getting the wrong idea.

I think about how Jonas and I appeared to others. A perfect couple. A happy one. How wrong that image was. Is.

"He's got someone upstairs but I'm sure he'll want you to go straight up." The elevator dings and he moves to open the front doors to another tenant exiting the building.

I thank him and a few minutes later, I'm riding the elevator up to Jonas' eighth-floor apartment, my hand closed around the photo in my pocket.

Making my way down the lavish corridor, I find two men in suits standing just outside Jonas' apartment door. They watch my approach but neither of them greets me. I'm about to say something when the door opens. I hear an unfamiliar voice and just as I stop a few feet from the door, the man turns.

I meet his gaze. And I freeze.

Because there is something very wrong about this man.

Jonas comes into view to see what's made the stranger stop. "Percy," he starts. "What are you doing here?"

"Percy?" the stranger repeats stepping toward me and holding out his hand. He must be my father's age and it takes all I have to keep my revulsion in check because I don't want to touch this man. "The fabled Persephone Abbot, I presume." He raises an eyebrow and I realize how awkward I'm being, so I slip my hand into his to shake it, but he brings it up to his mouth instead and brushes his lips against my knuckles. "More beautiful in person than your photos do justice."

"Where have you seen photos of me?"

"Oh, here, in your fiancé's home, of course."

Jonas still has photos of me around? I glance at Jonas who looks so small next to this man. So out of his league. I clear my throat and steel my spine.

"I'm sorry, I don't know you."

"Angus Scava. A pleasure to meet you."

I don't recognize the name and am grateful when Jonas interrupts. "I'll call you later about that matter, Angus."

The older man drags his gaze from me to Jonas. His mouth stretches into a smile that doesn't touch his eyes and when he releases my hand, it takes all I have not to wipe it off on my coat.

A moment later, he walks away, the two men flanking him, and I know as I watch them go that he's linked to the mafia. Maybe it's the Benedetti connection to my dad. I'm not sure, but I trust my instinct and right now, instinct is telling me to beware.

"Who is he?" I ask Jonas once Angus Scava is gone.

"No one," Jonas says, looking me over.

"What is that?" I ask, gesturing to the large envelope he's holding.

"Nothing." He doesn't even look down but sets it on a side table near the door. "I never expected to see you here again."

"Me either."

"How's your head?" he calls over his shoulder, his tone flippant.

I don't bother to answer him. He's trying to rile me up. It's what he does.

He walks into the living room and I follow. It's the first time I've been here since the breakup.

"To what do I owe the honor of your visit?" he asks sarcastically, taking a seat on the couch without offering me one.

I perch on the chair across from him, remembering the other night at the fundraiser. Remembering how violent he'd been. That was the second time he became violent with me and I wonder if it was wise to have come here alone, but I need to do this now.

I take the photo out of my pocket as he studies me, hands folded on his lap. I set it on the table and turn it, moving my hand so he can see it.

In that moment, I think he stops breathing. He just stares at it for a long, long time and I'm not sure what to think as I watch layer after layer of emotion sweep over him.

When I tuck it back into my pocket, he looks at me.

I'd never shown him the photo before. When I broke it off with him, I told him I knew what he'd done. I knew what he'd done with Nora. But that was all, and it was enough. He was guilty. But I hadn't known the whole story.

"She was pregnant," I say.

He's not surprised. I see it on his face. A fine layer of sweat breaks out across his forehead, his skin taking on that sickly sheen it does whenever her name comes up.

"Did you love her?" I ask.

He looks at me and I see the pain in his eyes. But he masks it quickly. "She was my sister. Of course, I loved her."

"Not like that. You know what I mean."

He swallows, gets up and walks to the windows. I watch him run a hand through his hair.

"No one would understand what we had," he finally says.

My eyes fill up and my throat closes and I think what a tragedy this is. What a tragedy for everyone.

"That's what you wanted to tell me." Except that when I refused to talk to him, he came to the house and he made sure I knew to keep my mouth shut. He thought I'd reveal his secret. "Why did you want to marry me?" I ask when he turns to face me, hand around his own throat.

"To be close to her."

"That's why you wouldn't touch me."

"You were just the closest thing to *her*. No one understands what we had. How we felt. How deeply we loved."

I'm not moved by his words. By his pain. "How old was she when you...touched her?"

Anger flashes across his face. "It wasn't like that. Don't say it like that. Make it ugly—"

"Answer my question!"

He shifts his gaze away and I'm not sure he will answer. "Thirteen."

"God." How? For three years? How didn't I know?

He shakes his head, coming toward me crouching down and taking my hands in his clammy ones. "It wasn't like that. Not dirty and wrong. She loved me."

I pull my hands free of his. "You were an adult. She was a child."

He straightens, backs away. "I thought out of everyone, you'd understand. Nora wasn't ever a child. Not like you think. You didn't know her."

"I know she was thirteen when she changed."

"Because she loved me. She changed because she loved me."

"She got pregnant. With *your* baby."

Was I unsure for a moment it was his? If I was, any doubt vanishes when I look at his face.

I wonder, suddenly, if he knew about my father and I know I can't ask. I don't want to ask.

"That's why she killed herself? Because of the baby?"

He tries for a smile that collapses instantly. "The pills were for the baby to die. Not her."

"She slit her wrists after taking the pills, Jonas. She wanted to die."

He rubs his forehead, squeezing his eyes shut and I see how his hand trembles. I wonder how long he's been holding onto this.

"She wasn't supposed to die. She told me. She promised she knew the pills would only kill the baby."

"*Your* baby. You left her alone to kill the baby you put inside her. She was a child. You were the adult."

He shakes his head again and his eyes get that strange look inside them, the one I remember after Nora died. The one I saw often while we were engaged. Like a deer caught in the headlights of an oncoming truck.

"She loved me. We loved each other."

I need to go. I don't want to be here for another second. "I need you to go away, Jonas."

"What?"

"Leave here. Disappear for a while."

"I can't do that."

"You have to."

"Why?"

"Because when I tell Hayden the truth, he's going to kill you."

32

HAYDEN

"I think you should come by the club, sir," Peter says nervously into the phone.

"Why?"

"Someone dropped off a package for you."

"Who?"

"I don't know. He didn't give his name, but I thought he might be with the gentleman with whom you met the other morning." It's like he can't bring himself to say Benedetti's name.

"I'm on my way to see Benedetti."

"Sir, I—"

"Never mind," I say. When Peter gets nervous, I've learned from experience it's best to manage it quickly. "I'll swing by on my way."

After disconnecting, I tell the driver about the change in plans just as another call comes in from the man I had watching Persephone and her sister.

"She's gone, sir," he says as soon as I pick up.

"Alone?"

"Yes. Tail is in place. He'll send you her location ASAP."

"Thank you."

I dial Persephone, who doesn't pick up. I don't expect her to, though. Her words from the night before echo: *"You don't know the whole story."*

She does. And I'm going to learn the truth today.

But I have to handle the Lizzie Abbot issue first. I don't have to think too hard to imagine what Scava will do with the compromising photos.

When we get to the club, I find Peter waiting for me just inside the entrance.

"Okay, where is this package?"

He lifts a large sealed folder out of a drawer in his desk and hands it to me. Although not thick, it's heavier than I expect. And I can guess what's inside.

I turn the envelope over. It's not addressed.

"Thank you, Peter," I say. I wait to open it, so I only do it when I'm in the back of the sedan and the driver is on his way to the restaurant where I'll meet Benedetti.

Lifting the flap, I peer inside, reaching in to take hold of the pages.

Three photos. Taken last night in that nasty hotel room.

I look at the first one, detaching myself. I move to the second. The third. There's a note scribbled on the back of the last one.

Drop the Benedetti contract or these go public.

"Mother fucker."

I don't take too kindly to being threatened and Scava clearly doesn't know I won't bend when blackmailed.

I tuck the photos back into the envelope as we pull up to the entrance of the restaurant. Carrying the envelope, I ascend the stairs and enter, heading straight to the far corner where Dominic Benedetti is sitting at a table with his back to the wall. He's talking to a dark-haired man whose face I can't see from here, but I do see that Dominic notes my entrance the moment I arrive.

Men in his business better notice, though. They won't survive long if they don't.

A soldier eyes me, holding out his hand for me to wait.

A moment later, Dominic gives the signal and I'm walking through the dimly lit but noisy restaurant. I notice the tables around his are empty.

Dominic stands when I get to the table as does his companion. The latter looks me over, his face remaining unreadable.

"Hayden," Dominic says. "Good to see you. "This is my brother, Salvatore."

"Dominic." I extend my hand to first shake Dominic's then Salvatore's. "Good to meet you. I didn't realize you still worked with your brother."

"I don't," Salvatore says, not adding more before turning to his brother. "Remember what I said."

"I'm sure you won't let me forget," Dominic says.

Salvatore nods and excuses himself, leaving the restaurant.

Dominic sits down and I toss the envelope onto the table between us as I take the seat Salvatore just vacated.

"What do you know about this?" I ask.

He picks up the envelope, opens it and eyes the photos. He looks displeased, to say the least, and after reading the message, his eyes are narrowed when he returns them to mine.

"Elizabeth Abbot?"

"How did you know?"

"I do my research. Just photos or..." he trails off.

"Photos. Although I'm not sure I'd say 'just'."

"No, I wouldn't either." He reads the back of the last

photo again but doesn't seem at all disturbed. "Although, it's not Scava's style. Didn't used to be at least."

"Well, maybe he's desperate. Didn't you say this building would seal your position in the city?"

He nods. "How old is the girl?"

"Fifteen."

"Like I said, not his style."

"Maybe he's changed styles." I lean toward him. "I'm not getting in the middle of a fucking mafia war."

His casual stance gone he leans toward me. "You'll get in the middle of whatever I tell you to get in the middle of."

"I don't work for you."

"No, we work together." He leans back. "We're business associates. Friendly ones, I hope."

"I don't like being threatened and I don't like being blackmailed."

"Well, I assume the former is directed at me and the latter at those responsible for these."

"There are more, I'm sure."

"I'm sure. You're certain Scava's behind it? Not your father?"

"The kid he paid to get Lizzie Abbot to New York City is a low-level drug dealer. I had a conversation with him this morning and he confirmed that he works for Angus Scava."

"Conversation?" Dominic raises his eyebrows, a smile playing along his lips as he sits back in his seat and picks up a piece of bacon from his plate. "He's not lying?" he asks, sticking it into his mouth.

"I don't think so."

He signals to one of his men who comes over and he whispers some instructions. The soldier is gone in a moment. "Do you want to put a stop to the project?"

"Like I said, I don't take kindly to blackmail but this

needs to be taken care of. These photos can't turn up anywhere. You take care of it and I'll think about our project."

"You'll *think* about it?" I see how one eye narrows. "You care about Quincy's daughter? Why? I thought you hated the man."

I shift in my seat. "I care about any child being violated."

The way he looks at me, I wonder if he knows about Nora and my mind wanders to the letter burning a hole in my pocket.

I can't lie to you anymore.

There was someone else. My sweet, innocent sister had two lovers.

Lovers. Plural. Even the singular doesn't fit. Doesn't make sense.

I love him.

Do I want to know who she loved? It's where Persephone's going. Something in that letter gave her all the pieces of the puzzle. Pieces I'm still missing.

"She's not the one I meant," Dominic says but I'm so wrapped up in my thoughts that I'm not sure I heard right.

"What did you just say?" I ask.

"I said I'll take care of it."

My phone buzzes in my pocket but I ignore it. "I believe the person responsible for these was also on my property last night."

"I can send soldiers."

"I'll take care of what's mine, but you take care of the mess you bring into my life and the lives of those I care about."

"Care about. Big words."

We study each other for a long minute. A waitress arrives with an espresso for Dominic.

"Would you like something?" he asks.

"No, thank you." I stand and my phone alerts me to a voicemail. I take it out of my pocket and see it's the guard watching Persephone and her sister.

I give Dominic a nod and walk toward the exit as I open the text. But the pinned location on the map doesn't make any sense. I dial him. "You're sure this is the address?"

"Yes, sir. She's been inside for a few minutes. Knew the doorman from what I could see."

"Any chance she knew she was being followed?"

"No."

"All right. I'm on my way. If she leaves, let me know right away."

"I will."

I disconnect the call and a sick feeling takes hold of me as I walk back out of the restaurant and climb into the back of my car.

"Take me to my stepbrother's house."

33

PERSEPHONE

I don't realize I'm almost running until I get out of the building and half-way down the street. I stop in the cold, sunny day to catch my breath, wanting to scrub my skin.

"Are you all right?" someone asks me.

I look up, meet the eyes of an old woman. I suck in a gulp of icy morning air and nod. "I'm fine. Just...it was too warm inside."

"Well, it's not too warm out here, is it? Take care of yourself, dear."

I turn to watch her go as she heads in the direction of Jonas' building. That's when I see him. The sun shines in through the windshield of the car and our eyes meet.

Hayden.

Watching me.

Shit.

The driver pulls out onto the street heading toward me. They stop. The cars behind them honk their horns as the driver gets out and wordlessly opens the back door for me.

I stand there for a minute looking at it, unable to see Hayden sitting on the far end.

Someone lays on their horn.

"Get in," Hayden says from inside.

I turn to the driver. "I have a car—"

Hayden opens his door and steps out, his expression hard, like he's not pleased. Not at all.

More cars honk, someone yells a curse. I don't think he cares, not even a little bit.

"I said get in."

Without a word, I get in. He climbs in on his side and both doors close simultaneously. Strangely, even in a time like this, my first thought is how good he smells. The aftershave he wears the same one he's always worn. His own scent just beneath it. One I'm attuned to no matter how subtle.

"I can explain," I start.

He holds up his hand.

"Club, sir?" the driver asks.

"No. Take us to the Abbot house."

"I took Celia's car. She needs it back."

He studies me. I guess he's trying to make sense of why I'm here. We drive in heavy silence to the house. Only then does he finally speak.

"Give me the keys to Celia's car," he says.

I reach into my purse and take them out, dropping them into his gloved hand.

"Make and model."

I tell him.

"Where is it?"

"Down the street from where you were parked."

He nods.

"My sister—"

"She'll be brought back to the club when she's ready to leave."

"I was just..."

I trail off when he turns to the driver, handing him the keys and telling him to get someone to drive Celia's car to the hospital. He then gestures for me to go ahead of him up the stairs to the front door. He reaches around me to unlock the door and allows me to enter first when he opens it.

We hang our coats by the door and he walks ahead of me toward my father's study. I slip my hand into my coat pocket and take the photo. I tuck it into my purse.

When he reaches the study, he opens the door and looks toward me.

I walk to the study and enter, feeling like a prisoner entering an interrogation room. I notice how Anna has cleaned up my plate from last night. The bottle of vodka and the glass are gone too.

I also notice the book on its velvet wrapping left open to the page where Nora had tucked the photograph.

Hayden looks at it, turns it over to read the title, touches the damaged corner.

Blood. Does he realize it's blood?

Did my father take it from the chapel and hide it before anyone else found her? Is that how he got hold of it? Is that why there's blood on the corner?

I remember the words written on the back of the photo in her perfect, pretty script. When she took the time, she had the prettiest handwriting.

I can't.

And I understand something. Understand this last piece of the puzzle. And I want to cry because I realize how alone she must have felt. How damaged she was. My best friend was hurting and I didn't have the first clue.

Hayden leans against the desk and folds his arms across his chest. He looks down at me sitting there and I can feel the raw emotion radiating from him. The barely contained rage. Because what could he have thought to see me coming out of Jonas' apartment building? About the fact that I snuck away to see his stepbrother, a man I was once engaged to. A man he despises.

"Talk," he finally says.

I swallow, feel suddenly chilled. I can't hold his gaze.

"You don't want me to."

He reaches down suddenly, gripping the collar of my shirt and hauling me to my feet so quickly that I'm too shocked to react.

"You don't know what I want," he says, the words seething, the rage behind them bubbling. If he knows...if I tell him, he *will* kill Jonas. I know it. I need to give Jonas time to get out. If he will get out. Not to protect Jonas but to save Hayden from doing something he can't undo.

It takes Hayden a full minute to loosen his hold on me, another minute before he releases me, and I see the effort it takes.

I take a step away, then another.

He grips the desk, his knuckles turning white. "Are you fucking him?"

The question catches me by such surprise. "What?"

"Are you fucking Jonas?" he repeats more slowly.

"No. God, no." I shake my head, look away. "It would be easier if I were."

And that is the wrong thing to say because he loses the battle against that rage he's barely been containing. His eyes go black and he stalks toward me and before I can turn to run, before I can take a single step, he's got my back pressed against the wall.

"Don't. Ever. Say. That." It's a roar, not a low, quiet threat, nothing remotely civilized about it. "Don't ever fucking say that again. Do you hear me?"

I nod. "I didn't mean—"

He cups my face with both hands, the pads of his fingers rough.

"You're mine. Not his. Not anyone's. And fuck any contracts. Mine. Only mine."

I nod again, and I touch his cheek, brush back his hair and I think he knows that something's about to change. That the thing he so desperately wants to know, I think he knows it'll kill him. And there's no way around it.

"I think there was a note," I say.

34

PERSEPHONE

Hayden leans his forehead against mine as a tear slides down my cheek.

I touch him, just his shirt, my fingers are light as feathers, and I swallow as my breathing levels out. I'm caged in this corner, his big body trapping me, but I'm the one who will hurt him when I tell him.

He draws back, looks at me and I think he knows. He must. He's guessed it, hasn't he?

In his eyes, I see what I saw when I first met him out there on the street when I was a little girl and he was my Hades. My dark hero. I see that sadness that was there then, too. Something broken inside him. Broken long before Nora killed herself.

I remember the bruise on his face, and I reach up to touch the spot now and I feel my eyes fill with tears again.

"I think she did leave a note," I say.

He doesn't speak, just watches me, waits.

"I think my dad took it when he found her." He was the first one at the chapel. I remember when he'd walked out there that icy morning, the frozen dew evaporating into mist in the sun creating a thick fog. How opposite the morning to the night before. It had rained for days that Halloween. Like something knew what she'd do. What she'd planned.

"I think I've had it all along," I finish.

When I move to slip away, he lets me, still silent. A silent beast.

I pick up my purse which is on the floor. I don't know when I dropped it. I open it, see that photo I wish I'd never seen.

Without a word, I set it on the table, face down.

Hayden is close again, I feel him. His fingers touch the curve of my neck and I turn to look up at him.

He's not looking at it yet. He knows this will change everything.

Nora wasn't who he thought.

She wasn't who any of us thought. She was too broken to be innocent.

I watch him shift his gaze to the desk, watch his eyes as he reads those two words.

I can't.

I put my hand on his shoulder when he moves his arm and he stops for a moment. Meets my gaze.

"That book, it's mine. I'd lent it to Nora a long time ago. I think she had it with her at the chapel. I think the stain in the corner...it's blood."

He clenches his jaw, still doesn't speak.

"You don't have to look," I try. One last-ditch effort. "You don't have to see." I'm crying now. Tears like a river down my face.

He shifts his gaze back to the desk and I know he will look. I know he has to see.

And I know the instant he's turned the photo over. I hear it in the sound that catches in his throat. See it as he processes, even though I think some part of him knew.

But maybe it's different when your stepbrother is sleeping with your sister. His sister. Maybe it's different if it's your family.

After that moment that stretches into an eternity, I feel him tense, like he's coiling up, readying. I look back at his hand on the photo, see that it's becomes a fist. The photo inside it, one that my father managed to preserve for all these years, is crumpled in that fist, destroyed.

It's not so easy to destroy history, though. Once you see, you can't unsee.

"Hayden," I start as his eyes harden, as his whole body hardens. No pain here. Rage. Only rage.

"Why?" His voice sounds like it's been caught in his throat for decades.

I shake my head, put my hand on his shoulder.

He grips my wrist and I gasp with the force of it. He'll snap it if he's not careful.

I hear him force a breath, and it takes him a long time to release me.

"Why?" he asks again.

"I'm sorry."

He steps away, turns and stalks to the door.

"Stop, Hayden!" I run to catch up to him, grabbing hold of his arm, my hand too small to wrap around the thick muscle as I try to stop him from leaving.

In an instant, he has me backed up against the wall and this Hayden, this seething, raging Hayden, he's dark and dangerous and when he leans his face close to mine, my heart pounds, pumping adrenaline through my veins, telling me to heed his earlier warning. To not become his enemy.

"You're going to get hurt. Again," he says.

"You can't go to him," I force myself to speak. "Not now. Not when you're like this."

"Do you think I'll be some other way soon? Do you think I won't kill him if I wait five minutes? Five years?"

"You don't know the whole story."

"I know what I need to know."

"She wasn't innocent, not like you think."

He grits his teeth, his jaw tight as he presses a fisted hand to the wall.

"Don't defend him—"

"I'm not defending him."

"And do not condemn her," he continues like he doesn't even hear me. "She's in the ground. He's not. It should have been him in the fucking ground. Not her."

"Hayden—"

"No one should die at sixteen! No one should die like she did!" He slams his fist into the wall, and I jump. I see the effort it takes him to step away, both hands now fists at his sides. "Stay here."

He turns to the door and I follow. "You can't go to him. You'll kill him!"

"Maybe he deserves to be dead." He opens the study door and I grab his arm.

"Hayden, please."

He turns to me, takes my hand off his arm. "Stay. Here."

"No."

"Yes." He walks out the door and before I can reach it, he closes it and I hear the lock turn and his footsteps recede.

"Hayden!" I try the door, but I'm locked in. "Let me come with you at least! You can't go to him. Not like this!"

My hands hurt from beating on the door, but he doesn't come back and a few minutes later, I hear the front door open and close.

35

HAYDEN

S hane is smoking outside when I open the front door. He takes one look at me and tosses the newly lit cigarette.

"Where to?" he asks.

I shake my head. "I'll drive myself." I start down the stairs but he's on my heels.

"You don't look like you're in any condition to drive. Where to?"

I suck in a breath, nod. He's right.

"Jonas." I can barely get the word out. I feel sick at the thought of it and the photo I've crushed in my hand singes the skin of my palm.

"He just headed out of the apartment. Let me see where he's going." Shane puts the phone to his ear as he starts the engine. A minute later, he disconnects the call. "Headed to the office."

"Mother fucker." I'm going to kill him. I have to.

Persephone's words circle my mind. *"She wasn't innocent, not like you think...Nora gave me the drink that night. Told me to finish it. Not Jonas..."*

I grit my teeth and fist my hands. "Drive. Faster." Fuck. I should have driven.

Shane nods and accelerates but fuck, it's not fast enough.

"She told him to do it. When he hesitated."

She told him to rape Persephone?

No. No fucking way.

The image of what I saw when I walked into the chapel that night invades my mind as if arguing against me. Against what has to be true.

How strange they all looked with Nora holding Persephone down. How could she hold her down? She wasn't strong enough, not if Persephone didn't want to be held.

But she was drugged. I saw that for myself.

"She told him to do it. When he hesitated."

Fuck.

Fuck.

Fuck.

No. I shake my head, clear these thoughts. She was fifteen. Just turned sixteen. A child. He was a man.

It's sick, when I think about it. I feel sick at the thought of it. Of them together. Jonas and Nora. Jonas and Nora naked together.

I force myself to look at the photo, at the back of it. I've crushed it so badly, it's hard to read the words but I know what they say.

I can't.

I wonder when she'd written the letter to Abbot. When she'd decided to do it, to end her life. Did she know on Halloween? She'd been more distant those last weeks, but I'd had my own shit to deal with. Fuck. If I'd known she was in trouble would I have been able to stop it?

"Fucking drive faster!" I slam my fist into the dash and

when, a few minutes later, we pull up to the front entrance of the Montgomery office building, I open my door and I'm out before the car comes to a complete stop.

I don't bother to greet anyone in the lobby this time. I don't bother to speak a word. I just get on the elevator and ride it up to the top floor. I register the look of shock on the receptionist's face when the doors open and she doesn't get a word out before I'm stalking to Jonas' corner office, my hands fists at my sides.

I see him through the glass wall. See him with my father who's pacing and looks pissed as fuck.

Jonas sees me before I'm inside and his face goes from that sickly jaundiced look he sometimes gets to one of surprise and then panic as I push in.

"Are you fucking insane? She's a fucking kid! You've gone too far!" my father yells.

"You goddamned piece of shit!" I throw the crumpled photo at Jonas, watch it bounce off his chest. I close my hands around his throat before he can utter a word and slam him against the wall so hard, there's a dent where his head hits.

"What the fuck?" My father tries to drag me off, but he's no match. Not by a long shot.

"Get off me, old man, or I swear I will kill you too."

I hear the door open, hear a woman gasp.

"Maryanne, call security," my father yells.

I don't turn around. "You raped her. You fucking raped her."

Jonas is trying to shove against me. I'm stronger than him on a normal day but today, today is special. Today, the murderous rage erupting like a volcano inside me makes me invincible.

"Hayden!" my father is still trying to get me off Jonas.

I turn to him. "I said get off me." I shove my elbow into his gut and hear his grunt as he stumbles backward.

When I shift my gaze back to Jonas, I look at him, see him for maybe the first time ever. I've always hated the son of a bitch. He's always been an arrogant mother fucker. But what I see now, it's different. It's worse.

"You're sick, you know that?" I release his throat, draw my arm back and punch him so hard, his head snaps to the side and he stumbles, only staying upright because he catches the edge of his desk.

I grab him by the collar and shove him hard against the wall again, watch his dazed expression as he bounces off it, a second dent right beside the first. I slam my fist into his face and follow it up with a hit to the gut before two men grab hold of me and drag me backward.

"You sick son of a fucking bitch! She was your sister. Your own fucking sister!"

"Shit." My father's face is that of a ghost in my periphery as I shove one set of arms off me only to feel a fist in my kidney when I lunge toward Jonas again.

It takes me a second to recover but all I see is red when I look at Jonas. All I see is a raging fury of red. Of blood to pay for blood. Of life to pay for life.

Too late, though.

She's gone. Long gone. Dust in the earth. No amount of blood will bring her back.

I break free and I'm going again, and I get hold of him, kneeling over him as he blinks, tries to focus his eyes, one of which is already swelling, and I get one more hit in before something hard smashes the back of my skull. I'm dazed and my arms are dragged behind my back and I'm forced into a seat, handcuffed to it.

"Call a fucking ambulance. Fuck!" Jeremiah looks at both of us and it takes me a minute to focus, my head heavy.

"Should I call the police too?" Maryanne asks, and I hear the shock and fear in her voice. But I don't care about her. I don't care about anyone or anything right now. I just need to kill that son-of-a-bitch.

My father bends to pick up the crumpled photo. He sets it on the desk, smooths it out as Jonas rolls onto his side and pukes, then groans.

I notice the dark stain at his crotch. He pissed himself. I'd laugh if I could. If I didn't have murder on my mind.

"Jesus Christ," my father mutters and I look at him, and I swear the color drains from his face as he takes in the significance of that photo. He drops into Jonas' seat behind the huge, modern desk, eyes wide on that damning picture.

"Sir?" Maryanne asks.

He looks at her, shakes his head. "No. No police."

She nods, obviously not agreeing with his decision but still backing out of the office to make the calls she needs.

My father is watching me when I turn to him, his expression one of horror.

"Did you know?" I ask.

He pushes his hand into his hair, leans the weight of it on his elbow as he mutters the words Jesus Christ again.

"Did you fucking know?"

He shifts his gaze slowly up to mine and all I have to do is look at him to know the answer.

36

PERSEPHONE

T wenty minutes pass and I'm still banging on the study door yelling for Anna. I don't know where she is, if she's even in the house. My throat is hoarse by the time I hear footsteps running toward the study and a moment later, she pushes the door open, alarm on her face.

I didn't think I'd ever be glad to see her.

"Are you all right? I just came in when I heard—"

"I'm fine. Just got locked in." I wouldn't be surprised if she tried to restrain me if she knew Hayden had been the one to lock me in.

I'm about to run from the room but see my purse, turn to pick it up. I manage to drop half the contents on the study floor until I find my phone.

Scrolling, I find Jonas' number and push the button to call his cell. No answer, though. He's either got it powered off or muted because it goes to voicemail right away. I hang up but try again and the second time, I leave a voicemail.

I notice the missed calls and the messages, but I don't have time to look at those now. I need to find Hayden before he does something he'll regret. I rush toward the front door, grabbing my coat on my way. I step outside while sliding my arms in, the brisk air welcome.

I fumble for my keys, cursing when I don't find them in my purse. They must have fallen out when I was looking for my phone.

I'm walking back to the front door when I hear a car on the driveaway. I turn to see who it is. Lizzie maybe? But they wouldn't bring her back here. They'd take her to the club.

My heart races as the unfamiliar car comes to a stop just a few feet from me. When I see that inside is Hayden, I breathe a sigh of relief. But when the door opens and he smiles, I realize it's not Hayden.

"Ares?"

"Glad I caught you at home."

"Why? What are you doing here?"

"I need you to take a ride with me."

"What?"

"Come on. Get in the car." He walks around the front of the car toward me.

"What's wrong?"

"I'm sure it'll be fine."

"Is Hayden okay?" Am I already too late?

He gives me a strange nod and opens the passenger side door. "Get in."

I do because I don't know what else to do.

He closes the door and a moment later, he's in the driver's seat, his focus almost entirely on the road, the smile having vanished from his face and replaced by something harder.

"What's going on?" I ask as he pulls out of the driveaway.

He glances over at me. "You've got some influence with my brother," he says, slowing for a traffic light, his words making no sense and something telling me I shouldn't be here with him.

"Where are you taking me?"

He gives me a smile again and I think how easily he smiles.

"Dominic Benedetti wants to meet you."

My throat goes dry as I remember who Dominic Benedetti is. As I recall how adamant Hayden was about me staying away from him.

"Why?"

"Because my brother isn't being very smart."

The light turns green, but the car in front of us doesn't move. Ares touches the horn and, without thinking, I take hold of the door handle and I'm about to open it when his hand closes over my knee just a little harder than it needs to be.

"I wouldn't do that," he says.

A moment later, traffic begins to move, and he moves with it. He shifts his gaze to the road, and I study him in profile, his expression hard. He and Hayden may be identical twins but right now, he doesn't look anything like him.

37

HAYDEN

"Get these off of me," I tell my father once the EMTs have taken Jonas out of the room and we're alone. I'm still cuffed to the chair.

"Not yet. Not until you're calm."

"Fuck you."

"You think I wanted this?" His lips are tight. "I loved that little girl like she was my own."

"And we all know how well that keeps turning out. Did you know all along?"

He shakes his head. "What kind of monster do you think I am?"

"I don't know. You tell me."

"I found out a few months ago...Christ. To see it..." he glances at the photo, rubs the back of his neck.

I remember the argument I overheard him and my grandfather having the night of the fire. Remember how my grandfather had said something about *that filth* being allowed to enter his house.

"Did Grandfather know? Is that what you were arguing about that night?"

"I don't know. Maybe." He shakes his head. "We didn't get that far. He hated both Jonas and Nora. Never accepted them as part of his family. Blood mattered to that old man. And that's all that mattered." The look in his eyes when he meets my gaze again is harder. Like how I look at him. "You didn't know him. I did. I know what he was capable of. What he'd do for his own blood. What he *did* do when your mother wanted to take you and Ares away."

"What does that mean? What did he do?"

"Your mother didn't walk away like he wanted everyone to believe. She would never have abandoned you or Ares. She loved you." He pulls at his hair again and I hear him mutter a curse.

"What the hell are you saying?"

He shakes his head. "Ancient history. Everyone involved is dead and gone. Dust. Let them lie," he says through his teeth, like he's just barely keeping it together. "You hate me, and you have every right to, but I grew up with a monster too."

We stare at each other for a long, weighted minute.

"Sir?" One of the security guards enter. "You want us to take him?"

"Just uncuff him."

"Sir—"

"Do it and go," he tells the guards, sounding weary. He walks to the window, one hand on his hip, the other rubbing the back of his neck.

Once I'm free, I stand. I look out the window too, watch the blinking lights of the ambulance disappear and something tells me not to ask what he means. Because I think whatever it is might change the past and I can't have any more of that.

"Why did you stop me?"

He turns to me and he looks a mess. Like he's aged ten years in the last ten minutes. He shakes his head, moves to the nearest chair and sits down.

"I thought it was Abbot. I thought he was the one who'd gotten Nora pregnant." He struggles with the last word. "But then, after Jonas and Percy got engaged, that's when I found out the truth. He threatened Jonas. Told him to walk away from his daughter or he'd expose him. Said he had proof. Jonas came to me then. Told me."

"And you protected him?"

He looks up at me. "What could I do? She was dead and gone. And you don't know how he was. How messed up—"

"Oh, I know how messed up he is. How sick."

"I'm sorry," he starts, suddenly breaking down into sobs. "I'm so fucking sorry. I'm sorry for all of it."

I stop because I have no clue what to do or how to react. I've never seen my father shed a single tear. Right now, he looks like a broken man.

But a few minutes later, he manages to pull himself together, at least a little. "I was young when I became a father."

"Is that your excuse?"

"No. I have no excuse. I'm sorry for what I did to you. I'm sorry I was a shit father to you and Ares."

"If you want me to tell you it's okay or you think you're somehow going to clear your conscience, then save your breath, old man."

He looks at me, shakes his head. "I don't say it to alleviate my guilt. I am guilty. And I live with the knowledge of what I did to you and your brother daily."

I grit my teeth, this admission causing a lump to form in my throat.

"I fucked up with you and I'm just glad I didn't fuck you up completely."

"Who says you didn't? I've made it my life's mission to destroy you."

"That's only after Nora. How long have you known about Jonas?" he asks.

"I thought it was Abbot. I thought that old man was raping her. I only found out today about Jonas."

"They're not related by blood—"

I'm at the desk in an instant and I slam both fists into it. "Don't you fucking dare!"

He doesn't recoil. Just sits there looking defeated and pathetic. Not the man who raised me with an iron fist. Two iron fists.

"She was going to be my redemption," he starts, pulling his hands away from his face, his eyes red and puffy, complexion blotchy. "She was older when I took her in. Had been through some pretty bad shit. 'Not adoptable' is what the case worker told us. Three homes had sent her back. Bad news. They tried to talk us out of it and Carry was against it. She wanted a baby, a toddler maybe. Someone she could raise and mold. But me, I wanted someone I could help. Someone whose life I could make better after I fucked so royally with you and your brother."

I remember he'd stopped drinking by the time he adopted Nora. Maybe the year before.

"They never did tell us what it was. Abuse, sexual and physical, abandonment issues. But there was more. There was a mention of sealed records and I know there was an older sibling, a brother who had died, but I never did find out what it was. Something was never right about her. As sweet as she was, there was a darkness she battled, and I think she was more troubled than I ever knew. She never trusted anyone, not really, not fully. I think if she had, she'd be here today. If she hadn't felt like she had to battle her demons alone." He shakes his head. "I didn't do right by her, either, did I? Not by any of you."

Fuck.

In all these years, this wasn't what I expected from my father. It's easier to hate someone when you know they're evil. But looking at him now, he just looks old and tired and sad.

"I need to get out of here," I say, my voice hoarse and thick as I take a step toward the door.

"There's one more thing, Hayden. Something you should know."

I stop, turn to find he's standing.

"Quincy Abbot's accident...I was protecting Jonas."

Fuck.

He nods then shakes his head eyes downcast as if he's having a conversation in his head simultaneous to this spoken confession. "You asked about my relationship with Angus Scava. Well, he took care of it. And we went into business together. Or that was the plan with Abbot out of the way."

"I need to get out of here." I open the door.

"Where are you going?"

"I don't know." I don't. "Not the hospital, don't worry."

"I'll get him help, Hayden. He needs help."

"I don't care what the hell you do." I'm about to walk out when Maryanne rushes into the room.

"Mr. Montgomery, I'm so sorry to interrupt but I thought you should see this." She starts moving things around the desk until she finds the remote control to the TV mounted on the wall across the room.

"Now isn't the time," my father says.

Ignoring him, she switches on the TV and a CNN correspondent's voice carries over the aerial recording of a man being taken away from a restaurant in handcuffs. I can't tell who it is.

"What the fuck?" my father says, taking the remote from Maryanne and turning the volume up as he walks toward the TV.

"Angus Scava, a local businessman with known ties to the mafia, has been arrested on various charges including running a child pornography ring."

I blink, read the same words the reporter just spoke on the ticker just below the image of Scava being hauled away in handcuffs.

My phone buzzes in my pocket and I reach absently for it.

"My god," my father says.

I answer the phone, my eyes still on the TV.

"Hayden." It's Ares. "You see the news?"

"Watching it now," I answer, not sure what his interest in this is.

"Dominic wants to see you."

I turn away from the TV. Ares suddenly has my full attention as I put two and two together. "I didn't realize you were his errand boy."

"I'm just making sure you don't do anything stupid."

"By stupid you mean pulling out of the deal."

"He's taken care of the photos. Like you asked."

"And taken the competition out of it. Two birds one stone."

"Possibly three."

"What do you mean?"

"Jonas was the one Scava conspired with to get those

photos. You've made it pretty obvious you have an interest in the Abbot family."

"What are you talking about?" I ask, turning to the desk, seeing the envelope on it as I do, recognizing it. I pick it up. It's thicker than the one I got. The flap is open, and a quick look inside tells me it's the same as what someone delivered to the club with just a few photos of Lizzie Abbot inside. This one, though, has a few dozen. "Jesus Christ."

"Christ had nothing to do with it."

"What's going on, Ares?"

It's quiet for a moment and when he comes back on the line, he's speaking more softly. "He wants to make sure the deal's still on. You need to come. And you should know that Percy's here. I brought her earlier."

PERSEPHONE

"How did you meet my father?" I ask Dominic Benedetti who is sitting across from me studying me with eyes that are at once curious, mischievous and mostly dangerous.

"I've known him a while actually. We were most recently reacquainted when he ran into financial difficulties."

"You mean he came to you for money?"

He shakes his head and smiles. "He came with a business proposition."

"Why would he do that?"

"I don't know the details of his financial situation. I only know that it made sense for us to work together. We each had what the other needed."

"He never mentioned you."

"I was sorry to hear about the hit-and-run."

Ares walks back into the room then and I watch Dominic who raises his eyebrows, the question unspoken.

"He's on his way," Ares says.

Hayden.

I glance at Ares who leans against the wall and folds his arms across his chest.

"Is that why I'm here?" I ask. "Bait to lure Hayden?"

"Are you afraid, Persephone?" Dominic calls me by my full name, and I don't like it. That name is reserved for Hayden. Only Hayden.

"No," my voice comes across more confident than I feel.

His eyes narrow a little as he tilts his head to the side and studies me. "You're safe," he reassures me anyway. He must see right through me. "No one will hurt you."

I glance at Ares who gives me a wink. What a jerk.

"Turn on the TV," Dominic says to the man standing at the far wall and a moment later, the TV's on and a reporter on CNN is talking about a man known to be linked to the mafia being arrested for various charges, including child pornography.

I turn from the TV to Dominic and take in his pleased smile.

"Who is that?"

He looks at me. "Angus Scava."

It takes me all of a second to place the name and I glance at the TV again just in time to see the face of the man I met at Jonas' apartment flash across the screen. He appears cool and collected and he's looking straight into the camera with a grin on his face like he's looking right at me.

Or, I turn to Dominic who grins back, right at Dominic.

"He's an enemy of my wife, my family," Dominic says, shifting his gaze to me. "And your enemy as well."

"What?"

"But it's taken care of now."

"What are you talking about?" I ask, but he doesn't get a chance to answer because just then, the door smashes open and Hayden stands hulking in the doorway like an animal that just escaped captivity. Even with two men on his heels, they can't hold him back.

"Hayden!" I'm on my feet.

He looks me up and down, ignores Dominic and lunges for his brother.

I stumble backward, knocking my chair over. Dominic shakes his head to stop his men from pulling them apart but other than that, he doesn't move, just watches as the brothers take each other by the collar, faces inches apart.

"What the fuck did you do?" Hayden spits at Ares.

"Relax, brother. I did you a favor."

"Favor my ass," Hayden roars, drawing his arm back, hand fisted.

I scream.

Dominic finally gives his men a nod and three of them are on Hayden dragging him from Ares.

Ares adjusts his collar, goes right up to Hayden and I think he's going to be a smartass or punch him or something, but he just gets in his face and tells him "I'm on your fucking side, asshole."

"Calm down, boys," Dominic says.

I look over at Dominic and think how strange it sounds, him calling them boys. I'd guess them to be about the same age.

The brothers turn to him. I see Hayden force a breath in as his gaze shifts to me.

"Are you hurt?"

I shake my head.

He nods then turns to Dominic. "Get your men off me and tell me what the fuck you think you're doing."

Dominic gestures to the men with a quick jerk of his head.

Hayden straightens his sleeves and collar and walks

back to Ares who stands his ground. They're well matched and I get the feeling this isn't their first fight.

"You and I will talk later," Hayden says.

"I look forward to it," Ares taunts with a wide smile and I think if he's not careful, Hayden will knock those pretty white teeth out of his mouth.

Hayden comes to me, looks me over again as if checking for himself that I'm not hurt.

"Why is she here?"

"I wanted to meet her," Dominic says.

"I'm guessing she didn't come of her own free will."

"She was encouraged, it's true, but I've been a generous host, haven't I, Persephone?"

I feel Hayden tense beside me, and I answer quickly. "It's fine. I'm fine." I touch his arm, slide my hand into his.

"We need to discuss some things," Hayden says.

"Right down to business. I like that," Dominic says.

"Shane," Hayden calls out and his man appears at the door. "Take Persephone to the car."

"If it's business, I want to hear," I say.

I feel Dominic's eyes on us, but it's Hayden who speaks.

"You'll wait in the car. Period."

Before I even open my mouth, I'm ushered out by Shane, the door closed behind me.

39

HAYDEN

I slam my hands on Dominic Benedetti's oversized desk.

"You do not touch what's mine."

"Got your attention, didn't I?"

"I mean it, Benedetti. You do not touch what's mine." I'm so angry, my voice is hoarse and raging.

"Sit down," he tells me, the cockiness of a moment ago replaced by something darker.

When I don't move, he stands, sets his hands on his desk and leans toward me, the threat clear.

I don't scare so easily though.

Just then the door flies opens. "Did you see it?" Gia Benedetti asks as she rushes in with a child of about two following close behind her.

She stops the instant she sees us. Sees how we're facing off. The little boy runs behind the desk straight at Dominic's legs who, without a moment's hesitation, almost like flipping a switch, bends to scoops him up.

This is his son. The Benedetti heir.

It's strange to see him like that. To think of him as husband and father.

"I made a drawing for the baby, daddy!"

"Did you, Franco?" Dominic asks to the boy, his tone that of a father, not the mob boss he is.

He looks to his wife.

Gia clears her throat. "I didn't realize you were busy."

"It's fine."

"You want to see it?" the boy asks.

Dominic turns to his son. "Later. When I'm done with my meeting," he says, setting him down.

Gia rushes to take his hand and there's a moment where the pair exchange a look and I see her mouth the words, "Thank you."

Dominic reaches out to tuck a strand of her hair behind her ear and she momentarily lays her cheek in his hand and then she and the child are gone.

When the door closes, I sit.

He does too.

Seeing this side of him casts him in a different light.

"I've taken care of the *mafia war*, as you called it. And the photos of Elizabeth Abbot will never see the light of day."

"Was it Scava or my stepbrother who arranged for them to be taken?"

"Jonas Montgomery made the arrangement with Angus Scava. Scava was no less eager."

I grit my teeth, fisting my hand which is sore after beating up Jonas.

"Detectives found compromising photos on his computer, apparently. Elizabeth Abbot's were among others. It's disgusting, really."

The way he says it, I know he's responsible. I know he

planted evidence and tipped the authorities off, but Scava earned it.

"We resume construction on the property in two weeks," I say.

"I'm glad to hear it. And Senator Hughes?"

"Won't be a problem."

"Good."

40

PERSEPHONE

ayden settles into the back of the SUV. He looks disheveled. Tired. And when he closes his hand over mine on the seat, I notice his knuckles are red.

"Take us to the club," he tells Shane and Shane nods. "Are you okay?" he asks me.

"Yes. Are you?"

"Been better."

"What happened?"

"With Jonas or in there?"

"Both."

He rubs the back of his neck, glancing out the window. His forehead is creased when he turns back to me.

"Well, Jonas is in the hospital." He gives me a strange smile. "And we're going on with the Benedetti project. Those photos of Lizzie will never get out." He looks away again, shakes his head. "My father knew."

"You mean about Jonas and Nora?"

He nods heavily.

I touch his cheek, brushing the scratchy growth of a few days on his jaw.

"All along?" I ask.

He looks at me, and I can't quite figure out what he's thinking, why he seems to be hesitating. But then he shakes his head.

"No, only recently," he says finally. "I'm glad you're okay. I'm sorry I scared you." He smiles but he looks sad and we don't talk again until we're at the club and he's ushering me up to his office, and through it to the living quarters and finally to his bedroom. Once we're there, he takes my face in his hands and he looks at me for a long minute, then kisses me and it's the softest kiss we've shared.

He draws back, he looks at me again, his eyes dark and when he starts to strip off my clothes, he's controlled, not rushed.

I undress him too, closing my hands over soft skin and hard muscle and as our kissing grows more urgent, he walks me backward to the bed and he never breaks that lock of our mouths as he pushes inside me, one hand cupping the back of my head, the other my cheek as he kisses me.

I wrap my legs around him, and I move with him and when he breaks our kiss and I open my eyes, I find him watching me and there's something strange about the way he's looking at me. Something tender.

"He had to let her go every year. Let her be in the light."

It takes me a moment to realize what he's talking about. Hades and Persephone. The myth of them. Of us.

"I can't do that," he says as if he's still in his head.

"Hades." I see pain in his eyes and mine water.

"You're a piece of me." His thrusts are deeper, his cock thicker and I know he's close. "When I'm not with you, I feel it. It's like a gaping hole I can never fill. And I can't have that anymore. I can't be without you anymore."

I touch his cheek, kiss his mouth and hug him tighter with my legs.

"I want to steal you away. Hide you. Keep you." He's moving faster, the fucking harder. The frenzy is coming.

We kiss again, our mouths open, tongue on tongue, hands gripping.

"I want to fuck you day and night. And I'm going to do just that. Lock you in this room. Tie you to my bed. Never let you go."

"Kiss me, Hades."

I gasp with the last of those words as he kisses me, lifting me a little, shifting our position a little, just enough that he hits that spot and I'm coming. I'm coming and my breath is his name and our eyes are open and he's not alone in this, in wanting me like he does because I can't be without him either. What have I been without him?

"I love you, Persephone. I love you." The words are a rumbling breath as he stills inside me and we watch each other as we both come and he's so beautiful. He's the most beautiful thing I've ever seen.

"I love you, Hades," I tell him, pulling him close when he collapses on top of me and I feel his heart racing against my chest. "I've always loved you. Only you."

41

PERSEPHONE

I hear the muffled sound of a phone ringing in the distance. I open my eyes, groggy as I try to make out where I am.

Hayden is beside me, his arm heavy across my chest.

The ringing stops and I turn my head to look at the clock. It's late afternoon. Is it only afternoon? This day has stretched too long.

I look at Hayden whose eyes are closed. I'm not sure I've ever seen him sleeping. The few times we've slept together I've always fallen asleep first.

I watch him, think how beautiful he is, how fiercely protective. Possessive. Two sides of the same coin. One aggressive toward the object of its obsession, the other toward any threat to that object.

The ringing starts again, and I turn my head to see my purse at the far end of the room under our clothes. When I move, hoping to slip out without waking him, he groans, pulls me to him.

"What are you doing?" he asks.

I turn to find his hazel eyes on me, more gold than green right now.

"My phone. Someone's trying to call me."

"You'll call them back." He pulls me closer, but then his phone rings too.

I get out of the bed first but by the time I locate my phone in my purse, the call has gone to voicemail. I look at all the missed calls. Most are from a number I don't recognize but a notification tells me someone left a message.

"What is it?" Hayden asks.

I turn to him, thinking he's talking to me but he's on his phone. I'm about to click in to listen to the voicemail when the phone rings again. Same number.

Without hesitating, I answer. "Hello?"

"God, Percy! Where have you been?"

"Lizzie? What's happening?" Panic makes my voice higher.

"I've been calling and calling." She doesn't have her cell phone which explains why I don't recognize the number.

"I'm sorry. I—"

"You have to come now." A brick drops in my belly. "Come to the clinic now, Percy."

"What's happened?" I ask and hear Hayden mutter a curse from behind me.

"His heart stopped." She chokes on the words and my heart breaks. "He," she sucks in a sob. "I thought maybe..."

"Oh God."

"They have him on a ventilator, but it's bad."

"I'm on my way," I say, already pulling on my clothes as I drop the phone back into my purse.

"Persephone," Hayden starts behind me.

"My father," I say, pulling on my pants as I turn to him and I see from his face that he already knows. "You know?"

"That was the driver who took you and your sister this morning. I'll call down for a car."

We get to the clinic in record time and I rush to my father's room expecting to find a team of doctors working on him, a buzz of activity as they try to save his life, but I'm surprised when the only person in the room is my sister.

I look at my father, at the new machine he's hooked up to in addition to the others. I listen to the sound of the ventilator operating his lungs.

Lizzie wipes her eyes and stands. I hug her and for a long minute, we just hold each other. We just stand like that and hold each other until I hear the door open and Hayden enters along with a doctor.

"Where's Celia?" I ask when Lizzie pulls away.

"Her daughter's school called. She wasn't feeling well so Celia left a few hours ago."

"Ms. Abbot?" the doctor walks over to me. "I'm Dr. Nicholson. I was here when your father took a turn this afternoon."

"What happened?"

"I thought he was going to wake up," Lizzie says. "I thought—"

I take her hand, squeeze it and pull her to me. Dr. Nicholson looks at her with an expression of pity. This isn't the first time he's seen something like this.

"His heart gave out," he says to me. "It's not uncommon for a man in his condition. We were able to revive him, but he hasn't been breathing on his own since." He puts a hand on my shoulder. "You'll need to think about what you want to do."

I look at my father lying there, and he looks old and frail and so small.

I already know what I have to do. As much as it will

break our hearts, I know. It's what I should have done already. What I know he would have wanted.

"I'll give you some time alone," Dr. Nicholson says and turns to exit the room.

"Doctor?" I call out.

He stops and turns to me, eyebrows raised.

"There's no chance he'll wake up from this, is there?"

"No, Ms. Abbot, outside of a miracle, I don't believe so. I'm sorry." A moment later, he's gone.

Hayden puts his hand on my shoulder, squeezes it while Lizzie brushes her fingers through our father's thinning hair.

"We should let him go, shouldn't we?" she asks, surprising me. She drops into the chair she was sitting on earlier. "He'd hate this."

I nod, my eyes still on my father.

42

HAYDEN

Quincy Abbot died two days later with his daughters holding his hands.

I stood back and watched and I can't say that I felt anything for him. No sadness or regret. Justice, maybe? What he did with Nora was wrong any way you slice it. He's guilty of that.

I don't care about what happened to Quincy Abbot. But I do care that Persephone is suffering.

And I know that that suffering is on my father's hands.

I stand beside Persephone at the cemetery now and I still don't feel anything as I watch the casket lowered into the ground. Persephone wanted a private ceremony for family and close friends only but there are still reporters along the periphery because he was a senator, after all.

Irina turned up for the funeral, which I guess shouldn't surprise me because the reading of the will would follow directly.

She's a pariah. A bottom-feeder.

Quincy Abbot hadn't updated his will before his accident. In fact, he hadn't changed it since his fortune began to collapse. So, when their attorney reads his final wishes, it's a moot point. Because the house is mine. Controlling shares of the company will remain mine even though each of his daughters will receive an equal division of his shares. And there's not much fortune to speak of.

Irina would receive an allowance out of his estate, but since said estate is no longer financially viable, she will get nothing.

I watch her from my place at the back of the room when she hears this and, exactly as I expect, she huffs and puffs and leaves in a flurry, her rage overriding any grief she may have pretended to feel.

I watch Lizzie as her mother throws her tantrum. Persephone isn't affected but I see her watch her sister too and as much as Lizzie tries to pretend she doesn't care, she does. She's hurt. I see it. I'm sure Persephone does too.

When it's over, Shane takes them home. I don't accompany them. I have to take care of one thing first. Digging my phone out of my pocket, I call my father and, without even a greeting, tell him to meet me at the hospital.

When I enter Jonas' room, my father is already there.

Jonas is sitting up on the bed, his face swollen and bruised, both eyes black one arm in a cast and bandages circling his torso. He gives me a hate-filled look, but I don't miss the fact that he presses himself deeper into the bed at my approach.

"You fucking asshole. Look what you did to me." He seethes, his rage a palpable thing.

"Shut up," my father tells him before I get a chance to. "What's this about?" my father asks as the door quietly closes behind me.

"Quincy Abbot's death makes that hit-and-run a homicide."

My father's jaw tightens, and Jonas looks the other way.

"I have a question," I say. I wait to speak until Jonas turns back to me. "Why did you leave that letter for Persephone to find in the chapel the other night?" I'm actually not certain it's him who did it, but he's the one with the most to gain from it. She'd know her father was involved with Nora to the point that he'd thought he'd impregnated her. She'd know her father tried to pay for an abortion. Maybe she'd see that Nora loved Jonas? The thought still sickens me but in his twisted mind, maybe it made sense.

"I wanted her to know if she told anyone what she knew, her father would also be implicated."

He was covering his own ass. Hardly a surprise.

"Like I said, he's dead now." I turn to my father. "Homicide." I pause to let that fact sink in, although I'm sure he's already figured it out. I shift my gaze to Jonas. "You commissioned the photographs of Lizzie Abbot." It's not a question.

"He wasn't thinking—" my father steps in.

"I'm not asking you," I tell him.

"It's not like you can commission something from the fucking mob. I told Scava about your relationship with Percy. He wanted to take her, but I wouldn't let him touch her. It's because of me he didn't take your *precious Persephone*."

My father steps toward me, puts a hand on my shoulder. He must feel the energy it's taking me to keep control of myself.

"I should thank you?" I ask Jonas.

"Son," my father starts. "Please."

"First Nora, now this. You're fucking sick, Jonas. A predator."

He blinks several times, finally turning his gaze away. Guilt? No. People like him don't feel guilt.

"Nora's gone," my father says. "I don't want her name dragged through the mud. You can't go public. For her sake, not his."

"So, he should walk away scot-free? And what about you? Should you for your part in this?"

"My part? You don't care about Quincy Abbot whatever you feel for his daughter. Remember, he played a role in Nora's downfall too."

"I haven't forgotten."

My father backs up a couple of steps, drops into the seat in the room. "It's too late to make this right."

It's too late for a lot of things.

He looks up at me. "What do you want me to do?"

I turn my gaze back to Jonas because ultimately, he's at the heart of this. He's the cause of it. And Nora's part, she's paid her price. So has Quincy Abbot. The only one who hasn't is this piece of shit.

"You're gone. Disappear."

"What?"

"Today. Tonight." I turn to my father. "Make it happen. Make sure I never see or hear from him again. Make sure he doesn't come near me or what's mine. Or believe me." I stalk to the bed and Jonas cringes away. "If there's a next time, you won't survive it."

43

PERSEPHONE

I t's late when Hayden walks into my father's study that night. I don't even realize he's in the house. It's not like he rings the doorbell or anything.

I'm sitting behind the desk after having gone through most of his things to separate anything personal.

"Hey," I say, looking up at him, feeling strangely relieved that he's here. I think about what he said about how he feels when I'm not around. I have the same with him. My mind wanders to that afternoon before my sister's call came in. To what he told me. To those few moments after.

He loves me.

Hades loves Persephone.

"Hey." He comes inside and closes the door. I see the black envelope in his hand and remember the last time I had one of those delivered to the house. He sits down on the chair across from the desk, his stance casual. He's still wearing his dark suit that he wore to the funeral.

"Where's your sister?"

"She went to bed. She's exhausted."

"I think we all are. How are you holding up?"

I shrug a shoulder. "Okay, I guess. I have to be there for Lizzie now."

"You lost your father, Persephone. You also have a right to grieve."

"It's weird," I start, looking at the few stacks I've made. "I think a part of me knew he wouldn't wake up, and you'd think I'd be ready, but I wasn't. Not even close." I wipe a stray tear.

He's up on his feet and pulling me into his arms. He holds me to him, touches my cheek gently.

"I don't think you can ever be ready for death." He sits down, sets me onto his lap and I lay my head on his shoulder.

"I'm glad you're here," I tell him.

He smiles down at me.

"Where did you go? After the funeral?" I ask.

"I needed to take care of some things."

"What things?"

He brushes a strand of hair behind my ear and gestures to the envelope.

I glance at it then back at him. "I remember the last one of those envelopes that was delivered."

"Open it."

I pick it up. I open the flap and take out the sheets of paper inside. I read the first sentence but sit up to re-read it as it requires all of my attention.

"What is this?"

"What you think it is."

I read the words again, turn back to him. "You're giving me back the house?"

He nods once.

"But..." I turn the page, read a few more lines but I don't follow all the legal terminology.

"We'll sign the papers tomorrow."

"I don't understand."

"The house and everything inside it are yours."

"What's the catch?"

"No catch."

"Why?"

"Why no catch?"

"Why are you doing this?"

"Because look at all that's happened. Because I've won and look where it's left all of us. The ones lucky enough to be standing that is. To be alive. I'm finished, Persephone."

I feel my face drain of color.

"There's more in the envelope."

My hand trembles as I reach inside to pull out the two torn sheets I recognize.

Our contract.

When I turn to him, he's watching me.

"Are you finished with me?" I finally find my voice to ask.

He seems momentarily confused then shakes his head, pulling me close. "I will never be finished with you. And what I want," he starts, then pauses to amend, "What I'll *have*, well, it's not the right time. Not today." He picks up the contract again. "You may have missed the part about me moving in permanently." He points to it.

I laugh and I think it's the first time I've laughed in a very long time.

EPILOGUE 1

HAYDEN

Six Weeks Later

Jonas disappeared that night after my visit. I neither know nor care how my father pulled it off but he's gone. He sold his apartment and my father put out a press release about his starting a new venture and he's gone.

I've actually seen my father twice in the last six weeks and we somehow haven't killed each other. I'm getting to know the man he is, not as my father, but as a man. And maybe I can forgive him his past. It's strange how much I want to. Like the boy inside me still misses the father he should have been. Still seeks his approval.

But now isn't the time to think about that, not when the elevator doors slide open and Persephone walks into my office holding one of those black envelopes.

"I was *summoned*?" she asks, one eyebrow raised.

I look her over, appreciating the short skirt she's wearing

that hugs her hips and shows off her slender thighs. She slips her coat off her shoulders and saunters to the desk, perching on the edge of it.

I pick up my whiskey and take a sip as she glances at the city out of the glass wall at my back.

"It's pretty with the Christmas lights."

I run a hand down her thigh. "You look good."

She turns to me as I stand, situating myself between her legs. "I didn't know you were back." I'd gone away for two nights mostly for business.

"Just got in a few hours ago." I kiss her mouth, winding my fingers through her dark hair. She cut it a few weeks ago so it just touches her shoulders. A new beginning.

She kisses me back, violet eyes shining up at me as she undoes the top buttons of my shirt.

"Drink?" I ask her, holding out my glass.

She shakes her head. "I like licking it off your lips," she says, doing just that before kissing me.

"You drive me crazy you know that?"

"I hope so." She bites her lip as I lift her to push her skirt up and her panties down and off.

I pull her toward the edge of the desk and look down at her spread legs, her open pussy as I undo my pants. I push her backward a little so she's on her elbows, and enter her.

She exhales with the intrusion, like the breath is being forced from her.

"Fuck," I lean down to kiss her. "I missed you. I missed this."

"Me too."

"You feel good. So good."

"Harder. Do it harder."

"That's my girl." With a grin, I slide her off the desk and turn her over, bending her over my desk and taking hold of her hips to spread her open and look at her. I lean over her. "You want it hard?"

She nods, gripping the edges of the desk and pushing her ass into me.

I slide into her wet passage and bring my thumb to her asshole. "You're going to have to take my finger in your ass too, then." I hook her asshole.

"Fuck, Hades."

I push her hair off her neck and kiss her before I straighten, to look down at her like this, my cock buried in her pussy, my finger in her ass and her squirming, dripping and when I slide my other hand between her legs and rub her swollen clit, she calls out my name as her walls throb around me, pushing me over the brink, making me grunt with my release as I fill her up, fill her with my seed.

And when we're spent and I slide out of her, I lift her off her feet and carry her to the couch. From the bathroom, I bring a towel with warm water and clean her, then adjust her skirt as she lies back, fingers playing with my hair.

I look at her when I'm finished. "You look even more beautiful after you're fucked."

"You're such a romantic."

I chuckle and reach into my pocket to pull out the tiny velvet box.

"You want romantic?" I ask.

Her eyes move to it, her mouth opens, and she shifts her gaze back up to mine, looking suddenly very nervous.

I smile and wipe the fresh tear that drops from her eye, then open the box and turn it so she can see it.

"Hades." Her hand comes to her mouth and more tears slide down her perfect face.

"I told you I'm going to keep you. Keep you forever. Marry me, Persephone."

EPILOGUE 2

3 Months Later

The sky is clear and the air crisp as I step out of the limousine that drives me to the church where Hayden and I will be married.

Enveloped in lace, I shiver in the cold, turning my face up to the sun to let it warm me.

I think about the story of Hades and Persephone. I think about what Hayden said to me during our first meeting. That Hades stole her simply because he wanted her, not to save her. I don't think he'd forgotten the detail that I reminded him of that day. That Hades loved Persephone. I think he knew it all along.

Did he love me all along?

I smile at Lizzie as she hands me my flowers, a bouquet of calla lilies of burgundy and red. Together we walk to the church where two men open the heavy doors.

A hush falls as soon as light penetrates the dark cavern,

a moment of stillness before the pianist begins my wedding march.

I look up to the altar where Hayden, dressed in a dark gray suit with a vest and a calla lily matching my bouquet that's so red, it's almost black in his lapel. When he sees me, I see him stop for a moment, like he's struck. He looks me over, meets my eyes and when he smiles, I think I'm going to cry.

"Percy?" Lizzie whispers.

Hayden sees it too because in the next instant, he's walking down the aisle toward me and he takes my arm. He tucks it into his and holds me close to him.

"You're beautiful," he whispers.

I smile faintly. "You said something once." I don't know why I bring it up now, but I have to. "You said he knew he'd condemn her when he gave her the pomegranate, but she ate it willingly, even knowing the cost because then she would be his. Truly his."

"And you're mine. You've never not been mine."

I see notes of sadness in his eyes even as he smiles, but that's the past, even if it will always be there. He leans down to touch his forehead to mine as I cup my free hand to his cheek.

"You said, too, that it's naïve to expect to be happy as adults. You're wrong on that because I'm happy. I'm so happy, Hades."

"Me too. I love you, Persephone. I have always loved you."

The End

THANK YOU

Thank you for reading *Descent!* I hope you enjoyed Hayden and Persephone's story. If you'd consider leaving a review at the store where you purchased this book, I would be so very grateful.

If you're new to the Benedetti Mafia World, keep reading for a sample from *Salvatore: a Dark Mafia Romance.*

If you've already read the Benedetti series, check out an excerpt from Stefan Sabbioni's story, *Collateral: an Arranged Marriage Mafia Romance!*

Make sure to sign up for my newsletter to stay updated on news and giveaways! You can find the link on my website: https://natasha-knight.com/subscribe/

Like my FB Author Page to keep updated on news and giveaways!

I have a FB Fan Group where I share exclusive teasers, give-aways and just fun stuff. Probably TMI :) It's called The Knight Spot. I'd love for you to join us!

EXCERPT FROM SALVATORE

A DARK MAFIA ROMANCE

Salvatore

I signed the contract before me, pressing so hard that the track of my signature left a groove on the sheet of paper. I set the pen down and slid the pages across the table to her.

Lucia.

I could barely meet her gaze as she raised big, innocent, frightened eyes to mine.

She looked at it, at the collected, official documents that would bind her to me. That would make her mine. I wasn't sure if she was reading or simply staring, trying to make sense of what had just happened. What had been decided for her. For both of us.

She turned reddened eyes to her father. I didn't miss the questions I saw inside them. The plea. The disbelief.

But DeMarco kept his eyes lowered, his head bent in defeat. He couldn't look at his daughter, not after what he'd been made to watch.

I understood that, and I hated my own father more for making him do it.

Lucia sucked in a ragged breath. Could everyone hear it or just me? I saw the rapid pulse beating in her neck. Her hand trembled when she picked up the pen. She met my gaze once more. One final plea? I watched her struggle against the tears that threatened to spill on her already stained cheeks.

I didn't know what I felt upon seeing them. Hell, I didn't know what I felt about anything at all anymore.

"Sign."

My father's command made her turn. I watched their gazes collide.

"We don't have all day."

To call him domineering was an understatement. He was someone who made grown men tremble.

But she didn't shy away.

"Sign, Lucia," her father said quietly.

She didn't look at anyone after that. Instead, she put pen to paper and signed her name—Lucia Annalisa DeMarco—on the dotted line adjacent to mine. My family's attorney applied the seal to the sheets as soon as she finished, quickly taking them and leaving the room.

I guess it was all official, then. Decided. Done.

My father stood, gave me his signature look of displeasure, and walked out of the room. Two of his men followed.

"Do you need a minute?" I asked her. Did she want to say good-bye to her father?

"No."

She refused to look at him or at me. Instead, she pushed her chair back and stood, the now-wrinkled white skirt falling over her thighs. She fisted her hands at her sides.

"I'm ready."

I rose and gestured to one of the waiting men. She walked ahead of him as if he walked her to her execution. I glanced at her father, then at the cold examining table with the leather restraints now hanging open, useless, their victim released. The image of what had happened there just moments earlier shamed me.

But it could have been so much worse for her.

It could have gone the way my father wanted. *His* cruelty knew no bounds.

She had me to thank for saving her from that.

So why did I still feel like a monster? A beast? A pathetic, spineless puppet?

I owned Lucia DeMarco, but the thought only made me sick. She was the token, the living, breathing trophy of my family's triumph over hers.

I walked out of the room and rode the elevator down to the lobby, emptying my eyes of emotion. That was one thing I did well.

I walked out onto the stifling, noisy Manhattan sidewalk and climbed into the backseat of my waiting car. The driver knew where to take me, and twenty minutes later, I walked into the whorehouse, to a room in the back, the image of Lucia lying on that examining table, bound, struggling, her face turned away as the doctor probed her before declaring her intact, burned into my memory forever.

I'd stood beside her. I hadn't looked. Did that absolve me? Surely that meant something?

But why was my cock hard, then?

She'd cried quietly. I'd watched her tears slip off her face and fall to the floor and willed myself to be anywhere but there. Willed myself not to hear the sounds, my father's degrading words, her quiet breaths as she struggled to remain silent.

All while I'd stood by.

I was a coward. A monster. Because when I did finally

meet those burning amber eyes, when I dared shift my gaze to hers, our eyes had locked, and I saw the quiet plea inside them. A silent cry for help.

In desperation, she'd sought *my* help.

And I'd looked away.

Her father's face had gone white when he'd realized the full cost he'd agreed to; the payment of the debt he'd set upon her shoulders.

Her life for his. For all of theirs.

Fucking selfish bastard didn't deserve to live. He should have died to protect her. He should never—ever—have allowed this to happen.

I sucked in a breath, heavy and wet, drowning me.

I poured myself a drink, slammed it back, and repeated. Whiskey was good. Whiskey dulled the scene replaying in my head. But it did nothing to wipe out the image of her eyes on mine. Her terrified, desperate eyes.

I threw the glass, smashing it in the corner. One of the whores came to me, knelt between my spread legs, and took my cock out of my pants. Her lips moved, saying something I didn't hear over the war raging inside my head, and fucked up as fucked up can be, she took my already hard cock into her mouth.

I gripped a handful of the bitch's hair and closed my eyes, letting her do her work, taking me deep into her throat. But I didn't want gentle, not now. I needed more. I stood, squeezed my eyes shut against the image of Lucia on that table, and fucked the whore's face until she choked and tears streamed down her cheeks. Until I finally came, emptying down her throat, the sexual release, like the whiskey, gave me nothing. There wasn't enough sex or alcohol in the world to burn that particular image of Lucia out of my mind, but maybe I deserved it. Deserved the guilt.

I should man up and own it. I allowed it all to happen, after all. I stood by and did nothing.

And now, she was mine, and I was hers.

Her very own monster.

Available in all stores now!

EXCERPT FROM COLLATERAL

AN ARRANGED MARRIAGE MAFIA ROMANCE

Gabriela
Present Day

It's almost one in the morning when we drive up to the house in the posh Todt Hill neighborhood of Staten Island. The tall iron gates stand open, which surprises me. Security isn't something my father takes lightly.

As we slow to a stop, the guard greets the driver then shines his flashlight in through the open car window.

I turn away from the bright light when he flashes it in my face.

"You're to take her directly to her room. She's to stay there," he tells the driver.

Translation: lock her in.

"What's going on?" the driver asks.

I catch the guard's eye. "He's got company."

The driver nods then pushes the button to close the window and we drive toward the house. It's a beautiful mansion, one many people stop to look twice at, but I've always thought of it as more of a prison.

And tonight, I'm being brought back like an escaped convict.

Two SUVs I don't recognize are parked alongside the circular drive. I can see from here there's a driver sitting inside each one. Cigarette smoke wafts out of the open window of the first vehicle.

"Who's here?" I ask.

Neither my driver nor John, the man my father sent to retrieve me, answer. Instead, we pull to a stop and John climbs out, opens my door.

I step out, grab my duffel bag.

He takes it from me in one hand and closes the other around my upper arm.

"Don't touch me," I tell him.

He neither lets me go nor bothers to reply. Why should he? He doesn't answer to me. He answers to my father and he knows what happened to the other soldier who tried to help me. I'm sure they all know.

Tonight, an example was made to show what happens when someone crosses Gabriel Marchese.

Guilt makes me nauseous. He made me watch. Part of my punishment. Only the beginning of it, I'm sure. I'll take what I have coming but Alex didn't deserve what they did to him. That's on me.

We climb the stairs to the wide portico, John's grip harder than it needs to be as I walk along, my steps slower than his. I'm in no hurry to get inside.

The men stationed at the door open it, only sparing me a quick glance because I don't matter, even if I am the daughter of the boss. I'm just a pawn and everyone knows it.

Once inside, I glance down the hall toward my father's study. Two men I don't recognize stand just outside the door.

They don't work for him. I know it just from the way they're dressed.

When we near the stairs, the study door opens and my father's attorney, Mark Waverly, steps into the hallway. He takes a few steps toward us, studies me for a long moment before turning to John.

"Bring her in here," he says.

"I was told to take her upstairs."

"Change of plans." He gestures to the study with a quick sideways nod of his head.

My father doesn't often call me into his study and certainly not when he's doing business.

When I don't move, John tugs at my arm.

"Gabriela," Waverly says. "You'll want to *walk* in."

"Then tell my father's goon to get his hands off me."

Waverly gestures to John to let me go.

I brush my hair back, steel my spine. I try to ignore the splatters of red on my white T-shirt. My father ordered the beating, after all. I'm sure his business associates will neither be surprised nor offended by the evidence of such violence.

But as I near the study, I feel my heartbeat pick up. I force a bored expression on my face. I've worked on it for years and still, I don't know if they see right through it.

When I'm a few feet from the door, I take a deep breath in, hoping it will calm me. It doesn't.

I take two steps into the dimly lit study and stop. John and Waverly enter behind me and close the door.

There's an older man I don't recognize sitting in one of the armchairs. He's dressed in a three-piece suit and I wonder how he's not burning up even with the air-conditioning. But maybe it's anxiety that has me sweating.

My father is seated behind his huge desk leaning back in

his chair. If he's trying to look relaxed, it's not working. I see how the corner of his left eye is twitching. It's his tell. I wonder who else has picked that up.

I watch as he scans my face, takes in my shorter hair. I cut about six inches off since he last saw me. I hated to do it, but I didn't want to risk being found.

And still, I was found.

But disappearing when you're Gabriel Marchese's daughter is not an easy thing.

On the upside, I do like my new bangs, although they're a little too long and I keep having to tuck them behind my ear.

I shift my weight to one leg and look back at him.

He eyes my dirty T-shirt, shorts and army boots. It's not my usual attire, and I know he hates it. There are expectations for how his daughter should be seen, after all.

"Gabriela," he says, his voice elegant and rich. "How's Alex?"

"You know how he is."

His reply is a mean grin.

"I'm tired. If you don't mind, I'll go to bed. You can punish me tomorrow if that's why I'm here."

For as close as I was to my mother, so am I distant from my father.

Someone clears their throat and my head snaps to the far-right corner.

There's a man standing there, leaning against the wall. I hadn't realized there was anyone else in the room. I can't tell who it is. His arms are folded across his chest and his face is hidden in shadow.

He's tall, and built. I can see the thickness of his arms, his wide shoulders. He's dressed in a dark suit and from here, I can see his shoes are expensive.

He moves, unfolding his arms, checking his watch. When he drops his hand to his side and I see the ring on his finger, I gasp.

I know this man.

"The McKinney deal is off," my father says, forcing me to turn my attention to him.

"What?" I ask, my gaze shifting back to the stranger.

To his hand.

To that ring on his finger.

What's he doing here? In my father's study in the middle of the night?

"McKinney. The contract with the boy. It's off," my father says.

I face my father, confused. By contract, he means my forced marriage because to my father, everything is business, even his daughter's life.

Not that I'm surprised.

And that *contract* he's referring to is why I'd run.

I've had to do a lot of things in my life that I didn't want to do, but I won't marry someone just because my father deems it good for business.

"Waverly has drawn up a new contract."

"What are you talking about?" I ask. I can't seem to process what he's saying.

There's a sound behind me and I turn to find the man stepping out of the shadows. He's adjusting the cuff of his shirt and a gold cufflink glints in the lamplight.

I can't seem to drag my eyes away from his hands. From that ring.

And I don't want to look up. I don't want to see his face.

"The marriage will take place in one month's time," my father's words are slow to sink into my brain because I have to do it, have to look up at this man's face. "In the meantime, you'll be taken to the Sabbioni estate in Sicily for safe-keeping."

Still, the words, they're like physical things. Like they're lining up, waiting just outside my ears for when I'm ready to hear. To process. Because he can't be saying what he's saying.

"Mr. Sabbioni," Waverly says, his tone neutral.

Mr. Sabbioni.

Stefan Sabbioni.

"We'll need your initials on this modification," Waverly continues. He must have moved around the desk when I wasn't paying attention.

The man—Stefan Sabbioni—takes a step forward and I have to look at him now. I have to meet his strange hazel eyes. And when I do, I think they're darker than they were that night. Or less bloodshot. Maybe it's just that tonight, he's not drunk. Not raging.

"What's happening?" I ask. I don't know who I'm asking as I can't drag my gaze from Stefan Sabbioni.

He gives me a smirk and when he moves past me, I don't know if it's on purpose that his arm brushes my shoulder. I smell his cologne and I remember how he smelled that night.

God, I don't think I'll ever get that smell out of my head.

He stands taller than all the men here and I watch him lean down, pick up my father's favorite fountain pen. I see my father's jaw tighten and I know Stefan did it on purpose, choosing that particular pen.

Before signing, he reads the text, nods, then quickly puts his initials down.

"Dad?" I ask, because I'm starting to understand what my father meant when I watch Waverly turn the page and Stefan puts his signature in the designated spot.

He hands the pen to my father and I take a step backward.

"*Dad*," Stefan says, his tone mocking me or my father or both of us.

My father takes the pen and turns the document around to sign it.

When I move backward toward the door, John grips my arm. Maybe he knows that I'm about to bolt, even though I know there's nowhere for me to go.

"Gabriela," my father says, holding his pen out for me to take it.

I shake my head as all the men turn to me and my eyes are drawn to Stefan's. He's watching me with such intense curiosity I feel like he can see right inside me, see the chaos, the panicked beating of my heart.

"We need your signature, Gabriela," Waverly says.

Sweat collects under my arms and beads on my forehead. "I'm not—"

"Bring her over here," my father orders John.

John begins to drag me to the desk, and I know it's useless, but I dig my heels in and try to pull him off.

"Get off me!"

Waverly and my father watch, expressionless. I can't see the other, older man's face. Stefan's blocking him. But Stefan's eyes narrow as they zero in on where John's hand is digging into my skin.

"Let go!" My voice is higher, thinner than usual, and I hate that they must hear the panic in it.

Stefan steps forward almost too quickly for me to process and an instant later, he clamps his hand over John's wrist. At first, all I can do is look at that ring and remember that night. Remember him the night of my sixteenth birthday.

"Let. Her. Go." He pauses between each word as if each is its own command.

"How chivalrous," my father's words are pierced with a strange sort of laugh, but I can't drag my eyes from Stefan to look at him now. I can't look away from Stefan's face as he cows my father's soldier.

Stefan squeezes his fist and John's grip on me loosens. Then it's gone, and he's got a pained expression on his face as Stefan twists his arm.

"You don't touch her again, am I clear?"

"John," my father interjects.

But Stefan doesn't relent. "Am I clear, *John*?"

"Fuck. Yes."

Stefan shoves him backward, releasing him, then shifts his gaze to me.

I watch his eyes drop to my blood-splattered T-shirt then back to my face. I touch my cheek, wondering if there are specks of blood there too.

I can't read him. He's completely closed.

He steps to the side, making a path for me to move toward the desk.

"Your signature is required," he says, tone level, the words cold.

I turn to Waverly, to my father.

"Don't be fooled, Gabriela," my father starts. "He's not going to save you. He's the beast in whose bed you'll sleep."

An icy chill runs down my spine.

I don't know if my father means to insult Stefan with his comment but if that's his point, then he fails. Stefan just smiles, checks his watch for the second time that night, then looks at me.

"Sign," he says, like maybe I'm keeping him. Like maybe he has somewhere else to be.

I turn to my father and for a moment, I see something I have never seen before. It's fleeting and I know no one else sees it, but for the first time in my life, and for as awful as he is, I'm scared.

Because that look on his face, in his eyes, it's defeat.

"Daddy?"

He blinks and it's gone, and I don't remember the last time I called him daddy when I wasn't being sarcastic. Maybe when I was five.

Before I can think, Stefan's back at my side and his grip, I think it's harder than John's. Or it can be, at least. Maybe he's letting me know it can be.

He takes me by my wrist and walks me to the desk. Snatching the pen out of my father's hand and pushing it into mine, he closes his fist over my fingers, forcing my signature on the contract and I feel that rage inside him again, like I did that first night I met him in the shadows of my bedroom. I feel that terrifying, deep hate.

"Dad?" I ask.

But it's done.

Whatever this is, it's done.

And my father with all his power can't save me now. I know it. I'm sure of it.

Because Stefan Sabbioni is more powerful.

Stefan drops my hand and I have moments to look at the scratchy signature, at the blob of a teardrop that lands on it before he collects the pages and the other stranger in the too-heavy suit stands.

"I'll be back for you early in the morning. Be ready," Stefan tells me.

Then, without another word, the two of them are gone and all I can do is watch the empty space. I listen to the sound of their retreating footsteps and remember his whispered promise from two years ago.

"Tell your father I'll be back to take something precious too."

Tonight, Stefan Sabbioni made good on his promise.

Available in all stores now!

ALSO BY NATASHA KNIGHT

Collateral Damage Duet

Collateral: an Arranged Marriage Mafia Romance

Damage: an Arranged Marriage Mafia Romance

Dark Legacy Trilogy

Taken (Dark Legacy, Book 1)

Torn (Dark Legacy, Book 2)

Twisted (Dark Legacy, Book 3)

MacLeod Brothers

Devil's Bargain

Benedetti Mafia World

Salvatore: a Dark Mafia Romance

Dominic: a Dark Mafia Romance

Sergio: a Dark Mafia Romance

The Benedetti Brothers Box Set (Contains Salvatore, Dominic and Sergio)

Killian: a Dark Mafia Romance

Giovanni: a Dark Mafia Romance

Descent

The Amado Brothers

Dishonorable

Disgraced

Unhinged

Standalone Dark Romance

Deviant

Beautiful Liar

Retribution

Theirs To Take

Captive, Mine

Alpha

Given to the Savage

Taken by the Beast

Claimed by the Beast

Captive's Desire

Protective Custody

Amy's Strict Doctor

Taming Emma

Taming Megan

Taming Naia

Reclaiming Sophie

The Firefighter's Girl

Dangerous Defiance

Her Rogue Knight

Taught To Kneel

Tamed: the Roark Brothers Trilogy

ACKNOWLEDGMENTS

Cover Design by CT Cover Creations

Cover Photography by Wander Aguiar

Cover Model Zack Salaun

ABOUT THE AUTHOR

USA Today bestselling author of contemporary romance, Natasha Knight specializes in dark, tortured heroes. Happily-Ever-Afters are guaranteed, but she likes to put her characters through hell to get them there. She's evil like that.

Want more?
www.natasha-knight.com
natasha-knight@outlook.com

Made in the USA
Middletown, DE
01 July 2023

34300452R00182